Nobody
Dies a
Virgin..

Life Screws us All

Nobody Dies a Virgin..

Life Screws us All

Sanjay Kumar Shukla

Srishti
PUBLISHERS & DISTRIBUTORS

SRISHTI PUBLISHERS & DISTRIBUTORS
N-16, C. R. Park
New Delhi 110 019
srishtipublishers@gmail.com

First published by
Srishti Publishers & Distributors in 2012

All Characters in this book are fictitious, and resemblance to real persons, living or dead, is coincidental.

Typeset by EGP at Srishti

Dedicated to my alma mater
IIT Kanpur,
College of Technology, Pantnagar,
Campus School, Pantnagar

Acknowledgements

Behind every story's success, there are many characters. I would like to thank those characters from my life who have played a pivotal role in bringing this book to fruition.

Mere words cannot express my gratitude towards my parents Shri Ram Narayan Shukla and Smt. Usha Shukla. Whatever I am is all their effort and perseverance. And thus, they are directly responsible for any mistakes herein. Being impartial, the other sins committed in this work are those of my siblings, Neetu and Amit.

I would like to thank Ashish, Nanda and Dr. K.L. Mishra, whose generous criticism has been instrumental in bringing the work to its current state. Their meticulous editing of numerous drafts and creative ideas has made this work a lot more interesting than what was initially written.

Karthik has been beside me since the time I picked up the pen, figuratively. This story would have never seen the light of the day if not for his constant motivation and belief in me.

Neha's rave comments sparked the craving in me to reach out to a bigger audience.

The time spent with Anirudh, Chintan, Mayur, Pankaj, Rajesh and Shiva at IIT Kanpur is unforgettable. Before any of them sue me, here is the disclaimer, "All the incidents plotted in this book are fictitious, and any resemblance to the real life experiences of our stay at the IIT campus is a mere coincidence".

Asim, Mitesh and Harsh, my childhood friends are a great sounding board to me. Poor souls, they had no choice but to listen to me rant. I appreciate their candid feedback about all my endeavors.

Ashok, whose execution abilities soaked in humility and humor have always impressed me, is the secret behind I being able to manage this work.

My destiny has crossed paths with two iconic historical figures through this work. The title and its tagline are a gift to me from the great Kurt Cobain and Michael J Trent.

I would like to thank Terrafugia Incorporation (www.terrafugia.com). This story is inspired from their innovation in the flying car technology.

A token of thanks to sourceforge, whose configuration versioning system WinCVS I have extensively used to manage between different versions of my book.

If God grants me a wish today, I would like to thank Bill Gates in person for his 'Microsoft Word' for its inbuilt editing and comparison features.

Many thanks to my publisher Shri Jayantakumar Bose, loving Da, for having shown faith in me and for publishing my work. I am thankful to the entire team of Srishti Publications for working assiduously towards publishing my book.

And above all, I would like to thank you, the reader, who has picked up this book. I truly believe that you will not be disappointed.

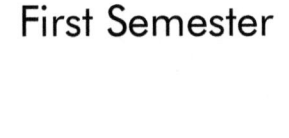

First Semester

VETERAN'S BATTLEFIELD TURNED AMATEURS PLAYGROUND

25ᵗʰ July 2005

Auditorium, IITC

Orientation for the master's program had just finished when the students admitted for the course were hijacked by the volunteers from the 'student counseling service'. Pulling together a sightseeing tour of the campus, the volunteers navigated the bus through the spots of importance in IIT Cawnpore (IITC). Inside the bus, all but a pair of curious eye balls watched the things around. Those lonely eyeballs were engaged in excavating the distant past.

'Aadi, I have lost my father. My family is going through a tough time,' said Sakshi. She coughed as she continued. 'I don't want to invent problems for my family. My brother doesn't like you and he can never accept our love.'

'Sakshi, I am not asking you to lie to your family. I just want you to hang on for a while. Once I have a job, I can talk to your mom and brother about our marriage. Your brother ...,' Aadi was not even done when Sakshi interrupted. 'Aadi, this relationship can't work.'

'Sakshi, give me a second chance.'

'It's not possible Aadi,' replied Sakshi coldly.

'Hi.' A voice echoed inside the institute bus bringing Aadi back from his haunting past. 'I am Tapan.'

Aadi shook the extended hand and studied the stranger

closely. A sober looking guy, Tapan had a lean body framed to a tall structure. He had big black eyes, a pointed nose and clean well combed hair that gleamed in the natural light. A tailor made red colored shirt hung loosely on his body. His wheatish complexion gave him a charismatic look.

After due scrutiny, came the reply. 'I am Aadi Malhotra.'

'The orientation program has been quite hectic. I fear how the real academics are going to be,' said Tapan.

Aadi smiled indifferently and turned back, his thoughts ready to taxi for a flight to his troubled past. Before he could take off, Tapan asked, forcing him to abort. 'Which Hall are you in? I am in Hall 8.'

'I am also in Hall 8,' replied Aadi.

'Did you meet anyone else from our class?' asked Tapan.

'No,' replied Aadi curtly.

'How are you finding this place?' asked Tapan.

Aadi replied with his silence but that wasn't enough to deter Tapan who filled in his comments. 'This place seems to be boring.'

Aadi was determined not to fuel the talk. He cast a gloomy glance upon Tapan. Collecting the cue, Tapan leaned back on his seat. After about fifteen minutes the touring bus came to a stop. Students flanked by the volunteers were brought to the air strip.

Grabbing the attention of new joinees, a volunteer spoke. 'Friends, you all would be glad to know that IITC is the only institute in India to have an airstrip of its own. We conduct detailed aerodynamic experiments for a number of institutes who visit us regularly throughout the year.'

Looking through the dozens of gliders kept in the hangar, the volunteer continued. 'I am sure you all would love to fly on these beautiful birds.'

The student volunteer deliberately paused to read through the faces in the crowd. Having failed in his attempt to fish any response, he unscrewed the water bottle in his hand before continuing. 'If interested, you can have the flights by registering with the gliding club.'

The glider was certainly an attraction as it pulled everyone towards it. Students were on their toes to get the details of the glider while ensuring that they don't cross the yellow cordon line.

Hypnotically, Aadi moved ahead crossing the cordon line. He now stood close to the glider. Like a couple on their maiden night, Aadi caressed his hands on the glider's naked body. Attraction is the first step on the road of love. Aadi was now alone in the crowded hangar. He felt with his hands every rivet and nook on the body of the glider.

'Hello buddy,' said the student volunteer tapping on Aadi's attention.

Coming back to his senses, Aadi came out of the cordon.

The student volunteer irrigated his wind pipe with a shot of water and continued. 'We will now move to see a few more places in the campus. Our next halt is at Student Activity Centre, SAC, as you would know it from now on. We shall next visit institute's shopping centre and the last stop in our itinerary will be the medical centre.'

The rest of the sightseeing tour went according to the plan. By the time students were dropped at their respective halls, the sun had already hung his boots and called it a day. But it was not yet over at IITC campus.

'IITC campus never sleeps!', a colloquial phrase was true to its words. At IITC, it was not unusual to find floodlit lawn tennis courts occupied mid night with enthused players. In the dark of the night, students in pajamas festooned the classroom ajar with 'Gymkhana-Club' lectures. Mid-night cricket matches, endless bulla (talking about nothing) sessions, 'no-reason' parties in front of Hall 4 canteen and the list goes on and on. It was the entire life that ran through the night. How could have IITC campus slept?

5ᵗʰ August 2005

Lecture Hall Complex (LHC), IITC

The first day of any lecture would generally start with a terse introduction from the students and a brief introduction of the course to the students. The mathematics course was different as it spoke symbols. Without indulging in trivialities, Dr. Anubhav dusted the chalk powder and started putting arbitrary symbols on the blackboard. Symbols were jumping all over the board in frenzy as the professor waged a war against a mathematical problem. To him, symbols were soldiers, mere pawns of his intellect to win the battleground. Many soldiers died, some even camouflaged themselves, some forts got inverted and finally all the symbols settled diagonally breaching the last surviving fort in the war. On a triumphant note, the professor turned to face the students.

'Students, you just saw a method to evaluate the eigen vectors. You should resolve the matrix in triangular form to solve the problem.' Dr. Anubhav turned his back to the students, waging his next war.

'Hi Buddy!,' a whisper interrupted Aadi.

'Hi!,' Aadi gave an unwelcoming reply.

'Are you taking notes?'

'Yeah, but I find it really hard to digest the stuff,' replied Aadi.

'Check my Solitaire score,' said Harsh extending his iPod.

Peeking into the notebook that lay brazenly blank in front of Harsh, Aadi asked. 'Why are you not taking notes?'

'This is my highest score till date.'

Aadi's expression successfully revealed that it was hardly the answer he was expecting. Comprehending correctly, Harsh came again. 'I am bored of copying.' Closing the notebook, he continued. 'Later, I will borrow your notes. Do you know which book the prof has suggested for the course?'

'Kreyzig.'

'Crazzzzzyig! It is a nice name for the author dwelling on such a weird subject.' Putting his mental stethoscope on Aadi's interest in the talk, Harsh continued. 'I hope you don't mind me leveraging your notes.'

'Not at all, but I think you should concentrate on the lecture. The professor has already completed three derivations,' replied Aadi.

'All have been bouncers to me,' snorted Harsh, keeping the iPod in his shirt's pocket.

'He is moving pretty fast. I don't know if he cares whether we understand.' Aadi gushed out his anguish and turned back to his notebook. Without understanding the motif, Aadi cranked his phalanges and waged an operation, rescuing the soldiers of war to his notebook.

'Excuse me!' a voice fished Harsh's attention. 'Can I borrow your pen? I can see you are not using it'

'Yeah sure.' Looking around embarrassingly, Harsh extended his pen. 'By the way, I am Harsh,' he said.

'I am Tapan,' the other guy replied.

'If I don't understand it, I can't get it in the pages too,' said Harsh in an apologetic tone.

'I have heard that professor Anubhav is quite strict in grading,' a student sitting next to Tapan commented. At the first glance, it confused Harsh whether the student was a boy with a girl's voice. Also, the boy cut hair and the manly face confused him. Stealing a furtive glance at the ample breasts stocked inside a baggy T-shirt, Harsh settled his doubts.

'Are you also in the Mechanical Department?' asked Harsh.

'Yeah,' the girl replied.

'May I know your name?'

'I am Jaswinder.' Before Harsh could have introduced himself, she added. 'And you are Harsh.'

'Yeah.' Puzzled, Harsh asked. 'How do you know my name? um.. Did you see it in my notebook?'

'No, I overheard the conversation between the two of you,' said Jaswinder switching her attention to Tapan. 'If I am not wrong, you were the topper in the entrance exam.'

'Yeah ... ... but that was unintended,' said Tapan plastering a terse smile on his face. Stealing his eyes, he went back to work.

After Dr. Anubhav concluded the class, Aadi rolled his notes and tossed it in the parallel pocket of his trouser. Along with Tapan he walked out of the classroom. Aadi was a tall guy with an athletic build. His wheatish face rested comfortably on the broad shoulders. His chiseled features even included a well-defined philtrum. Toned muscles, ruffled hair and a casual outfit added to his carefree, 'I don't give a damn' attitude.

'Where are you going?' asked Aadi as Tapan turned his steps in a different direction.

Flashing a key, Tapan replied. 'I have a bicycle.'

Aadi now stood in his position. Bearing a smirk on his face, he said. 'So, you were the topper in the entrance exam.'

'I don't think it's funny,' said Tapan. With a scowl on his face and arms crossed, Tapan stood, staring at Aadi.

'Being outstanding is just like being pregnant. Everyone congratulates you but no one knows how hard you got screwed,' said Aadi on a lighter note.

'I thought you didn't have any funny bones.' The lines of surprise from Tapan's face had evaporated. The territory was now seized by a complacent and friendly smile. Dropping his guard against Aadi, Tapan said. 'Come on, I can give you a ride to the hall.'

25ᵗʰ September 2005

Swimming Pool, IITC

IIT Cawnpore boasted of an Olympic size swimming pool. Apart from feeding billions of microscopic organisms, the pool also fed a staff of 10. With 3 life guards and a trainer, the pool was a safe haven for the beginners.

Completing his set of laps, Harsh came back to the edge of pool where Aadi and Tapan were bobbing. 'Aadi, Is everything fine?' asked Harsh joining the two. 'I have been observing for the last few days, you are always preoccupied with yourself,' he explained.

'Everything is fine,' replied Aadi tersely. Slipping on his goggles over his face, he plunged in water, dodging further questions.

Combing water out of his hair, Harsh looked towards Tapan as he spoke. 'Stop practicing at the edge and take a leap in the pool.'

'I don't know how to swim,' replied Tapan.

'You can't drown in five feet of water. Give it a try,' exhorted Harsh.

Seeing Tapan's hesitance, Harsh walked towards him. Continuing his guru-gyan, he said. 'You should know that your girlfriend can only give her fifty percent to the unity while this elixir of life contributes seventy.'

'What do you mean?' asked Tapan, his face contorted.

'Don't be afraid; rather try living this amorous experience of lying half naked on your 'more than a girlfriend'. Enjoy the waves thumping on your body. Allow yourself to sway with them in an unsaid rhythm. Surrender yourself to water as if you are in the arms of your girlfriend.'

'I didn't get what you said but I will give it a try. I would rather drown than listen to your junk philosophy,' said Tapan donning his goggles.

'Either way, my friend is getting enlightened,' shrugged Harsh. Upholding Tapan's faith, he continued. 'I will keep a watch on your movements. Just go ahead and you can do it.'

The water splashed as Tapan dived in. Panic-struck, he furiously beat his hands in the water, obviously that did no good to him. Finally he came out gasping for breath and funneling water from his mouth. 'I can't do it.'

'Leave it. I don't think you are ready yet,' said Harsh. Catching up with Tapan who was now walking out of the pool, he asked. 'Is Aadi facing any problem?'

'I don't know,' replied Tapan.

'I think there is some serious problem with him,' said Harsh. Looking towards Tapan, he asked. 'Are we leaving?'

'Yeah,' replied Tapan.

Aadi stood at the other end of the pool. With hand signal, Tapan asked him to call it a day for swimming.

It was a tough walk to the shower. The exhausted muscles had already succumbed to the gravity. The shower helped in washing off the bleached water of the pool but didn't plug the sweating pores. Once they were back in the hall, Aadi's room became the rendezvous ground. Harsh was fast enough to claim the territory of a cot while Tapan had to manage with a wooden chair. Aadi sat on the computer table checking his mails. After a blissful silence, Harsh hurled his question to Aadi. 'What's that burning you from the inside?'

Surprised, Aadi looked towards Harsh. Rescuing Aadi's doubts, Tapan anchored his words in the conversation. 'It's apparent from your behavior that something is bothering you. You can share your problems with us. If possible, we would like to be of some help.'

'At least, we can offer a consoling shoulder,' added Harsh.

'Let me find you some sweets.' Evading the topic, Aadi pulled out the chest kept below his cot. As Aadi unzipped the mouth of his bag, it vomited the clothes that it had gorged earlier. Picking up the box of sweets, Aadi extended it to Harsh. 'Have some sweets.'

'Is it a matter of the heart?' asked Harsh taking a piece.

'Yes,' replied Aadi. Heaving a deep sigh, he went back helping his bag which suffered from indigestion.

After cleaning the stomach of his helpless bag, Aadi closed its mouth and pushed it under the cot. Retiring to one corner of the room, he continued. 'The relationship is almost at its end.'

'Share something that you like,' said Harsh, peeling away another layer of Aadi's emotional reticence. Coming close to Aadi, he said. 'Tell us about how you proposed to her.'

With a quaint smile on his face, Aadi continued. 'Sakshi and I graduated from the same college. I developed an instant liking for her from the very first day. After two years of silent admiration, I mustered the courage to ask her to meet me in the university library…' Aadi rolled back his imagination in time and space to enjoy those fleeting but fulfilling moments of his life.

3rd November 2003

Library, Pantnagar University

Covering the word 'sexy', engraved blatantly on the table, Aadi slipped a book over it. On his first date with Sakshi, Aadi found himself uncomfortable under the vigilant eyes of the thousands of books around him. Adding to his woes were the indecent graffiti etched all over the furniture. Though he had scrambled plenty of volumes on the desk, he was still short by a few to cover them all.

'Aadi, what is it you want to talk about?' Aadi looked up at Sakshi. Mesmerized by her beauty, he gazed at her. Sakshi waited for Aadi to speak up but finding no answer coming her way, she tapped gently on his hand.

'What?' asked Aadi, holding the book on the taboo characters.

'Weren't you listening to me?'

'I am sorry. Can you come again?'

'Why did you call me here?' asked Sakshi looking around. A slight eye contact was enough to confront the intruding eyes of the other students sitting in the library.

'Sakshi, I love you,' said Aadi looking straight into her eyes.

'You can't just propose to me with those three magic words. You need to do some more work,' said Sakshi stealing her eyes.

'I don't see many bollywood movies. Please manage with those three words only,' said Aadi pushing back the ball in Sakshi's court.

'Then, you can't get me,' replied Sakshi with a mischievous smile.

Aadi didn't want to lose the game point. Hesitantly, he asked. 'Do you want me to propose to you in front of everyone?'

'If you can dare so,' replied Sakshi.

Taking stock of witnesses around, Aadi mused for a while. Before he could have mustered the courage, Sakshi asked. 'Who is going to propose?'

'I will propose,' said Aadi taking a resolve.

There were two students, sitting too far to eavesdrop in their conversation. Aadi dropped his book, loud enough to grab their attention. He bent down to pick up the book, and from the corner of his eyes observed the unwarranted heads rolling towards him.

Aadi waited as the heads rolled back, finding nothing unusual. Aadi took Sakshi's hand in his and knelt before her.

In a tone too low to travel beyond a few steps, Aadi proposed. 'If I were a painter, it's only you that I would have drawn. As an actor, it's only you that I would have romanced. If I was a robber, I would have stolen you forever. But then, I am none of these.' Unsure, Sakshi listened keenly as Aadi continued. 'I may not be someone special but my heart beats for you. I may not paint or act but would like to explore every bit of you as you are the oil to my engine and it runs only for you.'

'*Dhat, reh gaye na engineer ke engineer*. Anyways, you are my superhero,' said Sakshi lifting Aadi's hand up. 'Stand up! It was not a military drill.'

'The superhero never gets the girl.'

'But, I am all yours and you are mine,' whispered Sakshi.

Standing up, Aadi dusted his trouser. While Aadi was slapping the side of his leg, Sakshi spoke. 'Aadi, I admit that I like you but...' After a brief pause, she suddenly asked. 'But, I want to know what you want to do with me.'

'Do with you...what sort of question is this? I love you,' said Aadi sitting back on his chair.

'That's true. I also like you, but I want to know how far you want to take this relationship.'

'I love you and I want to live my life with you. Would you like to?' asked Aadi.

'I already accepted your proposal,' replied Sakshi smiling impishly. She went back to fiddling with her nails.

The silence between the two deepened as Aadi was busy leading a crusade against the indecent graffiti on the table. Claiming victory, he looked up to face another combatant. Aadi found himself nervous under Sakshi's piercing gaze. He hesitantly picked up one of the books covering the graffiti. 'From the windows on this floor, there's a great view of the campus. Would you like to take a look?' asked Sakshi.

Aadi nodded in agreement.

'Come with me.' Sakshi held Aadi's hand and led the way

to the corner of the floor. Aadi was intrigued. Many questions echoed hard on the walls of his mind when finally he got to the windows on the library's wall.

Aadi had no clue when windows of human size got planted on the walls covered up with bookshelves. Aadi started admiring the height of the windows. They were large enough to let a beam of light equivalent to 40 tube lights into the room. Aadi was lost in these calculations when Sakshi gently pressed her lips against Aadi's and gave him a warm hug.

In no way was Aadi prepared for what was happening to him. Sakshi now stood in front of him with a sparkle in her eyes.

'What now?' asked Aadi in a trance.

Sakshi said nothing but closed her eyes.

Was she waiting for him to kiss her? Unsure, Aadi waited for another cue. Before he could have concluded, Sakshi dropped her books. Aadi bent down to collect the books while Sakshi moved forward, her eyes closed. A moment elapsed before Sakshi opened her eyes to find Aadi collecting the books that she had dropped.

'What?' asked Aadi, looking up. Sakshi's expression had turned sour but it was enough to give him a kick for what she waited. With his heart pounding on his ribs, Aadi moved forward and took her in his arms. Before Aadi could have locked his lips with Sakshi's, his eyes got stuck on a graffiti sketched on the wall. 'Wrap it in foil, before checking her oil,' said the graffiti.

'What are you thinking?' Sakshi swiveled her head in the direction of Aadi's sight but before she could have caught a glimpse of the graffiti, Aadi grabbed her face. 'I love you, Sakshi,' said Aadi smacking her under his lips.

'So, was there anything beyond kissing?' Passing a mischievous smile, Harsh winked at Aadi.

'Shut up Harsh!' snapped Tapan. Looking towards Aadi, he asked. 'Why did you break up?'

'Here's a piece of advice for free.' Looking straight in Aadi's eyes, Harsh continued. 'Move on in your life. Don't brood about the past.'

Bringing the conversation to an abrupt halt, the door to the room opened with a thud. It was Sid. 'What are you guys doing?' asked Sid. He advanced towards the undressed sweet boxes inviting him amorously.

Siddhartha aka Sid was a South Indian boy with a charismatic personality. His face bore a visceral innocence of adolescence that hinged with a moustache in his adulthood. Born with a silver spoon in his mouth, Sid hailed from a business class family. Innately talented, Sid held command on six regional languages and with admission at IITC he had Hindi in his crosshairs.

Looking away from the boxes kept on the cot, Sid dove for the sweets with his dirty hands. He ravenously plundered the sweets, gorged his mouth till it pleaded to save it from choking. He was now in no position to fire another question. 'What were you guys doing?' Puffing the sweets out of his mouth, Sid repeated his question.

'First eat, then ask,' suggested Aadi hiding his annoyance.

'Have you guys ever been to NASA?' asked Sid puffing even harder this time. 'I was there last month.'

'No,' replied Aadi. Shuffling a few books on the bed, Aadi slyly swept the sweet boxes undercover.

'You guys should hang out there sometime. It's a really nice place.' Sid gnawed his nails to savor the last stock of sweet cached behind his long yellow colored nails. Licking the last bit, he continued. 'Are you guys not coming for Mukherjee's class?'

'Oh Shit, we had totally forgotten that,' said Tapan jumping from his chair. 'Hurry up guys.' Parking their discussion, the group moved towards the 'New Lecture Hall complex'.

THE GLOVES ARE OFF

22ⁿᵈ October, 2005

'You love me, na?' Sakshi's eyes gleamed in the dim light inside the room.

Aadi looked around for eavesdroppers. With a deep breath and a pounding heart, he spoke. 'Please don't rhyme your 'I love you' jingle now.' Bringing his tone down, he continued. 'We will get into trouble if someone overhears that.'

'You Love me or not? I want to hear from you,' asserted Sakshi. She played dare devil sitting in her room.

'God damn, please don't speak so loudly. If your mother overhears us, then we are dead,' said Aadi clinching his teeth.

Sakshi's demand was like a spark on the pile of explosives. Before Aadi could have doused the spark, an explosion happened. Razing down the kohl, tears from Sakshi's eyes seized the territory till her cheeks.

'Sakshi, those ugly tears rolling down your eyes can even crush a stone, then where does my little heart stand. Save me,' said Aadi spreading his arms around Sakshi. 'I do love you.'

Sakshi blushed and a mischievous smile ran across her face. Adding to the beauty were her hazel eyes. 'Why did God make her so beautiful?' thought Aadi. He tried to ignore the thoughts and looked away from her, browsing through her notebook which she had brazenly inked with 'I Love You Aadi' claims.

'What would you do if you were the Prime Minister of India

for a day?' asked Aadi changing the course of the discussion. Looking up from the notebook, he turned to face Sakshi. Before he could have realized, Sakshi pasted a sweet kiss on his cheek. It came as a total surprise to Aadi. If he was the Prime Minister of India for a day, he surely would have given her the 'Red and White' bravery award.

The kiss broke the last boulder of self-restraint. Also, the privacy in the room stoked the fire. Mesmerized, Aadi got closer to Sakshi. Slowly he moved his face close to hers. Locking his lips with hers, he smacked them tightly. Aadi felt a current rushing through him like an electrical surge. Licking her lips, Aadi moved his tongue inside her mouth. She felt soft and moist. Before Aadi could have explored further, Sakshi pushed him back.

Hesitant, Aadi was frozen in his place when Sakshi took his hand and placed it on her bosom. With a shaking hand, Aadi opened the first two buttons of her shirt and unhooked the blouse. He stood gazing at her round smooth breasts. Grabbing it with his hand, he went ahead to devour his feast when the dim light escaping into the closed room turned into an avalanche, catching Aadi and Sakshi unguarded. Though Aadi quickly moved back, he was a split second too late. Sakshi's mother stood in front of them, her jaw dropped to the ground.

Aadi was caught red handed with his hand inside Sakshi's shirt. Coming out of his momentary stupor, Aadi pulled his hand back. A button popped off her shirt. Spinning on the floor, it came to a stop after a while but the eyes of Sakshi's mother still wobbled in her sockets.

Instinctively, Aadi picked Sakshi's blouse and tried to cover up the mistakes.

'What were the two of you doing?' asked Sakshi's mother. Bringing the situation under control, her mother continued. 'Sakshi, you go into the other room.'

'Auntiji, you are getting it all wrong,' said Aadi wiping off his wet lips.

Picking his books, Aadi stood up. With a rage visible on her face, Sakshi's mother bawled. 'My brother is the Superintendent of Police. You are now going to rot in jail for years.' She was not done when a few police men with their faces painted and holding machine guns stormed inside the room. Leading them was Sakshi's maternal uncle.

'Kill this bastard,' retorted the uncle.

Raaat...raat.....raat, between the noises of rounds fired from the machine gun, Aadi raced in the mine laden battleground. Suddenly, assaults from the sky lit the dark night and the bombastic sound pierced through his ears. Rivulets of sweat broke out from tens of thousands of pores, flooding his face. An assault from the sky found its way in front of Aadi and he jumped to his last fall ... from the bed.

'What the fuck was that?' Tapan jumped from the computer chair to the floor where now Aadi was lying. 'What happened to you? You are sweating like a pig.'

'I had a dream. It felt scary,' replied Aadi. His heart still raced at light speed.

'What was the dream about?' asked Tapan handing Aadi the water bottle.

'I had a dream about her,' replied Aadi.

'I thought she was beautiful.' With a conspicuous smile, Tapan continued. 'At least, I never expected her to be scary.'

'I had a good time with her. But then her mother came in,' explained Aadi.

'Tell me your dream,' asked Tapan. 'Not as in ... uh ... your good time with Sakshi, but your troubles with her mother.'

'Her mother tried to bully me.' Yawning, Aadi continued. 'Sakshi's maternal uncle is the Superintendent of Police.'

'I am out of this game then,' said Tapan impishly.

'Leave this nonsense,' snapped Aadi. Rubbing his eyes, he continued. 'I can't tell you how vivid the dream felt.'

'Dude, do something.'

'What can I do when she ...'

Patting on Aadi's shoulder, Tapan spoke. 'Ask her to come back into your life. You can't run away from your past.'

Aadi pondered for a while and then spoke. 'That's it. I need to give it one last try.' Looking towards Tapan, he continued. 'I will meet her on 21st November. It's her birthday.'

After a second's pause, Tapan said thoughtfully. 'But, we would be having our final term exams during that time.'

'I will manage,' said Aadi.

'Love is a chemical cocktail that makes the world go round,' said Tapan whirling his fist in the air. With a contented smile on his face he moved out of the room. Aadi followed him.

8th November 2005,

CAD Lecture, Lecture Hall Complex (LHC), IITC

'We will continue with Bezier Splines in our next lecture,' Dr. Subbarao kept the chalk on the table and dusted his hands.

'Get ready for your roll call,' said Dr. Subbarao opening the attendance register. In the laboratory of his mind, Subbarao had invented a strange philosophy of taking attendance at the end of the lecture. He believed it kept a check on the proxies.

'Reddy'

'Yes Sir'

Subbarao's call to Reddy had not even died down when a muffled sound echoed in the back benches. 'Steady and go.'

'Shut up Aadi, Subbu will hear that.' Exchanging a stern look, Tapan returned to his notes.

Dr. Subbarao bore a self-pompous personality. He often stumbled with the words and whenever he stammered his eyes fell in a blinking fit. His tummy brazenly bulged out increasing his share of space. On a fair face, Subbarao had fluffy cheeks which bordered a small round nose resting on a thick moustache. While nasal hair falling below the line of nose gave his face an abandoned look, balls of mucus rendered it haunted. His little pair of eyeballs never gave others enough room to read through his mind.

Completing the attendance, Dr. Subbarao distributed the second mid semester answer sheets. The stock of answer sheet on his table reduced as the size of the queue in front of his desk increased. Other than Sid, everyone in the class stood in the queue, dissatisfied with their marks.

'What is it that you want to discuss?' asked Dr. Subbarao.

'Sir, my answers are correct but I have got only partial marks.' Aadi held his dead hopes in one hand while his other hand rested casually on Tapan's shoulder.

'Check out Sid's answer sheet. That's the way I expect answers from you all,' said Subbarao signaling Aadi to get back to etiquette. Bringing back decorum to the class, Subbarao continued. 'Sid has elaborated every step involved in solving the problem. An answer should be such that anyone can understand.'

'Sir, what would an explanation do if we haven't answered correctly?' asked Harsh. Subbarao found Harsh's cold sneer discomforting. Quibbling with words, he asked. 'Can you explain your answers to my mother who is totally technologically illiterate?'

Harsh didn't reply but the expression on his face clearly revealed that he was ready to lock his horns. Dropping the arms, Subbarao asked. 'Harsh, why are you giving me that look? I don't know why you guys suspect my grading.'

After a brief moment of silence, Harsh spoke. 'Sir, I don't know about the explanation thing but I have answered the question. I should get the marks.'

'Will my mother understand that? I have already mentioned that my mother is technologically illiterate. I want an answer that could be understood by my mother,' retorted Subbarao. Taking a pause, he said. 'Now, I am not dealing with the doubts over the grading anymore.'

'But sir,' blurted Aadi.

'Take my mother's cell number,' said Subbarao handing his 'Nokia 1100' to Aadi. 'Tell her your solution and ask if she understands that.'

'Sir, I don't think that IITC appoints the faculty from the road side,' interrupted Harsh. 'We wrote the answers for a professor to understand and not for someone's mother.'

Harsh had dropped the bomb shell which exploded into a pin

drop silence. Subbarao stood dumbfound with his jaw dropped on the ground. The silence continued for a while which Subbarao broke, signing a truce. 'Submit your answer sheets and I will take another look. Since I am grading again, marks can swing both ways.'

Collecting the answer sheets, Subbarao sat at the desk. Looking through the faces in the class, he asked. 'Will it be okay if we reschedule the end semester exam for an earlier date? What about 21st November?'

'Sir, I am not in campus. Can we look for some other date?' It was Aadi to exercise his veto against the proposed date.

'Why are you not in campus in the middle of end semester exam?' asked Dr. Subbarao.

As Aadi could not have revealed his plans, he kept silent, rigid on the raised veto.

'I think you are not taking your studies seriously. You screwed up your mid semester exams and are ready to bet against the final. What are you up to?' Before Subbarao could have continued, a bell rang, saving Aadi of further probing questions. Resolving the conflict, Dr. Subbarao spoke. 'We will have the exam on 25th November as per our original schedule.' Picking up the answer sheets, Dr Subbarao marched out of the classroom.

'Harsh, do you understand what you said in the class about that mother thing?' asked Tapan joining Aadi and Harsh on the way to the bicycle stand.

Harsh held back his words. Once they reached the bicycle stand, Harsh took cover against a column and lighted a cigarette. Puffing out plume of smoke, he spoke. 'How can he penalize us for not filling the sheets when we had got the answers correct?'

'It would have been embarrassing for him,' added Tapan.

Harsh sucked the end of stick harder. Holding an inebriated expression, he smiled. 'He had pissed me off. The exam was not meant to educate his mother.'

On a tall frame, Harsh held a heavy face that rested on broad shoulders. Inside the red branded T shirt, he had a broad chest and a flat abdomen. Manned by bushy eyebrows, Harsh had sharp eyes and a chiseled nose. His complexion was overly fair for his skin to hide blood running through his veins. With pink chubby cheeks, Harsh had a juvenile look.

'You better throw away that cigarette. If any professor sees it, we all would be in trouble,' said Sid wiping excess water from his face using his shirt's sleeve. He had come out for drinking water when he saw the group and took a detour.

'Don't worry.' Diverting the flak of unwarranted suggestions, Harsh questioned. 'How much did you score in mathematics?'

'Not much! I think I scored the lowest in the class. I scored 18.' With a confused state of mind Sid emphatically asked. 'What's your score?'

'I scored 10.'

'By the way Sid, I haven't opened my innings yet,' said Aadi joining the conversation.

'Did I hear you right?'

'Yes, you did.' Aadi continued slowly with a gloomy sneer. 'What the shit am I? For a zero, I painted 20 odd pages.' Aadi sadly pulled the paint cracking off the column.

'Don't worry. Anubhav also did a pretty dirty whitewash,' giggled Harsh.

'You shut up,' Tapan elbowed. Consoling Aadi, he said. 'I am sure you will do well in the next exam.'

Throwing away the cigarette stub, Harsh cranked open his bicycle lock. 'Is anyone joining me to the hall?' Harsh looked up for an answer but had to catch a question hurled at him by Tapan. 'Are you not attending Mukherjee's lecture?'

'I am coming with you. With this shit in hand I can't take lectures anymore,' said Aadi offsetting the balance in favor of Harsh.

'Mukherjee sir can schedule the surprise quiz today,' Tapan mumbled.

'He always keeps the pressure up by assignments and these surprise quizzes,' Harsh said as he moved his glance furtively at the tall lady passing by them.

'Surprise Quiz … bullshit,' mocked Aadi. 'No questions ever

get asked from the parts we prepare for. Every other exam is a surprise to us. There's nothing new with the surprises.'

'But he may schedule the quiz today,' reiterated Tapan, his eyebrows squeezed together.

'*Chhod Na*! Today, he can't schedule the quiz.'

'Who gave you the crystal ball?' asked Tapan.

'It's plain simple logic. In a class of 9 students, if 3 are missing, then do you think Mukherjee will schedule the quiz and deprive one-third of the class from the surprise?' reasoned Harsh.

'Man, you can sell the dirt to a ditch digger,' said Tapan putting his heart before his mind. Bunking the class was nothing new for others but Tapan certainly felt a tinge of excitement.

MOVE ON

21ˢᵗ November 2005,

Coffee House, Pantnagar

The weather had turned rogue as Aadi waited in a sprawling lawn in front of a coffee house near the library. The air was moist and laden with the smell of damp soil. Shoving the sun back, the dark clouds loomed; their shadows large on the ground. It had been a calm sunny day when Aadi started from his house, but it seemed to him that weather was playing a conspiracy to keep him away from his love.

Aadi could feel his heart pounding as he saw a lady in black kurti a few meters away. He constantly gazed at her as she walked towards Aadi. Her charming face left Aadi with a wish to melt in her arms. The smack of the first kiss still rested on his lips. Aadi had lived a life admiring the beauty in those few steps that Sakshi made towards him.

'Hi Aadi,' said Sakshi picking up the chair.

Aadi took a brief moment before moving his eyes from her mesmerizing face. 'Hi Sakshi,' he gestured. Extending a chocolate bar, Aadi said with a smile on his face. 'Wish you many happy returns of the day. Happy Birthday, Sakshi.'

Sakshi took the chocolate bar and kept it to one side. She fiddled with her nails while Aadi struggled for words.

'Aadi, you wanted to talk to me?' asked Sakshi stoking the conversation.

'Would you like to have coffee?'

'Yeah, a coffee will do.'

Aadi ordered the coffee and with his eyes down on the table continued. 'Thanks a lot for seeing me on such short notice.'

'Aadi, we both have gone through a rough phase in our life. I want to help you, and that's why I came over.'

'Sakshi, I tried really hard.' Heaving a sigh, Aadi continued. 'With every single breath of mine, I tried to get over your thoughts but I failed miserably each time…'

Air blowing came to a standstill as it tried to listen to the conversation between the two. Aadi didn't care for the eavesdropper. Engrossed in his thoughts, he continued. 'Please come back into my life. I can't live without you.'

'Aadi, I want to help you but first you need to help yourself. What you are asking for is impossible.'

'Why is it not possible? What's the problem?' asked Aadi punching his fist on the table.

'I am leaving,' said Sakshi standing up.

'Sakshi, I am sorry. Don't you think you owe me at least an explanation? I love you,' Aadi's voice sunk as his heart yelled in pain. His words had not only tamed the weather but had won over Sakshi as well. She sat back.

Sipping the coffee, both of them kept silent. Today, there were no graffiti on the table that Aadi had to keep an eye on. Rather, there was graffiti on his heart that he wanted to show to Sakshi. Aadi had his sound box choked. His emotions were ready to brim over. Breaking the silence, Aadi said. 'Let's give our relationship a second chance.'

'I don't want to get into a relationship again. I am getting engaged.'

'Sakshi, marry me.' With a pause, Aadi continued. 'I am doing well in my studies and will surely settle with a good job.'

'It doesn't matter now.' Composing herself, Sakshi continued. 'I have already given my consent for the marriage.'

'You remember, once you said that it's hard for a girl to forget her first love while boys easily can.' With his voice cracking, Aadi continued. 'I can't forget you.'

'Aadi, if you try you can forget me easily,' said Sakshi lowering her eyes which had already gone wet. Moving her hand quickly, she smudged the moist eye with her first finger. Looking up, she said. 'You will get a girl better than me.'

'Why can't I get you?'

'Aadi, why don't you understand, this relationship has no future. It's dead,' shrieked Sakshi. Looking earnestly towards Aadi, she continued. 'After so many difficulties, I have settled down in my life. Please don't create trouble for me.'

The moist eyes now had full grown tears in them. Aadi could have kissed her tears but now they were not his. 'Sakshi, please don't cry.' Grabbing her hand, he said. 'You know it very well that I can't create trouble for you.'

'What are you doing now? Don't you think you are troubling me?' said Sakshi snatching her hand back.

'Remember one thing. I can't trouble you and I love you,' said Aadi, his face numb. Aadi took out his wallet and fetched the bill. Putting it on the table, he left. His heart yelled to look back at his love one last time. His eyes yearned to let them steal a glimpse of her, but Aadi moved on. He didn't look back till he reached his house. Time heals all pain but when it pains, it pains. His eyes were filled to brim as they had seen the castle of his dreams being shattered to pieces. The weather also commiserated with his feelings, the clouds roared and winds howled. Thick drops of water poured from the skies. The universe around him cried in sympathy. Aadi left all of them alone, locked himself in his study and switched off the lights.

25th November 2005,

Mess, Hall 8, IITC

In the simmering oil, the cook added chilli, cumin and mustard seeds. Sweeping the pan in the air he flushed the hot oil even on the seeds' head. They spluttered in resilience as the oil caught flame. With a sleight of hand, the cook doused the flame with the onions and ginger garlic paste. After the onion turned red, he added mashed potato, turmeric and myriad of masala powders. The fried potato substitute got ready in two minutes while Tapan waited by the side of the open kitchen in the mess. Holding his dinner plate in one hand and fried potato dish in the other, Tapan took the table with Harsh and Aadi.

'This fried potato is the only salvation on Wednesday.' Like a gourmet, Tapan whiffed up the aroma of the fried potatoes.

'Guys, can I sit with you?' asked Sid like a gentleman, his pronunciation slurred.

'We don't shit while eating. Come back in the morning,' said Harsh sporting an infectious smile. Sid didn't ask again and joined the table.

Eating in silence for a few minutes, Sid asked. "*Kiholo babu moshai*', You guys are eating as if someone is dead. Why is no one talking?'

'Sid, what is the meaning of *hiholo*,' asked Tapan pushing hard the mix of poori and dal in his mouth.

'It's *kiholo* not the way you pronounce *hiholo*. The way you pronounce it seems as if it's the language of nomads.'

'It's simply 'key and hole',' snapped Harsh.

'*kiholo*,' Tapan chuckled.

'That was nerdy,' commented Sid.

'Nerdy was when you said that you have been to NASA,' smirked Harsh. 'We all were in awe till we learned that it was nothing but a boys-booze out place.'

'I thought you guys would be aware of the happening places in the campus.'

'Forget it,' said Tapan. Extending his plate to Sid, he said. '*Babu moshai*, have some fried potato.' How could Sid have denied? He had earned it. Taking his share, Sid began a conversation with Aadi. 'Whom are you planning to take as supervisor?'

Doodling with the food, Aadi replied in a muffled tone. 'I am not sure which topic to pick.' His eyes locked on a tiny speck on his spoon as he continued. 'I have always been interested to work in the field of aerodynamics.'

'Dr. Dutta would be a good choice for you. One of the best professors in the Aerospace Department, he has some really interesting research projects under him.' Sipping water from his glass, Harsh continued. 'You should talk to him at the earliest. He would be on the radar of the students from both Mechanical and Aerospace departments.'

'How do you know so much about Dr. Dutta?' asked Tapan, cocking a quizzical eyebrow.

'During his bachelors, he worked in the Aerospace Department on a six month project. He ..' Interrupting Sid, it was Tapan to toss a question. 'At IITC?'

'You are right. He was one of the three students selected across India,' explained Sid.

'Thank God! I am not an endangered species,' said Tapan exhaling a deep breath.

Tracking the discussion back, Harsh continued. 'As Dr. Dutta belongs to Aerospace Department, you can have him only as a co-supervisor. You need to have a main supervisor from Mechanical.'

'I will suggest you to take Dr. Mukherjee as your main supervisor,' added Tapan.

'Are you suggesting Dr. Mukherjee because you have him as your supervisor?' asked Harsh.

'Dr. Mukherjee is a nice and resourceful man. Aadi just has to meet the rules. Dr. Dutta is the one who he needs.'

'What about you Harsh? Have you taken some pain to finalize your supervisor?' asked Sid.

'*Chhod Na!*'

'Guess what Harsh would have said to the nurse helping his mother during his birth?' asked Sid. It was his chance to settle the score.

'What?' asked Tapan.

'*Chhod Na!* Why are you pulling my leg? I am comfortable inside,' chortled Sid.

Everyone on the table fell in peals of laughter while Harsh blushed pink with embarrassment. Aadi's eyes gleamed and a smile meandered its way through the facial muscles to his lips. The joke from Sid was able to rediscover his lost smile.

Completing the dinner, the group came out of the cafeteria. While washing his hand in the basin by Aadi's side, Harsh whispered. 'I am glad to have you back with us.'

Moving out of the restroom, Harsh slipped his hand on Aadi's shoulder. Grabbing his shoulder, he advised. 'The faster you lose your scary past the lesser you lose from your present. Just because of one bad experience, you can't stop living or admiring the good part of your life.'

'I can't lose my life for what I never had. Rather, I will live it for the ones I have,' said Aadi exchanging a brief smile.

'That's more like my Aadi,' said Tapan throwing his arms across Aadi. Cuddling both of them tightly against his gaunt frame, Harsh skipped a brief moment before speaking. 'Ease out friends. We will have lots of time for emotions, but now we should be studying.'

29th November 2005,

Aadi's room, Hall 8, IITC

A thin column of light gazing through the glass window and escaping the shield of curtains found its way into the room. The column penetrated Aadi's eyelids and got registered in the photosensitive ganglion cells. Trekking its route through the labyrinth of nerves it activated the visual cortex. Doors to Aadi's brain got a knock. His brain which was involved in supporting a surreal fantasy world crashed with the storm of signals. Irritated, he covered his face with a pillow and turned his back to the column of light.

'Oh shit!' Aadi woke with an impulse. He picked his mobile to fetch time in the day. 'It's 911!' Aadi stood up thumping his fist on the cot. The Mathematics exam was to start at 10 and he had slept more than what he had planned.

'Tapan, why didn't you wake me up?' Tapan was studying

when Aadi dashed inside the room.

'It seems that you have been sleeping till now. What happened? Didn't you set the alarm?' asked Tapan.

'I had set the alarm but was not able to get up.' With a flush of disappointment on his face, Aadi continued. 'I had to revise lots of stuff.'

'There's no benefit in regretting now. Get fresh, we need to leave in some time,' said Tapan.

Aadi rushed to his room. Short of time, he covered the mundane chores in haste. Every second seemed valuable and Aadi didn't want to lose any. By skipping his breakfast and borrowing from Tapan a ride to the examination hall, he traded in some time to study.

The exam had already started when they entered the examination hall. Picking up the question paper and the answer sheet they settled in the seats marked for them. For a few pregnant minutes, the faces went blank. The symbols in the paper appeared strange. As seconds ticked away, efforts to salvage every possible mark started. The three hours were no less than a nightmare. A bell rang concluding the examination.

'Students, please submit your answer sheets,' Dr Anubhav stood up from his chair. The silence in the classroom broke with his slippers rubbing ears of the floor. He stood in front of a student scribbling in frenzy on his answer sheet. Being considerate towards his effort, Anubhav waited for another minute.

'Stop writing and submit your copies.' Dr. Anubhav pulled the floor beneath the dancing pen. The sound of crack followed as the answer sheet tore apart in two pieces. Further, the job became easy.

Submitting his answer sheet, Harsh trashed the question paper into his pocket. Looking towards Aadi, he asked. 'How did you do?'

'I solved two questions. Rest is on the luck!' replied Aadi, puffing out a deep breath.

'I have tanked,' said Harsh.

Dr. Anubhav rattled his throat, seeking the attention of the students who had already started discussing. Under the gazing eyes of the students, he said. 'There was a sad incident that happened today. A student from our department met with an accident. He has been rushed to the hospital.'

'Is he alright?' asked one of the student in the class.

'His condition is not known,' replied Dr. Anubhav. Taking stock of the reaction from the class, Dr. Anubhav continued. 'Media is at the front gate of the department. I will request you to avoid the media and leave to your hostels immediately. Use the back gate.'

Instructing the students, Dr. Anubhav left the classroom. The students had reached the bike stand when they saw dozens of media people standing behind the human barricade put up by the institute's guards. Media people tried to break through the barricade but with no success. Picking their bicycles, the students left the place, away from the media's eyeball.

'Why is the media trying to cover such a small incident? Accidents happen. What's the big deal in it?' asked Aadi in a surprise.

'It wasn't an accident. It was a suicide.' Spilling the beans, Sid continued. 'The student is dead.'

'What?' snorted Tapan. 'Why is the institute hiding this?'

'It would be stupid of them to fuel the media fire,' replied Sid.

The tender sunlight that felt good a few seconds ago was now itching. With a burning desire to light a cigarette, Harsh took the pack out. Igniting his cigarette, he asked. 'When did all this happen?'

'It happened last night. The student had earned *fuckka* twice in a mandatory subject and was about to be terminated,' shared Sid. In IITC's lingo *fuckka* stood for an F grade and it had rightly gained that alias as that grade f***ed one's career.

Belting out another detail, Sid said. 'Before killing himself, the student had googled for the easiest way to commit suicide.'

'What the hell was that?' asked Aadi, raising his eyebrows.

'Lying down on the railway track and getting killed by a train.'

Taking stock of the stunned faces around him, Sid added. 'In the wee hours, the student's body was found on the tracks, his head was chopped off.'

'Holy Shit!' With passing second, Harsh flung out the question troubling him. 'Shouldn't we tell the truth to the media?'

'No, we should not,' replied Tapan. 'Don't think anything crazy. We have our careers in front of us.'

'But, this is not fair,' said Harsh puffing harder on the cigarette.

'Harsh, you are coming with us,' said Tapan, grabbing Harsh by arm. Pulling him on his bicycle, he directed Aadi to follow.

THE TURMOIL

28th December 2005,

Aadi's room, Hall 8, IITC

IITC campus was robbed of life the very day the semester came to an end. Students took the ticket off the hectic semester schedule and went on vacation. The cursed few left in the campus had either academic obligations or had no better alternatives. Aadi, Tapan and Harsh stayed back for their own good reasons. Tapan wanted to start his research work while Aadi was running away from his past. Engaging himself, he joined the gliding club and enrolled for the professional hacking classes. Harsh had as such no convincing reason except for his 'friends should be together' mantra.

Harsh and Aadi were watching a movie on the desktop when Tapan entered the room. His face looked visibly stunned and was panting hard. After greasing his wind pipe with a bottle of water, he spoke. 'Have you guys checked your mail?'

Holding the movie on pause and turning the lights on, Aadi asked. 'What's in it?'

'I got a mail from DOAA. It appears that I ran low in grades,' said Tapan. Wiping off thin lines of sweat on his forehead, Tapan stuttered, his voice cracking. 'What ... what is going to happen now?'

'Show us the mail,' said Harsh.

After Tapan opened the mail, Harsh took over. Scrolling through the list of addressee his eyes got stuck on a name. Belting his surprise, Harsh spoke. 'Shit man! I am also in the list.'

'How can I get the low grades?' Harsh was now standing. He lit a cigarette and puffed at it twice. Bearing a sober composure, he asked. 'How can we mess up so bad?'

'Check out the mathematics marks,' suggested Aadi.

A quick check on the online academic records helped in sizing up the situation. After a brief moment of silence, Harsh spoke. 'It's all because of Mathematics.'

In a muffled tone, Tapan asked. 'How can I get a *fuckka* when I have B grade in the assignments?'

'I don't know what the shit this is,' spoke Harsh. Tapping his cigarette ashes into an empty beer can, he continued. 'Anubhav has not considered the assignment marks.'

'What should we do now?' asked Tapan, coughing briefly.

'Let's ask Dr. Mukherjee. He can guide us better,' suggested Aadi.

Dr. Mukherjee was a veteran in the Manufacturing Science lab and one of the few professors loved by his students. Aadi held Dr. Mukherjee in high regard. He not only took Aadi under his supervision but also brought Dr. Dutta as co-supervisor, accommodating Aadi's interest.

'Aadi is right. Dr. Mukherjee can suggest us something. Firstly, he chairs the counseling service. Secondly, he is a nice man by heart. If nothing else, he can at least suggest the consequences of this mail,' said Harsh.

'But, Is it right to talk to him? He is my supervisor,' asked Tapan.

'Do you guys still have second thoughts? You guys are in the damn termination list,' said Aadi, his eyebrows arched up.

'Let's do it then,' said Tapan.

Smoke found a way to escape as the door opened and the three friends moved out. Biking their way across campus, they reached Dr. Mukherjee's residence in fifteen minutes. They now sat inside with Dr. Mukherjee, sipping the orange juice. Even in the hour of despair, they had to indulge in the formalities. The orange juice glass was only half done but Tapan was done with the wait.

'Sir, what can we do now?' asked Tapan biting his finger nails in anxiety.

'Tapan, there's nothing much that you can do. The termination and the warning cases are sent to DOAA and the panel looks into each individual case,' replied Dr. Mukherjee. Switching his attention to Harsh, he asked. 'What's your CPI?'

'6.4,' replied Harsh.

Sipping the orange juice, Dr. Mukherjee continued thoughtfully. 'In the case of termination, nothing can be done but in the case of warning, if DOAA committee approves, a student can continue with the course.'

'How does DOAA committee decide on the fate of a student?' asked Harsh.

'Decision is taken based on the feedback from the student and his supervisor,' explained Dr. Mukherjee. 'As you guys have grades higher than 6, you probably have been put on warning. If reinstated, you would be required to bring the CPI above 6.5 in the following semester.'

'When will this meeting happen?' asked Harsh.

'Hopefully, this meeting should be convened within next one week,' replied Dr. Mukherjee. Reading the question loosely hung on Tapan's face, he added. 'Tapan, I will surely support you in the meeting. I am really impressed by your commitment to stay back during the recess to work on your thesis.'

Tapan nodded in a silent acknowledgement. Looking towards Harsh, Dr. Mukherjee continued. 'You should meet Dr. Subbarao. Request him to help you with this.'

'I will do it sir,' replied Harsh.

'Sir, we should be going now,' said Aadi exchanging a brief glance with others.

'My best wishes are with you. Everything is going to be fine,' consoled Dr. Mukherjee. Seeing them off at the door, he added. 'Remember that there's a world beyond this institute and besides IITC degree.'

Coming back to the hall, Aadi, Harsh and Tapan stood in silence in the open balcony while the universe around commiserated with them. The stars twinkled in the clear winter sky to bring hope to the darkness that shrouded their life now. Chilling winds blowing from the north caressed through their faces, consoling them of what went wrong. The subsequent few days were pretty hard on everyone. There were a multitude of actions that they could surmise but the DOAA meeting's decision could only be binary, and they had to await it.

3rd January 2006,

Dean of Academic Affairs (DOAA) Office, IITC

Aadi longed for his cozy blanket and the comfortable cot while he waited with Harsh and Tapan outside the DOAA office. Three hours had passed since the meeting had started. It was a freezing day with dense fog. Basking under the warmth of 100 watt bulb, Aadi sat cross legged on a sofa kept in the waiting hall of the office. Aadi stretched his legs, crossing them at the ankles. He had a very strong urge to relieve himself and could wait no longer. 'I am going for a leak,' he declared, lifting himself off the sofa.

Aadi quickly hiked to the washroom. Standing in front of the urinal, he opened his zip. He moved his finger to bring down the underpants. He got a hold when a sound alarmed him. 'Sir, we also have some respect.' Aadi turned to find a lady inside the toilet. Was he in the ladies' toilet? No, his mind retorted looking to the urinal in front of him. What then was the lady doing in the gents' toilet? In a fraction of a second, he realized that the lady was a janitor. She was in her shift to clean the toilets. Aadi zipped his pant back, apologized and came out.

'Aadi, can you wait for a minute?' Aadi was striding towards the staircase when Dr. Subbarao's voice tapped him to attention.

'I expect better things from my students.' On full throttle, Aadi raced his mind, wondering what he did wrong. He had not travelled far when Subbarao came again. 'I never thought that I need to teach you manners as well.'

Instructing Aadi to follow, Subbarao went inside the toilet.

Aadi was perplexed what Subbarao was up to. Getting inside the gents toilet, Subbarao coughed, seeking attention of the janitor. 'Can you please go outside?' he asked.

Janitor furtively exchanged a glance with Aadi. With a terse smile on her face she moved out.

'Aadi, you take the other pot.' Subbarao had already positioned himself in front of the urinal.

Aadi hesitantly positioned himself against the urinal. He tried hard but was not able to squeeze a drop out. Contriving a relieved gesture on his face, he stepped back and waited till Subbarao was done.

Subbarao took another minute to flush out his body fluid. Zipping his trouser, he walked in front of the wash basin. Next, he rinsed his hands and dashed them in the water jet. Looking behind, he spoke. 'Aadi, I didn't see you wash your hands earlier. Now also you didn't care to do that. You should maintain proper hygiene. Wash your hands.'

Aadi was speechless, dumbfound and a little shocked. He followed Subbarao out of the men's room. Exchanging a terse smile with his pee-mentor, he paced towards the DOAA office. Inadvertently, his eyes met the janitor standing outside the men's room. Aadi stole his glance away from her but could not avoid listening to the conspicuous giggle, which added to his embarrassment.

Avoiding further troubles, Aadi didn't look back till he reached the DOAA office. He waited anxiously for Subbarao to get back to his office. As soon as Subbarao vanished from his sight, Aadi turned his feet back towards the restroom. 'Hey Aadi, I think the DOAA meeting is over. It was Harsh's voice that held him back.

Aadi walked towards Harsh as the door to the meeting room cracked open. Coming out of the conclave, a professor in the committee handed a paper to the clerk. Continuing the discussion, he walked out of office along with other members in the committee. It was Tapan's face, wrapped up in worries that warranted some attention. 'What's your name?' asked the professor.

'Tapan Shreiy'

'Go and prepare for registering yourself,' said the professor with a smile on his face.

'Are you sure sir?' asked Tapan.

'I was chairing the meeting,' replied the professor tapping on Tapan's shoulder.

Tapan's face was now filled with joy. He was all smiles when Harsh came to his side. 'Congrats dude,' said Harsh giving a hug. Looking towards the notice board, he said. 'Pray for me brother.'

'You will get through,' said Tapan.

'They are pasting something. Must be the circular,' said Aadi pointing in the direction of the notice board.

'Let's see!' Harsh rushed to the board but before he could have reached, it was already crowded. Struggling his way through, Harsh screened through the notice. 'I am in,' he cried out aloud.

"Can you check my name as well?' asked Tapan.

'You are also in. I can see your name,' replied Harsh.

'I knew nothing can go wrong,' said Aadi taking Tapan in a hug. If Tapan's lacrimal glands were stimulated, Aadi's rectum was ready to explode. Before a downpour could have taken over the upbeat mood, Aadi said coming out of the hug. 'I can't hold it back now.'

"What happened?' asked Harsh.

'I need to go pee.'

'Going by the frequency with which you are relieving yourself it seems as if you haven't urinated for years,' said Harsh cracking in peals of laughter.

'My emotions have found a different exit route. Now please don't hold me back,' said Aadi rushing towards the restroom.

Second Semester

A FRESH BEGINNING

9ᵗʰ January 2006,

Computation Fluid Dynamics (CFD) Lecture, LHC, IITC

On Dec 17 1903, the two brothers from Dayton, Ohio flew an air machine over the beach at Kittyhawk in North Carolina. The flight that lasted for more than a minute allayed the skepticism over the heavier-than-air human flight.

For several years, people across the world have been trying to defy the gravity and build a machine that could fly. But it wasn't turning out to be that easy. Nonetheless, Wilbur and Oliver after a long period of trial and error have found a formula that seems to work. The Wrights have been secretly working for several years using models and the wind tunnel designed by them. The successful first flight by the brothers is the start of a transport revolution. Their invention holds potential to make the world in many ways a much smaller and accessible place.

'You just saw the first controlled flight that shook the world,' said Dr. Anubhav killing the *YouTube* video. Strolling like a caged lion, he continued. 'It was after this event that scientists all across the world started studying aerodynamics with a practical orientation.'

All heads in the room followed Dr. Anubhav as he marched past the blackboard and stopped at the other end. 'Before we start with the lecture, I would like to talk about the term project for the course. Do I have your ears?' asked Dr. Anubhav.

Gathering the attention of every mite sitting in the classroom, he continued. 'For the term project, you need to simulate an aircraft model. I will teach you the theory and the software that you are going to use for the project.'

Dr. Anubhav searched for something deep down in his pocket. Picking from tail, he pulled out a frozen and wadded hanky. 'Am I sounding bells?' asked Dr. Anubhav as he blew his nose out in the hanky already dead with cold.

The class was silent as if in terror.

'You all have my ears. I am waiting for your answer.'

'Yes.' Combined acknowledgement of the students in the CFD course reverberated through the silence in the classroom.

Adjusting the spectacle on his nose, Dr. Anubhav said. 'The term project will be done in teams of two.' Interrupting him, a student safely placed at the rear corner of the classroom asked. 'Can we choose our partner?'

'No, I will not leave the choice with you guys. This term project doesn't need the comfort of friendship.' Dr. Anubhav sniffed his damp nostrils harder as he continued. 'Do you buy it?'

The class acknowledged the same with silence.

'I will randomly compose teams of two and mail you the details. Also, I will mail you the details of the problem and the underlying assumptions.' Dr. Anubhav explained the term project briefly and then started with the lecture. The one hour lecture turned out to be a marathon. Students came out of the classroom half asleep and bored. Completing their first half day of schedule, Aadi, Harsh and Tapan came back to the hall.

Shoving the bag off his shoulder, Aadi trashed it on the cot. Picking the water bottle, he flushed his throat and retired on the recliner chair. Heaving a deep breath, he asked. 'Harsh, are you not taking Mathematics?'

'This semester I will just concentrate on increasing my academic score. I will pick it up later,' answered Harsh sitting in front of the desktop.

'I have the same plan. This semester is just for building CPI,' said Tapan easing himself on the cot.

Harsh opened his mail box and skimmed through the mails.

Once done, he turned to face Aadi. 'What's going on with your hacking classes?' he asked.

'I got the certification,' replied Aadi.

'So, how much did you learn?' enquired Harsh.

'I can easily hack a server with level 2 security,' replied Aadi, his chest filled with pride. 'I tried once to hack IITC's server but didn't succeed. The security system here is quite complex. I will need some more time to crack it.'

'Don't stretch your luck too far. You never know when you run out of it,' suggested Harsh.

Avoiding further discussion on the topic, Aadi asked. 'Harsh, what exactly do we need to do in the term project?'

'We need to simulate an aircraft model in the software. Further, we need to test our design for its aerodynamics,' replied Harsh.

'Can we design an aircraft in a semester's time?' asked Aadi, gazing at Harsh with probing distrust.

'Designing an aircraft would not be easy but believe me; we are going to have fun.' Diving in his own ecstasy, Harsh continued empathically. 'The aircraft is one of the greatest inventions that have changed the course of human history. The world ...'

'You know too much about the aircrafts.' Aadi tried to put a lid but rush of Harsh's enthusiasm blew it off. 'The world would not have been the same if Hitler had used jet powered fighter aircrafts early in the Second World War.' Before Harsh could have propelled further, Aadi turned the sail. 'What are the design considerations?'

'There are about ten constraints that our design needs to honor. Given the constraints, we need to ensure that our simulated model actually flies. Anubhav has also given the list of software that we can use for simulation.' With a conspicuous smile on his face, Harsh added. 'Isn't it luck? You and I have been put together as a team.'

'That's great!'

'Leave it guys. Class is over,' grumbled Tapan. Hauling his ass off the bed, he asked. 'Aadi, where were you early in the morning? I was looking for you.'

'I had gone for gliding,' replied Aadi. Picking a cupcake from his desk drawer, he munched at it before continuing. 'You guys should also come with me. It's a really nice sport.'

'One day,' said Harsh smiling.

'How does it feel when you are airborne?' asked Tapan.

'It felt nauseating during the first few flights but now I have started enjoying the adrenalin rush.' Taking another bite, Aadi continued. 'Flying was one of my fantasies since childhood.'

'Childhood fantasies are real funny.' Picking up from where Aadi had left, Tapan continued with a gleam in his eyes. 'When I was a kid, I used to think that a plane flaps its wings to fly, just like birds.'

'And when did you see a plane flapping its wings?' snapped Harsh.

Before Tapan could have explained, Aadi said, picking on him. 'How could he have seen it? After all, the plane flies too high for him to notice.'

'It makes perfect sense. Now I understand why passengers are asked to buckle up.' Harsh waited for the cannonades of laughter around him to die down before asking. 'But how does the plane take off?'

'By flapping its wings, you idiot,' snapped Aadi.

'If you guys are so intelligent then why don't you design your own aircraft? Why the hell are you picking on me?' Exchanging a hard glance with Aadi, Tapan walked out, slamming the door behind him. He had not gone far when the room erupted in bouts of laughter.

15th January 2006, 6 A.M.

Airstrip, IITC

Aadi felt a shot of adrenalin rush as he stepped towards the glider. Every time he was about to board the flight, he felt nausea. He suspected whether the wings had sufficient strength to last the ride. The cloth wrapping the frame was never taut enough to uphold his faith. Nothing about the glider could allay his fears but he always came back determined for a flight.

Aadi's fear was not all unwarranted. Anyone would have felt the same about a small plane with one wheel to its stand. A person was required to hold the wing horizontal before the glider could sprint on the runway. Without an engine, the glider relied on the winch for its lift.

Aadi got into the pilot seat and the Captain occupied the seat behind. As the glider was meant for training, the rear seat had the overriding controls. As they locked their safety belts, the staff went through the standard pre-flight protocols. All the potential sources of accidents had been weaned out. The motor for powering the glider had a dry run to look in for fallacies. One of the staff engaged the locking head of the steel cable to the open hook beneath the glider's throat.

'Aadi, lock the hook now,' instructed the Captain. Once Aadi completed the orders, the Captain spoke into his walkie talkie. 'Mishraji remove the slack.'

The winch operator on the other side of the runway connected the clutch with the rotating spindle of the motor. The power from the motor got transmitted through the mechanical linkages to the cable drum held between fixtures. Spinning on its axle, the cable drum removed the slack in the steel cable connected to the glider. Taut, the cable vibrated in tension. Adhering to the instruction, the operator disengaged the clutch and retorted back on walkie talkie. 'Done'

'Mishraji, give us the launching power,' instructed the Captain.

Once again the winch operator engaged the clutch to the motor. The steel cable started winding up on the cable drum, pulling the glider by its throat. With each passing second the glider gained momentum. The captain pulled back the joystick. The pull further got transmitted by the mechanical linkages to the elevators, flapping its trailing edge upwards. The relative motion of the air above and below the wings provided the required lift and the glider got airborne.

The brain started pumping epinephrine followed by serotonin in the veins. The turbulence which resulted in wings vibrating in different modes stabilized with the ascent. The glider had gained an altitude of 800 feet when Captain instructed Aadi to disengage glider from the winch.

Disengaging the glider, Aadi took a panoramic view of the campus. He was trying to figure out his hall when the joystick moved to his left. He realized that captain had taken the overriding control. 'To take a turn you need to use the rudder together with the ailerons. Once you have coordinated the turn, you should come out of the roll while simultaneously applying rudder to counteract the resultant adverse yaw,' instructed the Captain.

'I am going to show you some aerobatics. We will go in a spin, will toss our glider upside down.' After speaking about the objective, the Captain filled in a word of caution. 'Spin can be dangerous. If you don't come out of it early, it may result in a disaster.'

Giving a positive right push on the joystick, the Captain rolled the glider to his right. A slight push on the joystick to the front brought the nose of the glider down. Thin lines of sweat trickled down Aadi's temple as the glider went into a spin. Aadi tried to wipe off any mark of fear from his face but suddenly his hand felt heavier. It felt as though lead had been pumped through his veins. He had to muster full strength to jack up his hand.

Coming out of the spin, the Captain stabilized the glider and now cruised smoothly. 'What you experienced was because of negative 'g'. Negative gravity field forces the blood out of the brain, resulting in markedly slow sensory response.'

The glider was hovering over the tarmac at a very low altitude when Aadi asked. 'Can we reduce the rate of descent?'

'I don't think so,' replied the Captain. Explaining to Aadi, he continued. 'The rate of descend translates to the speed for an unpowered glider. Below a critical speed, the glider goes into a stall.'

'What's the minimum cruise speed for our glider?' asked Aadi, stealing a gaze at the air speed indicator.

'40 knots, i.e. 74 kilometers per hour,' replied the Captain. Signaling Aadi to take a look at the altimeter, he continued. 'Now we should prepare for a landing. It's not advisable to continue flying once you have come down to an altitude below 400 feet.'

'You have the controls now. I will instruct you for the final descent.' Relaxing his hands on the controls, the Captain spoke. 'Aadi, you need to push the left rudder and move the joystick to your left.'

Aadi followed the instruction closely.

'Good, that's it. Now get out of the bank and kill the yaw.' Making it simple for Aadi to follow, he continued. 'Bring back the joystick to its neutral position, release the left rudder while picking up a bit on the right one.'

Aadi accomplished the task of heading the glider onto the air strip. Now he had full length of runway in front of him.

Once the nose of glider was aligned with the airstrip, the Captain instructed. 'Now move the joystick ahead, but do it gradually and slowly.'

The glider flew just a few feet above the ground. One more push on the joystick and the tyres were ready to kiss the tarmac.

'The glider now is no more than one feet above the ground. Pull the nose slightly up,' said the Captain.

Following the instructions closely, Aadi successfully landed the glider. Bringing it to a halt, he came out of the cockpit. On cue from the Captain a jeep rolled on the airstrip, towards the glider. Sitting inside the jeep, Captain extended his hand to Aadi.

After a formal handshake, Aadi asked. 'Sir, when can we have the next gliding class?'

'Gliding club is open throughout the semester. You can join us during our regular morning classes,' replied the Captain. Exchanging a warm smile, he signaled the driver to fire the engine.

Completing his gliding session, Aadi cycled down the street. In the cold Cawnpore morning his teeth chattered in their own rhythm. The smell of caffeine and the bon fire in front of a shop on the hostel road held him back. It was a T junction, where one arm of the road ran to hostels and other meandered to *Naankari* village. Aadi sat on a bench lying in front of a rustic tea shop. Commonly known as TIC (Tata Inter Continental), the shop was no way close to its name. Ordering a tea, Aadi reeled back his gliding experiences. Flying high, his thoughts drifted into the past. A smile sprouted on his face as he recalled the idea of the plane flapping its wings to fly.

'Isn't that possible?' thought Aadi. Pulling out his copy and pen, he sketched on it furtively. A wide smile spread across his face as he placed his notebook back in the bag and said to himself 'Flymoto'.

INCEPTION

28ᵗʰ January 2006,

Library, IITC

Sitting in the institute's library Aadi flipped through the pages of the journal on the flying car. The sun had long gone to sleep. The tube light above his head fell in spasm of flicks, pleading for some rest. His mobile flicked on when the tube light above flicked off. Receiving the call, he got interfaced to Tapan.

'Hey Aadi, are you done with your studies?' asked Tapan.

'Yeah most of it, I will come to the hall after some time.'

'Actually, we were planning to go to NASA. Would you like to join us?'

'I have some work at ShopC,' replied Aadi.

'Complete your work and come directly to the Insti gate. I will be waiting for you there with Sid and Harsh,' said Tapan.

Aadi switched the call off and, at the same instant, the tube light above him flicked on. Completing his work at ShopC, Aadi picked the main drive. Blood line of the institute's traffic, the main drive connected it to the outside city. The road ended in a T junction with its head butt against the national highway. On both sides of the national highway were grocery shops, photo studios, *theeke, dhabee* and myriads of shops selling myriads of things.

With the arsenal of four beer bottles, chicken kabab, peanuts and cold drinks, the group landed at NASA, the terrace of an abandoned building in front of the institute's gate.

Settling himself on the makeshift brick chair, Harsh opened

a bottle. Looking around, he said. 'This is the best place in the whole campus. Being surrounded by chaos and yet at ease is something that appeals to me.'

'Aadi, would you like to have beer?' asked Harsh frisking through the cellophane bag that he carried.

'Yeah, I can have one.'

Raising his bottle, Harsh said. 'Cheers to our friendship!' Bottles rubbed their shoulders and the liquid started its journey sating the thirst and finally mixing with the blood stream.

It's intriguing to see how people change with alcohol soaring in their veins. Inhibitions vanish into thin air. After gulping half of the beer, it was Aadi talking. 'What are we trying to accomplish in our lives? A mere degree to get us a good job. I feel ashamed that I am still a virgin. Look at Sid; he is at least trying to get rid of his virginity.'

'Virginity is a curse.' Lifting a leg piece, Harsh picked on Sid. 'What are your chances to get rid of your virginity this time?'

'Better than the chances I had with all my ex-girlfriends combined.' Catching the peanut thrown at him, Sid whacked his tongue.

'Are you going to marry your girlfriend?' asked Tapan.

'No,' replied Sid. Stuffing the last stock of nut in his mouth, he continued. 'There's a huge bounty on my head. I can't risk that.'

'How much dowry would you get?' asked Harsh, chewing noisily.

'Should be around two crores,' replied Sid.

'Two crores! That's awesome man,' said Aadi, stretching the last words. 'What will you do with all this money?' he asked with a fervent voice.

'I will join my family business,' replied Sid.

'Being self-employed is a bliss,' said Aadi, his eyes had a sparkle in them and an exuberant smile stretched across his face.

'It's also a big responsibility,' added Harsh.

'True,' sighed Aadi. A minute would have passed when he asked suddenly. 'Will you guys help me to prototype a concept?'

'What's the idea?' asked Tapan.

'Don't bore me guys. We came here to booze. Don't spoil the mood.' Sid emptied the beer bottle into his stomach. Throwing away the exhausted bottle, he asked. 'Is anyone in the mood for an ice-cream? I have a craving for 'Death by chocolate'.'

'Count me in,' said Harsh raising his hand.

'Come with me then,' said Sid standing up. Harsh and Sid rushed down the staircase while Aadi followed them along with Tapan.

'I am having death by chocolate and I am not sharing with you guys,' said Sid placing his order.

'I will have an ice-cream cone,' said Tapan.

'Me too,' added Harsh.

'Me three,' said Aadi.

Within minutes the order was ready. The conversation froze as ice-cream melted more on the hands than in the mouth. After a moment, Aadi spoke. 'I think there is some chemistry brewing between Tapan and Jaswinder.'

'That's the reason for the ice-cream cone. Is her choice vanilla or strawberry?' asked Sid impishly.

'If you are not dead by chocolate, I am going to kill you,' said Tapan clinching his teeth. Fuming, he went back licking his ice-cream cone.

Aadi smiled seeing Tapan compassionately eating his ice-cream. The pleasure on Tapan's face didn't last long. Bearing a nasty expression, Tapan said, staring sharply at his ice-cream. 'I think there's something wrong with my ice-cream.'

'Let me have a look.' Picking up the cone from Tapan, Aadi scratched the surface of the spot and exclaimed out aloud. 'Oh Shit! There is some sort of scrap in your ice-cream.' Pulling out the metal piece, he asked. 'Did you hurt yourself?'

'No, I am fine,' answered Tapan licking his hand.

'You come with me,' said Aadi. He race walked while Tapan followed him to the ice-cream shop.

'What is this?' Aadi bumped his fist on the counter. The ice-cream exchanged hands and now the shop owner was taking a look on the prima facie.

'Bhaiya, you can take another ice-cream,' said the shop owner completing his inspection.

'Okay, so what are you offering in your ice-cream this time? Something more deadly to score an instant kill,' barked Aadi.

'You are getting it wrong. This is not my fault. I had opened this stock in front of you only.'

'If this is not your fault then throw away the whole batch of product.'

'But, sir,' stuttered the shop owner.

'Discharge all the stock of this batch number from your shop. I want this whole lot to be thrown away, immediately,' asserted Aadi.

'You have said enough. We are not throwing anything. We have business to do,' said the shop owner slashing an authoritative tone, his moustache danced with his words.

'You are responsible for the product that is sold in your shop. You need to dispose of this lot,' insisted Aadi.

'We can't do this. This is not our product, this is *Yummylick* brand. We can't throw the whole lot but we can replace the one you have.'

'Let's leave Aadi,' said Tapan slipping his hand on Aadi's shoulder.

'No, I am not planning to leave.' Aadi switched his attention from Tapan to the shop owner as he spoke. 'Give back the piece of shit that I gave you.'

Picking up the ice-cream cone, Aadi came out.

'What are you up to? Let's leave this place. These things happen,' said Tapan shoving Aadi.

'I can't turn a blind eye to this,' snapped Aadi.

'What are you planning to do?' asked Harsh.

'I am dialing the customer care.' Aadi stripped the ice-cream cone and was now holding its cover. Reading through it, he picked the contact number of the customer care and placed a call.

'Hello, this is Sanya speaking. You are connected to customer care service of *Yummylick*. How may I assist you today?' came a soft voice from the other end.

'I am speaking from IIT Cawnpore. I am a student here and for my dessert, I was having a piece of death manufactured in your premises.'

'Sir, I couldn't understand you. Can you please repeat?'

'I got a metal scrap in *Yummylick's* ice-cream. I can't understand how this kind of mistake can happen in your quality product, when millions and millions of dollars are spent on commercials claiming '*Yummylick* - The toast of India ... synonym of purity'. How can your product pass the six sigma level, the de facto standard, when I get a piece of death from your product?'

'Sir, we regret the mistake.'

'What if I had been a victim of your product? I want an immediate and affirmative response for this gross negligence of quality standard in your product.'

'Sir, we will look into this issue immediately.'

'I want this whole lot to be immediately evacuated from the market, otherwise I will be seeking a legal recourse and this whole mess shall cascade to a big blot on the national brand name '*Yummylick*'. I am sure you don't want this whole affair to stretch so far.'

'Sir, I have noted down your complaint and we will get back to you within half an hour.'

'You better do. And yes, give me the complaint number.' After jotting down the number, Aadi hung up the call but the rhetoric had left every neck in the vicinity twisted in his direction.

'Aadi, let's leave. You have registered your complaint,' said Tapan pulling Aadi by his arm.

'I am not going to spare these guys,' said Aadi as the group left the shop.

Reaching his room, Aadi fired a mail to the company's top brass. He was planning to retire in his bed when a call from GM of the company took him by surprise. Within half hour the regional salesperson was there to remove the particular lot from the shop. The regional salesperson and the shop owner made a visit to Aadi's room in their effort to tie a piece of accord with a universal sorry. This time the voice of the shop owner had come back to the normal decibel levels. Collecting the photograph of the metal scrap, both of them left the room to let Aadi have a peaceful sleep.

10ᵗʰ February 2006,

Aadi's Room, Hall8, IITC

'Put the approximations correctly.' Harsh turned back his chair to face Aadi. Lighting his cigarette, he continued. 'We should first design an aircraft body with optimum volume to mass ratio. It's after that we should think about wings.'

Aadi and Harsh were lucky to be clubbed together for the CFD assignment. Heeding to the lesson learnt from the last semester, they started early on the assignment. The room was filled with smoke from the burning cigarette and brains smouldering over the problem. Supporting his spine on the toss pillow kept on the cot, Aadi asked. 'Where will we get the fluid properties?'

'I have those on my lappy,' said Harsh dragging his chair to the desk. 'I have already googled for that.' With books, notes, hair comb, water bottle, coins and pens struggling for breathing space, the desk looked no less than epicenter of an earthquake. Harsh dashed the books thrown on his desk to one side and revived his laptop.

'This place is burning. Harsh, can't you kill the smoke?' asked Aadi.

Extinguishing his cigarette, Harsh asked. 'Is everything alright? You look annoyed.'

'It's usual. Lab Stuff,' replied Aadi pensively. Exchanging a brief glance with Harsh, he continued. 'Will you help me prototype a concept?'

'What's that you want to do?'

On a low note, Aadi spoke. 'I want to build a flying car prototype.'

'Flying car is too optimistic a project. It has been in research for quite long without any success. It's going to be tough,' warned

Harsh. He stood musing for a while, before continuing. 'Why don't you talk to Dr. Dutta?'

'This project will require a collaborative effort. I can't handle everything on my own,' explained Aadi.

'So,' shrugged Harsh. 'Do you think Dr. Dutta can't get you a team?'

'I was thinking if Tapan and you can join me for the project,' proposed Aadi, his voice slurring.

'Aadi, we are already running low on grades. It would not be wise for us to neglect our studies,' explained Harsh. With an urge to smoke he took a cigarette out.

'I understand that,' said Aadi, heaving a sigh.

'You talk to Dr. Dutta,' said Harsh. Lighting up the cigarette, he continued. 'We will talk about it if nothing works out.'

A kindle of hope was enough to fuel the dream. Beaming with delight, Aadi said. 'That's now like a friend.'

Picking up the discussion from where he had left, Harsh said. 'We need to consider all the assumptions. We need to realistically account for the losses ...' Harsh was not able complete his talk when the door to Aadi's room swung open and Sid lurched forward. The strap on his slippers got hooked up in the door's foot rest and he tripped himself forward. Finally taking the support of cot lying ahead he killed the momentum. 'What's up guys?' Sid asked steadying himself.

'Ceiling,' replied Aadi curtly.

Smiling briefly, Sid asked. 'I hope I didn't disturb you guys.'

'Not at all, what brings you here?' asked Aadi.

'Can you translate a word for me in Hindi?' asked Sid. He now stood in front of the wardrobe mirror, hand combing his hair.

'What's the word?' asked Aadi.

With an inquisitive expression spread across his face, Sid asked. 'Assume someone is standing at Harsh's place. What would be the word in Hindi to call him to my place?'

'*Yahan aaooo,*' replied Aadi.

'And what if I want him to go back to Harsh's place?' asked Sid pointing to Harsh who now relaxed on a chair.

'You yourself go to Harsh's place and say '*Yahan aaoo*',' replied Aadi.

'Don't try to make a fool of me,' said Sid. Looking towards Harsh, he asked. 'Can you answer me honestly?'

'You will say '*wahan jaoo*',' replied Harsh.

'Thanks a lot friend. I will take your leave now,' said Sid rewinding his steps to the door.

'Where are you moving?' asked Harsh.

Sid quickly stole a glance at his wrist watch and then spoke. 'I am going to SAC.'

'What's at SAC?' asked Harsh.

'I am sitting in the relay hunger strike.' Taking stock of the faces around him, Sid said amusingly. 'Prop up my morale dude.'

'What are you protesting against?' asked Harsh.

'I am not aware of it.' Clearing the clouds of doubts, Sid poured down his clarification. 'I didn't want to let my girlfriend down. She has asked me to join the relay hunger strike.'

'Side effects of having a girlfriend,' shrugged Harsh.

Once Sid rushed out of the room, Harsh turned to Aadi. Taking a deep puff of the cigarette, he spoke. 'Why are you fucking the poor guy?'

'It's just my own private little entertainment with Sid,' said Aadi smiling.

Harsh shrugged his shoulder and belched out a plume of smoke from his mouth. The ribbons of smoke enlarged as they climbed high in the room. Aadi's hope too had ballooned up. After Harsh left the room, he got down to plan his next set of tasks to bring his dream to fruition. Whatever be the price, Aadi was determined to work on the idea that had stolen the sleep of his nights.

9th March 2006,

Sid's room, Hall8, IITC

'Hey get up. Go to the function, why the hell are you sleeping at this hour of the day?' said Sid shoving Harsh sleeping on his bed.

Slipping his foot inside the shoes, he now stood in front of the mirror combing his hair.

'Are you going somewhere?' asked Harsh, his eyes still drowned in the dream world.

'Yeah, I am going to the city,' replied Sid.

'Are you going to miss the party?' asked Harsh opening his eyes.

'I will return in two hours. I am just going for a dental appointment.' Moving his tongue on the decaying tooth stubbed in his mouth, Sid continued. 'I hate this root filling stuff.'

Sid pulled out the medical history of his tooth and stuffed it into his open bag. Zipping its mouth, he opened his. 'Did you invite your supervisor?'

'I did invite Subbarao. Courting him would be like hell,' spurted Harsh.

'You should be out in the ground. Guests have already started arriving.'

'Yeah, I will be going out in another ten minutes. I will just catch a quick nap,' said Harsh, pulling the blanket over his face.

'Alright, I am moving then. Keys are kept on the desk. Lock the room and keep the keys with you,' said Sid moving out for his appointment with the dentist.

The hall day was an annual function that every Hall celebrated. It was now Hall8's turn to celebrate. Festooned with flowers, paper streamers and fairy lights the hall was decorated profusely, like a venue for some grand wedding reception. Under the roof of a huge shamiana at one corner of the ground, a lavish buffet was arranged. A stage with a big bass audio system was set for hosting the events by the hall residents.

The evening was bubbling with excitement. After serving dance performances and plays as an appetizer, guests were treated to a sumptuous dinner. On the ground of Hall 8, the celebrations may have lasted only a few hours but on the turf of guests' memory it successfully made a lasting impression. After guests left the ground, the stage was converted to a dance floor. The big bass audio system now played rocks.

Completing their dinner, Tapan and Aadi burped in one corner of the ground. They were enjoying the music when someone tapped them to attention. 'The party is awesome.' It was Jaswinder, hiding her 'size zero–difference', 38-38-38 figure beneath her baggy clothes. An old SLR stuck between her bosoms struggled for breathing space. The only jewel that adorned her perfect body was an orthodontic brace gleaming in the dim light on the ground.

'It's great that you are enjoying the party. Is someone with you?' asked Tapan.

'I am with my friend Sonia.' Comprehending the complaints on everyone's face, Jaswinder continued. 'I will introduce her to you guys once I get a chance.'

'When will that happen?' asked Aadi.

'Have patience,' replied Jaswinder.

Jaswinder quickly twisted around to take stock of the party. The camera in her neck swung like a pendulum between her ample breasts. In an excited tone, she said. 'I am going on the dance floor. Will catch up later.'

Minutes after Jaswinder had left, Harsh walked in with Sid. 'Weren't you guys missing me? See how your faces have turned pale.'

'Where have you been? Subbarao waited for you before he left with Mukherjee sir. This would have been quite embarrassing for him,' growled Tapan.

'I was sleeping in Sid's room,' replied Harsh.

'Be more responsible Harsh,' said Tapan, belching out an indecent burp. Before he could have continued, Harsh interrupted. 'I can't take your verbal beating. There's already a battle going on in my stomach.'

'He can't ever be serious,' grinned Sid.

'I will go and get something for myself.' Holding his belly which now rumbled aloud in protest, Harsh asked. 'Sid, are you coming with me?'

'I can't have food,' replied Sid easing a hand on the cheek that covered the ailing tooth.

'What happened to your tooth?' asked Tapan.

'I got root canaling done on my tooth today. I need to go to the dentist once more for filling the cavity he created,' replied Sid.

'You can at least give me the company,' said Harsh pulling Sid with him.

Aadi and Tapan strolled to the row of chairs kept in front of the dance floor. Settling himself on a chair, Tapan asked. 'Aadi, did Dutta sir talk to you?'

Aadi's eyes were glued on the dance floor as he replied. 'Yeah, I got a chance to interact with Dutta sir. He mentioned about his one year leave.'

'What about your thesis?' asked Tapan.

Exchanging a quick glance with Tapan, Aadi replied. 'Mukherjee sir has put me under Subbarao's co-supervision.'

'How can Subbarao help you with the flying car project?' asked Tapan.

'I am not sure but Mukherjee sir has promised to help me with this,' replied Aadi, his voice trailing off. Tapan didn't realize when he lost Aadi from the conversation. Cruising alone, Tapan continued. 'Subbu's lectures have been a freeway pass from one ear to the other. A freeway pass, which never got taxed in the brain.'

Oblivious to the world around him, Aadi admired the beauty on the floor. Time seemed to have come to a halt. Minutes flew past without leaving a trail on his eyes which didn't even blink to leave the floor. He was charmed when someone tapped on his shoulder. 'Stop craning.' Aadi turned back to find Harsh standing in front of him with an ice-cream cone in his hand. Before he could have defended, Harsh asked. 'Who is the lady whom you want to steal away?' Clearing the doubts, Harsh continued. 'Boss, I am observing you since I came.'

'The girl in red,' replied Aadi, pointing to a girl on the dance floor.

'She looks nice,' said Tapan after closely inspecting the subject. Easing his hand on Aadi's shoulder, Tapan continued with a big smile on his face. 'So our Aadi is smitten by a beauty.'

'It's not like that. I was just admiring her. She looks great.'

'Stop fooling around. Go and talk to the girl,' said Harsh licking the ice-cream that dripped all over his hand.

'Are you sure?'

Harsh said nothing but smiled.

'Can you help me with this?' asked Aadi.

'Go and talk to her.' Harsh threw the cone to one side and rubbed his hands on his pants. Grabbing by arm, Harsh pulled Aadi up from his chair. 'I can't, it's not the correct time to do it,' resisted Aadi.

'Do you guys want to hear a song?' asked Harsh leaving Aadi from his grip.

Before anyone could have answered, Harsh slipped his way to the stage. Asking for D.J. to stop playing music Harsh took the charge and made an announcement. 'Friends, we have someone here lovesick by a beauty. Wouldn't you guys like to hear what he has in his mind? What are the thoughts that a young lover goes through?'

The crowd of students roared up as Harsh thumped his palm on the mike. 'I would like to call upon Aadi to express his feelings for the lady he is in love with.'

'What the fuck is he doing? I am not going anywhere. Ask him to come down and end this stupidity.' Perplexed with what Harsh was up to, Aadi stood up from his chair and started walking out of the ground.

'Aadi, listen to me.' Harsh jumped from the stage and came running towards Aadi. 'This is the time to bring back love into your life.' Holding Aadi's hand, he continued. 'Just think that you are proposing to Sakshi and do it. The girl will be yours.'

'I had asked for the help, not for the troubles,' grumbled Aadi.

'I am helping you dude.'

'Harsh but...,' said Aadi.

'No but. You better keep your mouth shut. Don't speak here but on the stage,' said Harsh pushing Aadi.

'Harsh, this is not the time.'

'There can't be a time better than this to express your feelings.'

Pushing Aadi on the stage, Harsh came back to his seat. He had settled comfortably on the chair when Tapan enquired. 'What the hell was that?'

'You just see the drama,' replied Harsh with a conspicuous smile on his face.

With the mike in his hand, Aadi stood numb, looking down at the ground. The crowd which had fell silent a minute before was now sending across a wave of murmur. Harsh was almost sitting on the edge of his seat, when Aadi spoke, his voice corny. 'I never have been good at words but there's a song that comes straight from my heart.' Taxing a brief pause, he added. 'I dedicate this song to the most beautiful girl that I have ever seen.'

'Make a wish and rock your stars,' a genie said walking out of his black car
He puffed at cigarette as I plead. 'It's the lady in red all that I need'
Before I could blink, the genie disappeared, putting a few words in my ears
'Your wish is on me but this I can't do. Behind me, you are in the queue'

The crowd roared in applause as Aadi finished his song. 'Mr. D.J. can you play a song for me?' After receiving a nod of approval from the D.J., Aadi continued. 'The song is 'lady in red'.'

Lights on the floor relaxed as D.J. meandered to a soft melody. Cheering Aadi, others also joined him on the dance floor. Aadi expected 'lady in red' to turn up but was surprised to find Jaswinder near to him. 'Would you like to dance with me?' asked Jaswinder.

'Sure,' replied Aadi. A few minutes would have passed when Jaswinder said with a conspiratorial wink. 'It's only Sonia in the party who is wearing a red dress.'

'What?' Aadi's face cheered up. Bringing himself together, he said. 'That's great then. Introduce me to her.'

'Don't be so excited,' said Jaswinder looking around. 'Wait! I will just pick up something for myself to drink.'

Jaswinder walked briskly down the dance floor. Aadi was all blushes when Sid joined him. Soaked in sweat, his white formal shirt licked his body. 'With these hot girls on the floor, mercury is not the only thing that is rising,' said Sid with a playful smile. Pointing to a lady, he continued. 'It seems as if she has got antigravity breasts. They are bellowing just like pennants perched on a fortress.'

Jaswinder was a split second too early. With anger on her face and her breasts sagged down to the ground she looked straight into Sid's eyes, the moment frozen and pregnant in nature. Sid stood paralyzed in his last dancing posture. '*Chappak!*' The sound of the tight slap died in the noise of discotheque but it reverberated hard in Sid's ears.

'You are such a sleazy scoundrel,' bawled Jaswinder. Stomping angrily on the floor, she left the party.

Once Jaswinder was out of the sight, Aadi put a comforting hand around Sid. Coming out of his momentary stupor, Sid slipped his hand on the cheek, hiding the imprint of slender hand. His cheeks burned like fire. He had another appointment with the dentist but that probably was not required now. With the slap Sid swallowed the tooth that he got treated a few hours ago. Looking towards Aadi, he said. 'Let's get in the room.'

AWAKEN THE GIANT WITHIN

7th April 2006, 5:30 A.M.

Airstrip, IITC

Harsh and Tapan stood at one end of the runway watching the preparations for the first gliding session of the day. Yawning, they cursed Aadi who had dragged them early in the morning to the airstrip.

Unaware of what went on outside, Aadi tested the rudder and the joystick sitting inside the cockpit. The Captain stood outside, still not sure if he should be flying that day. A crosswind during the morning hours was never welcome. It made the air heavy and also created problems during takeoff and landing. Betting against the odds, the Captain decided to fly. Accommodating himself in the rear seat, he closed the cockpit.

'Mishraji, give us the launching power,' the Captain retorted on the walkie talkie.

Everything in the surrounding sped past as the glider started rolling on the tarmac. Leveraging upon the power transferred from the motorized winch, the glider gained speed. After it had covered about half of the air strip, Aadi pulled back the joystick. Rocking heavily, the glider got airborne. As it climbed in the air, the turbulence subsided and the ride turned smooth.

'Aoounchu,' Aadi sneezed, his hand firm on the joystick.

'Today was not the day for taking the glider off,' said the Captain on the walkie talkie.

'Aadi, don't try your hands at the controls,' instructed the

Captain. 'The air is heavy and I don't think we can gain enough height to do some stuff. We will land immediately after we leave the winch.'

Cutting the speed further, crosswinds pushed the glider off the runway. With the steel cable at the helm, the glider swayed in the air. For the first time in his entire experience with flying, Aadi felt like a kite left at the mercy of the winds.

The glider had not even gained more than 200 feet when, with a sudden thud, its nose bowed down. The steel cable that gave the launch power now pulled it towards the ground.

'Aadi, disengage from the launch cable. It's broken,' yelled the Captain.

Aadi disengaged the launch cable but the glider had already left the airstrip and crossed the boundary wall of IITC. Beyond the boundary wall were paddy fields with a national highway running across them. Motorized vehicles plied speedily on the highway, unaware of what went on above in the skies.

'Hold yourself tight!' The Captain steadied himself and then seized the control of the glider. Maneuvering the aircraft for a full circle turn, the Captain whispered. 'God save us.'

The glider lost many feet while taking a complete turn. It was now headed straight towards the air strip but didn't have sufficient height to make it to the tarmac. The Captain took a call and prepared for a hard landing on the ground. Opening the flaps, he flared out to decrease the speed. With a shudder, the glider plunged to the ground. The Captain pushed the joystick forward and the glider made its contact with the ground. The brake plate mounted below the nose of the glider came alive, scratching the ground's head and screeching high on its volume.

The glider was now slipping under its own momentum. Inside the cockpit, Aadi and the Captain held on tightly to their seats. A sudden bump on the track and the glider bounced up in the air, throwing the passengers up from their seats.

Whoom! Whoom!, two simultaneous thuds got lost inside the cockpit but it left Aadi and the Captain rubbing their heads that swelled seconds after hitting the canopy. The glider slipped another hundred feet before coming to a halt.

'Hello! Hello! Mishraji, we aborted the flight for today. The launch cable has broken and we crash landed. Please send the jeep and the first aid kit,' said the Captain on the walkie talkie.

The crash from a height of 200 feet didn't prove fatal but it definitely left its victims with some scary moments. A cloud of dust belched out of the exhausted glider as Harsh and Tapan reached the crash site. 'Are you alright, Aadi?' asked Tapan, his breath accelerated from the run.

'I am fine,' said Aadi coming out of the glider.

After taking the first aid, Aadi pedaled back towards the hall with Tapan and Harsh. Crossing the Aerospace Department, the group had taken a left turn when they were put on guard. An approaching jeep rattled in front of them. The driver had lost the control and jeep seemed headed for a collision. Adrenalin rushed through Aadi's vein while his mind processed zillion possibilities in a split second. 'Jump to the road side,' yelled Aadi turning his bicycle's handle.

All of them had got on to the pedestrian walkway when the jeep hit the signage by the roadside. Though the signage had taken the blow, instead of succumbing to injuries it stood aplomb, instructing the rash driver, 'Don't ride over the pedestrian walkway'.

People on their morning walk rushed to the accident site and helped the driver who was bleeding profusely. Immediately an ambulance was called and the injured was rushed to the hospital. The group was safe but Harsh's bicycle was not able to escape the blow. Rolling down the hurt bicycle, the group got it admitted to a mechanic shop, near TIC, a small tea kiosk. It felt nauseating after witnessing two accidents in a row. Ordering coffee, the group tried to slow down the rush of blood.

'Life is so uncertain,' said Aadi sitting on the wooden bench kept in front of TIC. All his dreams and aspirations panned in front of his eyes. 'Life is too uncertain to push our dreams away any longer,' he added.

'What has happened to you?' asked Harsh.

'I have always dreamt of building a flying car,' said Aadi in a trance. 'I want to share the idea with you guys.'

'You want to discuss that now?' asked Harsh with a surprised overtone.

Uncertain, Aadi gazed at the vessel kept on the stove. Under the fire, the vessel burped the vapors of concoct brewing inside its belly. Aadi too was on fire. There were thoughts boiling in his mind that he wanted to release.

Even before the coffee could be served; its smell was well spread in the air. Along with the smell of caffeine, Harsh caught a whiff of thoughts running inside Aadi's mind. In a calm baritone, he said. 'We can talk.'

Mustering the confidence, Aadi spoke. 'I want to build a prototype for a car that can fly.' Exchanging a quick glance, he continued. 'I have already started the work on the conceptual design.'

'What about the aerodynamic considerations in the design?' asked Harsh.

'I haven't taken that into consideration yet,' replied Aadi. 'I am working towards a kinematically feasible design.'

The cold morning was sending a shiver down Tapan's spine. Taking a quick shot of hot coffee, he asked in a quivering tone. 'What about the propulsion system?'

'I haven't figured out the propulsion system and also I am not certain if the design can ever get airborne.' With conviction reflecting in his eyes, Aadi continued. 'With help from you guys, I want to take this effort to some logical conclusion.' Chirping of birds awakening from their slumber muted the discussion. It also gave Aadi's words a fair chance to sink in.

Two near misses, the early hour of the day and an inebriated discussion was enough to clout the mind. Harsh slowly sipped a caffeine rush bringing him back to sobriety. 'How will you pull out time from your thesis work to concentrate on this?'

'I am designing the flying car for my thesis work,' replied Aadi.

'Subbarao is not going to support you on this idea,' said Harsh.

'I can say this as I am doing my research under his supervision. I know him better than you do.'

'I have already asked Mukherjee sir to let me work on the concept.'

'As you told us, Dr. Mukherjee didn't commit to you a project for building a flying car prototype.' Forcing his words, Harsh continued. 'He simply can't. The institute will not allow a project which can't be mentored by any of its faculty. Had it been Dr. Dutta, it was possible, but none other than him can handle this.'

'Mukherjee sir has promised me a project for designing the flying car. He has already talked to Subbarao.'

'Yeah, that's what my point is. You can only create some funky sketches for your thesis. You can go nowhere near to building a prototype.' Taking the talk in his stride, Harsh continued. 'You do not understand the problem. Basically, Subbarao can only help you design but nothing beyond it. Moreover, he doesn't have the courage to try something new.'

'Let's assume that you get to design the flying car. But it doesn't end there. How are you going to build the prototype?' asked Tapan taking a deep breath.

'Carrying out aerodynamic experiments would be another big challenge,' added Harsh.

'I need you to help me out with that,' replied Aadi. 'We all know that no one is better than you in aero fundamentals. Your strength is aero'. Looking towards Tapan, Aadi continued. 'Your strength is manufacturing. I don't think that there's a machine that you can't fabricate. I need help from you guys to realize the dream of the flying car.'

'No one has ever gone beyond creating fancy designs. Why do you think that your design can fly?' asked Tapan.

Before Aadi could have answered, Harsh fired another round of shells. 'Let's assume that you have a design that can really fly. But, how will we convince the department to allow us to work together towards the idea?'

'No one will support us on that,' replied Aadi.

'So you agree to the point, huh,' said Tapan.

'I am not done yet.' Aadi took a deep breath as he continued. 'I said no one will agree with our working together on an idea that has been taken up by many without success. At the same time, no one would be bothered if we do as we are supposed to do and then work on our idea'.

'You mean to say that we do double the work?' asked Tapan.

'I understand that you guys have commitments but answer just one question of mine.' Aadi gazed blankly at the columns of sun rays. Dust particles inside the column danced to the tunes of the slightest disturbance. He didn't want to dance to others' whims. Breaking the clamor going on in his mind, he asked. 'What are you guys going to cherish after five years? The mundane thesis work that you anyway need to do, or working on an idea that no one has ever succeeded in.' Aadi's voice reached the highest pitch of crescendo before going for a free fall into silence.

A moment elapsed without a word. Killing the static, Harsh said in an annoyed tone 'You think your filmy dialogue will work on me'. Aadi looked at him losing all hope. Gradually Harsh's facial expressions broke into a warm-hearted benign smile. 'Yes it worked my dear. I am in the team,' said Harsh, extending his hand.

Aadi grabbed the hand and looked towards Tapan. Before he could have asked, Tapan spoke. 'I can't sit out and let you have all the fun. I am also in.'

The coffee kept on the table had already gone cold, but no one in the group required a kick anymore. Breaking the static, Harsh asked. 'Now, what is the plan?'

'I am not sure,' replied Aadi. Giving a brief pause, he mumbled slowly. 'We can pilot the idea on the CFD term project that we are doing.'

'How can we do that?' enquired Harsh.

'We have been asked to simulate an aircraft. Who said that we can't design a scaled down physical model of the plane?'

Harsh was able to read through Aadi's mind. With a brief smile on his face, he said. 'I think you are correct. We already have completed the hand calculations on the design. Better than designing things in the software we can design a flying model.'

'Where do I fit in this?' asked Tapan.

'You are the one who will fabricate the design', said Aadi smiling.

Further, the group ventured into the details of the execution. Hours fled past before they realized that the day had already started. They could not have afforded to miss the lectures. Picking up Harsh's repaired bicycle, they left directly to the lecture hall. There are times in life when fear can set you free. Aadi's misadventure with gliding and a near miss on the road had done something right. The dice had been rolled. How it turns up was left to the future.

12th April 2006,

Aadi's room, IITC

BSE Sensex crosses the 10000 point

The Sensex crossed the psychological barrier of 10,000 point mark riding on the policies and results shown by growing Indian economy. Buoyant emotions for the quarterly results from different companies took the shares to a new high. The view in the market about the Indian economy as a whole is quite optimistic. The Indian economy is bound to grow by close to double digit figures in coming year; an analyst said reacting to the question if the shares being traded were overpriced......

'What happened to you Aadi? You are reading Economics Times,' asked Harsh entering in the room. He held a coffee mug in his right hand and a wooden skeleton of the aircraft model in his left. Tapan was next to join with a coffee mug in his hand.

'I just thought of giving it a shot. Now, I realize it's not my cup of coffee,' said Aadi keeping the newsprint to one side.

'Are you going for the BIZ101 lecture today?' asked Tapan picking up the business club flyer lying on the cot.

Hiding his uneasiness, Aadi replied nonchalantly. 'I am thinking about attending it. Why don't you guys join me?' Aadi rolled his eyes around till they got locked on the aircraft model. With a gleam in his eyes, he took the model from Harsh's hand and inspecting it closely, asked. 'Have you started the work?'

'A journey of a thousand miles begins with a single step. I have added a step to our journey,' replied Harsh, sporting an infectious smile. 'When are you leaving for the business lecture?' he asked.

'Maybe in another thirty minutes,' replied Aadi.

'We may also join you,' said Harsh without asking Tapan.

The biggest of halls was falling short with the crowd which swelled with each passing minute. A lecture on investment had many suitors. The crowd settled into their seats as the podium was occupied by Avik and Sonia, instructors for the class. Avik was a first year Computer Science graduate, smitten by the business world. Sonia, a MBA student in her first year of academics was the live wire of the business club. On faded denim jeans, she wore a saffron sleeveless kurti with interwoven jari work. Her tight jeans and short kurti brought forth her curvaceous features. She held her hair in a pony and had smeared her big black eyes with mascara. She was a fair lady with a small chiseled face and a good height.

'Can you shift your omega?' Tapan exchanged a hard glance with Aadi as he signaled him to squeeze his butts, saving some space on the bench.

'You didn't tell us that Sonia was coordinating this lecture,' said Harsh, his voice inquisitive.

'I didn't know it either,' replied Aadi, in a plain tone.

Seeking silence in his class, Avik tapped on the mike. Taking stock of faces in the room, he continued. 'Friends, I am really glad to see such a huge response for this B Club lecture. I am Avik. Today, I will be delivering the opening lecture of BIZ101, an initiative of the business club.'

'We will first talk about investment. What is an investment and why is it so important?' said Sonia, writing the question in bold letters on the board. Avik switched over the talk and continued.

'After understanding why an investment is desired, we will talk about the investment options that are available to us.'

Throwing the chalk stub in the bin, Sonia picked up the mike. Looking deep into the audience, she spoke boldly. 'The most sought after field comes next, 'Stocks'.'

Sonia blinded the mike with her hand and stood at one corner of the board. Avik now led the show. 'We will have a discussion on stocks, markets, FII, FDI and other jargons that you would usually come across in any business talk.'

'Before devouring the business knowledge feast, let's brush up some basics,' said Avik loud on his voice. Dusting off the board, he scribbled.

Consumption........that's what we do all the time
Saving: The part of a person's income that is not spent on consumption.
Investment: An item of value purchased for income or capital appreciation (An increase in the price of the item).

'What are the threats that you can think we should be prepared for? How can a decent financial investment help us cruise through the troubled time?' Avik sowed a few questions with sweat pouring down his face.

Hands from every corner of the room sprouted.

'Yeah, you at the right corner … … by the back door. Sonia, can you hand him the mike?' asked Avik pointing to a hand shooting off the roof.

'A slowdown in the economy may lead to job losses. If sufficient funds are available to last the financial cycle, then one can easily push back the adversities.'

'You are right. Can you guys think of any other reason?' asked Avik wiping the sweat off his face.

'Tapan, can you think of something?' asked Aadi as he looked distantly towards Sonia.

'Not really, I share the same opinion as the other guy. Reasons can be many but I know we should be saving for our future.'

'Tapan, help me to put an impression on Sonia.' With a flash of brilliance something struck Aadi and he raised his hand.

'Yes, you in the middle of the bench,' pointed Avik. He signaled Sonia to get to Aadi and help him share his answer.

Aadi was awestruck with the beauty that Sonia unleashed in perfectly leashed dress of hers. He would have loved to invest his life in Sonia, if that was possible anyway. The glitter of her nail polish, her fragrance, everything about her had a magic.

Harsh and Tapan were still trying to guess what would have struck Aadi when Sonia extended the mike with her manicured hands. 'The money will rot if we keep it with ourselves for long. We have seen ...' Before Aadi could have finished, the crowd in the hall exploded in laughter.

'What kind of an answer was that?' asked Harsh looking discreetly towards Aadi.

Sonia came back to collect the mike as the laughter subsided. Instead of returning the mike, Aadi composed himself and spoke again, this time a bit louder. 'It's better to put money with the bank. The more money we have, the lesser value it takes. There was a time in Germany when people used to burn currency notes to cook their food and warm their homes. It was cheaper for them to burn currency notes than the coal.'

Aadi's answer was followed by a giggle and then a wave of murmur which was finally seized by the amplified voice of Avik. 'Actually, that's a good point. The phenomenon is called as inflation and it's caused by more money chasing fewer goods,' explained Avik.

The classroom fell silent. Breaking the static, Harsh and Tapan clapped fervently. Sonia was all smiles when she came to collect the mike from Aadi.

'Now as we understand why investing is a smart thing to do, let us explore the available investment options,' said Avik. Seeding a new topic, he continued. 'Now we will study about the stock market...'

Digging through the graveyard of stock market, Avik cremated the black board under the chalk dust. The lecture ended on schedule but was enough to tantalize everyone sitting in the room for the next surprise in line.

'If not an engineer, I would have been in finance,' said Aadi coming out of the hall with Tapan and Harsh.

'And close to Sonia,' said Harsh, passing a wink at Aadi.

'If nothing, I can at least be a monk,' said Tapan. Strolling leisurely towards the bicycle stand, he continued with a sigh. 'While joining Mechanical Engineering, I didn't know that I was choosing a path of celibacy for myself.'

'You have an option. Jaswinder will not mind being your girlfriend,' added Aadi with a mischievous smile.

'I need a girlfriend, not a non-male friend,' snapped Tapan.

Before Aadi could have added more, his mobile rocked inside his pocket. Picking his mobile, Aadi fed 'Hello' as an appetizer.

'Can I talk to Aadi Malhotra?' the voice on the mobile phone echoed.

'Yeah, speaking,' replied Aadi.

'I am Anil, General Manager Sales for *Yummylick* India Pvt. Ltd. We performed a root cause analysis for the complaint you lodged with us.'

'It's great to hear that. So, what did you find?' asked Aadi.

'We found a problem in our processing line. We had sensors all through the processing line, leaving a station where the product gets packed.' Coughing briefly, Anil continued. 'As we use aluminum foil for packaging, we could not afford to have a sensor at the packaging station.'

'What's your plan to negate such problems in future?' asked Aadi.

'We have changed our packaging material. We are now using paper instead of aluminum foil. This has enabled us to have sensors all through the processing line,' replied Anil.

'Good to know that.'

'Our company has a commitment towards the society. With support from our customers, we will bring our brand to the international level.' Taking a pause, Anil continued. 'From your mail I figured out that you belong to IITC.'

'Yes,' replied Aadi.

'I have an acquaintance at IITC.' The passing second was filled with silence. Fuelling the conversation, Anil spoke. 'You might know Dr. Bhaskar Saxena.'

'I am not sure if I have heard about him,' replied Aadi.

'Yeah, IITC is a big place.' Concluding the talk, Anil remarked. 'Anyways, please feel free to give me a call if I can be of any help. I owe you ... um ... You can save my number in your contact list. This is my direct number.'

'Yeah sure,' replied Aadi. Switching off the call, he left with others to the hall. His face bore a perpetual satisfaction of bringing some positive change to the society.

ROLLING THE JUGGERNAUT

4ᵗʰ May 2006

Manufacturing Sc. Lab, IITC

The Manufacturing Science lab was an old building with signs of constant reworks. It was one among the first few labs raised in the Mechanical Department. The musty and dark ambience of the lab bore a testament to its age. Flanking the walkway inside the lab was a cemetery of experimental setups and a small workshop. The skeletons of the experimental setups on its floor rendered the lab haunted while the workshop breathed its life with a lathe, grinding machine and a drilling setup. At the end of the walkway was a hermetically closed section that reared offices to the faculty.

In the dark of the night, the cemetery was ajar with a bulb hanging above the welding setup. Under the welding arc, Tapan fabricated the aircraft body. Cylindrical, with tapered nose and tail sections, the body housed a two-stroke engine with the propeller shaft coming out of its nose.

'Aircraft body is in shape now,' said Tapan inspecting the work. Satisfied with the model, he walked over to Harsh who was busy crafting the wings for the plane. 'How is it coming up?' he asked.

Measuring the wing's dimensions, Harsh answered. 'Here, we have the perfect pair of wings.' Harsh turned to his laptop which had a visual model of the aircraft. Feeding in the dimensions of the wings, he waited for it to refresh the structural details of the aircraft before continuing. 'If you have made the aircraft body as per the drawing then these wings should get it airborne.'

Shoving the mechanical tools and several other partially fabricated structures to one side, Harsh kept the wings on the table. 'Let me have a look,' said Harsh taking the aircraft body from Tapan's hand. He did some measurements on the aircraft before commenting. 'It's a nice piece of work. Though weight is slightly higher, rest all is fine.'

'I will size it up,' said Tapan.

'Also, attach the wings to the structure once you are done,' asked Harsh.

Removing extra material on the aircraft body, Tapan bolted the wings on its sides. Once Harsh approved, he fitted the rudder and elevators to the tail of the aircraft. Further, he accommodated two motors inside the aircraft and fixed a propeller on the engine's drive shaft.

It was Aadi's turn now. Giving feet to the aircraft, Aadi nailed two main wheels at the front and a small wheel at the tail. Next, he connected the rudder, elevators and ailerons to the motor sitting inside the aircraft's body. The motors were remotely controlled by the radio controller. Taking the aircraft in his hand, Aadi throttled the engine to its highest rpm. Soon, the lab was filled with the white smoke coming out of the engine's exhaust.

Switching off the engine, Aadi kept the model on the floor. Testing the control surfaces, he pulled back the joystick on the radio controller, the elevators flapped up. He switched on the engine and the aircraft propelled forward on the landing gears for a distance. The aircraft had travelled a few meters when Harsh picked it up. 'There's too much interference here. We will test it tomorrow in our Hall's ground. Let's go out for a coffee,' said Harsh patting on Aadi's shoulder.

'I have thought a name for her,' said Aadi coming out of the lab.

'What's that?' asked Harsh.

'Hell's Angel'

'That's nice,' said Tapan yawning.

Café Coffee Day (CCD) was a savior for the students working late hours. Located between the Mechanical and Computer departments, it served a decent crowd of students even at night. Picking up their order of maggi and coffee from CCD, the group now occupied the stone stools kept in front of the kiosk.

Sipping his coffee, Tapan asked. 'How was the meeting with Subbu?'

'Horrible! I am not sure he will allow me to work on my ideas,' replied Aadi.

'Subbarao is an eccentric guy. You better be careful with him,' suggested Harsh.

'I will take care,' said Aadi.

The conversation petered out as the group devoured the snacks. Breaking the static was the intermittent noise from Tapan slurping his maggi. After a few minutes Harsh asked, sipping his coffee. 'Now, when we have built an aircraft model, what's your plan about the flying car?'

'I was also thinking about it,' replied Aadi. Nibbling at the patty, he continued. 'Soon, we need to start the experiments. The design is complete. We should be fabricating the flying car model now.'

'I will handle that during semester recess,' said Tapan.

'So, we will be good to start our experiments by early next semester,' said Harsh.

'I forgot to talk about it earlier. We need money for all this stuff,' said Aadi.

'How much?' asked Harsh.

'About one lakh,' replied Aadi.

'What?' Tapan vomited maggi back in the bowl. With noodles half inside his mouth, he looked like a witch.

'Clean your mouth,' instructed Harsh.

Putting the bowl to one side, Tapan wiped his mouth using a tissue paper. Looking towards Aadi, he asked. 'How will we get the money?'

'We will take the computer loan,' replied Aadi.

'That's a nice idea. We can do that.' Musing, Harsh enquired.

'But, how are we going to manage the wind tunnel facility?'

'Frankly speaking, I don't have a clue. But, we will get it some way or the other,' replied Aadi.

'Okay, as you say,' said Harsh.

Completing their snack-break, the group left for the lab. They had lots of work left to complete on 'Hell's Angel' before it could take its first flight.

27th May 2006

CFD Lab, IITC

'Your bicycle should be banned.' Applying the brakes to catch up with Aadi, Harsh continued. 'Just imagine two skeletons having sex on a tin roof. That's the noise it makes.'

'Boss, this is Mach-1,' Aadi defended.

'This is a piece of junk. No matter how hard you crank the pedal it can't ever pick up a decent speed.' Taking stock of the time, Harsh continued. 'Today, we are going to get late.'

Aadi kept silent as there was no point in fueling the discussion. He rather burnt a few extra ATPs and cranked his bicycle harder. Reaching the lab, Harsh and Aadi parked their bicycles and moved inside. The entrance to the lab was crowded unusually. Students with their reports waited anxiously for their turn. Aadi and Harsh were in the corridor when Jaswinder came by. 'What is that you guys have got?'

Handing over the model to Jaswinder, Aadi replied. 'It's the aircraft model that we made for the project.'

'Were we supposed to prepare a model?'

'No, we thought of doing some practical,' replied Harsh with a flicker of smile.

'Hell's Angel,' said Jaswinder, reading the imprint on the aircraft's body. The wet paint on the body gleamed in the sunlight. Giving back the model to Aadi, she wiped her hands on her white salwar. She next picked the report from Harsh and after analyzing it briefly, spoke. 'Where is the software report?'

'We didn't use the software. It's all hand calculations that we relied on to design our model,' replied Aadi.

'You guys didn't use the software. So what's that you guys have done?' asked Jaswinder.

'Jassi, assignments are meant to educate. If we had used the software, we might not have understood the practical issues,' explained Harsh.

'You guys may be right. But, do you think Anubhav sir will be fine with that?' asked Jaswinder.

'I don't think we have the time to think about it,' said Aadi hearing his name being announced. It was their turn for the presentation.

'Best of luck,' wished Jaswinder as Aadi and Harsh rushed inside the office. Exchanging greetings with Dr. Anubhav, they took the seat in front of him. Making an entry for the new group in his notebook, Dr. Anubhav darted his glance around. His eyes met the model in Harsh's hand. Intrigued, he asked. 'What's that?'

'Sir, this is the aircraft model for the term project,' replied Harsh.

'Great, so you guys have prepared a physical model as well. I will certainly give you extra marks for this.' Writing a note in his notebook, Dr. Anubhav asked. 'Can I see your simulation report?'

'Sir, we didn't do the simulation. We relied on the hand calculations to design the aircraft model. All the calculations are in this report,' said Aadi.

'You guys haven't done any simulation?' asked Dr. Anubhav.

'Sir, we now know the physics behind the stuff. If we had used the software, we might not have got exposed to it,' explained Harsh.

'You are questioning my teaching,' said Dr. Anubhav

'No sir, we are not.' Offering the report, Harsh continued. 'We just tried to do the work in a way that appealed to us.'

'This is not what I asked,' said Dr. Anubhav trashing the report on his desk.

'But sir we have a working design,' argued Harsh.

Dr. Anubhav thought for a while and then spoke. 'How far can your model fly?'

'Sir we need to get out of the room to see its flight,' said Aadi cheerfully.

'I will like to see its flight and understand how executing the project differently has enlightened you better than the others,' said Dr. Anubhav standing up from his seat. He bore a magnetic personality and on a suite designed minutely to details he looked no less than a Hollywood star.

Students waiting for their turn spread far off as Anubhav marched out. Aadi and Harsh followed the steps which halted at one end of the open corridor.

'You can use this space,' said Dr. Anubhav.

Aadi looked around for any interference and then gently placed 'Hell's Angel' on the concrete walkway. He did a few checks before starting the show. Pulling the throttle, he raced the model on the concrete track. By slightly maneuvering the elevators Aadi got the model airborne.

Aadi enjoyed as 'Hell's Angel' flew higher. It was hard for him to hold back the adrenalin rush. The model was hovering at the building's height when using the radio controller Aadi banked it and maneuvered it for a turn. Aadi swiveled on his foot following 'Hell's Angel' but had his vision restricted by the trees. On his judgment, Aadi brought the plane out of banking. As 'Hell's Angel' showed up again, Aadi realized that it was headed for a collision. Aadi pulled back the joystick and the plane got its nose up. The vertical lift was not easy on the motors. The speed went down and soon the aircraft was in a stall. Spinning down, 'Hell's Angel' crashed on the ground.

Aadi scrambled to the accident site only to witness 'Hell's Angel' covered under dust. The motors were still on and bellowed dust around them. Switching off the motors, Aadi rummaged through the pieces of the aircraft. Picking up the remains of the aircraft from the wreck, he came back to Dr. Anubhav.

The wet paint on the broken aircraft still gleamed in the natural light. Looking towards Aadi and Harsh, said Dr. Anubhav. 'I appreciate that you guys have done something out of the league. But I can't give you marks for this. It would be injustice to the other students who have followed the instructions.'

'But sir…' Interrupting Harsh, Dr. Anubhav spoke. 'If you can submit me the simulation report in a week's time then I can reevaluate your term project.' Looking to the crowd of the students, he asked. 'Who is the next to present the term project?'

5ᵗʰ July 2006

Hall 8, IITC

The recess came to an end with some pleasant surprises and a few disappointments. For the semester Tapan stood as a topper with a grade of 10. Aadi savored the flavor of 8 while Harsh had to satisfy himself with a grade of 7.

'Bhoom …' Sid woke up with a thud on his room's door. Repetitive banging on the door didn't allow him to take stock of the time. He unbolted the door to find Aadi, Tapan and Harsh standing in front of him.

'Don your slippers. We are going to the terrace,' instructed Tapan.

'What's the time?' asked Sid.

'7:30'

'I dozed off for quite long.' Moving inside the room, Sid asked. 'Why are we going to the terrace?'

'Booze!' Harsh slipped the cover of his bag and four bottles glittered in the dim light inside the room. Judging Sid's skeptical eyes, Harsh clarified. 'Don't worry, no one comes there.'

'Is this a treat from Tapan?' asked Sid.

'This is a treat from all of us.' Counting on his fingers, Tapan started. 'This treat is for us completing the design of flying car, for me scoring a 10 and …' Before Tapan could have completed his list, Harsh interrupted. '… and for me screwing up again.'

'Get over it,' snapped Aadi. Harsh killed further discussion on the topic. Shoving his bag to Aadi, he said. 'Let's do the talking with the beer in hand.'

'You seem to be already boozed up,' said Sid picking up his mobile.

'I had a pint,' winked Harsh.

Before Sid could have locked his room, the group had already shot towards the stair case. Sid pulled himself up, trying to get past the evening nap that he enjoyed.

Reaching the terrace, Harsh opened the four beer bottles and kept it on the parapet. Leaning against the railing, he watched closely the sun which dived down to its slumber. The sky around it lay suspended, like a melted red hot iron. The current of air, which once charred the bodies, now relaxed in the evening.

'We never explored this area of our hall. It's awesome,' said Aadi taking a panoramic view of the landscape around the hall.

'It's cool out here,' said Tapan picking up a bottle.

'Where did you screw up?' asked Sid looking towards Harsh.

'We screwed up big time in the CFD term project. Otherwise, we could have scored more than 9 for the semester,' said Aadi sipping his drink.

'It was unfair of Dr. Anubhav. How could we have completed a semester project in a week's time,' growled Harsh.

'Harsh, where does your total CPI stand?' asked Sid.

'6.5'

'You need to take care of that. You are sitting on the border, a slip in the wrong direction can prove disastrous,' suggested Sid.

'Just like this,' said Harsh lifting himself on the parapet. He was now sitting precariously on the edge of the building.

'Are you insane? Get down immediately,' instructed Aadi.

'Nothing will happen,' said Harsh standing up on the parapet. He had struck a fine balance when Aadi grabbed his hand and pulled him down. Picking up the beer bottles, Aadi said. 'Let's not stand over here.'

Aadi walked down to the center of the terrace. Keeping the bottles on the terrace's floor, Aadi sat with his legs stretched. Sid and Tapan followed while Harsh still stood at the edge.

After sipping a few moments in silence, Aadi said. 'Harsh, my suggestion would be to take relatively easy courses for the next semester.'

'I am safe if I don't follow your suggestions.' Harsh picked the beer bottle cap and threw it at Aadi, he ducked. Smiling, Harsh strolled towards the group as he continued. 'If I had not fallen for your words, we could have scored well.'

'It's now past. Think about what we are going to do.' Opening a beer bottle for himself, Aadi said. 'We are now going to build a flying car.'

'That we are going to do,' said Harsh, clinking his bottle against Aadi's. Sitting down, Harsh looked towards Tapan who was unusually silent. 'What happened to you?' he asked.

'Did you hear that another student attempted suicide today?' said Tapan pouring a big gulp down his throat.

'Yeah, I heard that.' Sharing what he knew, Harsh continued. 'The student is alive though he has suffered some major injuries in the spinal cord.'

'I don't understand what can go so wrong that one has to kill himself?' said Tapan.

'The academics here are very tough.' Harsh took a deep breath and flushed a full beer bottle down his throat. 'The grading system here sucks,' he growled.

Not letting the spirit die down, Sid changed the topic. 'So, how is Flymoto coming along?'

'We are close to finalizing our design. Pretty soon, we will start building a prototype,' replied Aadi.

'Tell me something about how you guys conceived this idea?' asked Sid.

'Credit goes to Tapan,' Aadi winked at Tapan whose chest had already swelled with pride. 'It was his childhood belief that helped us develop this design.'

Sid had next question loosely hung on his face. Aadi easily picked it up and continued. 'When Tapan was a kid, he used to think that an aeroplane flaps its wings to fly.'

'How is that related?' Sid probed further.

'It was this point that helped us conceive the design.' Tucking his hand behind his head, Aadi continued. 'A flying car should be no other than a bird. It too should fold its wing on the ground and spread it wide while flying.'

'In the car mode, the wings of Flymoto fold up along the sides of its frame,' said Harsh, his eyes turned saucers and voice slurred. Zealously, he continued. 'In the flying mode, the mechanical lock at the joint arrests the wings in place. This enables it to bear the air loads.'

'I wish you all the luck,' said Sid giving a high five to Harsh.

'It's not done yet, the design has to fly and that will involve lots of work.' Aadi took a quick sip from his bottle before continuing. 'We need to create a physical model and have to do lots of experiments.'

'How will you guys get access to the wind tunnel facility?' asked Sid.

'I have some ideas but I am still not sure.' Aadi could read the same question in Harsh's eyes.

'Don't worry Sid. Aadi will solve this problem as well. He has a solution for all the problems.' Two bottles of beer had started kicking in. Harsh unbuttoned his shirt and relaxed his spine on the terrace's floor. Looking towards the sky, he said with a contented smile flushed across his face. 'Aadi may have an answer for all the questions. But, I bet if he can answer this.'

Harsh rolled on his side to face Aadi. 'What's hell and what's heaven?' he asked.

'He is boozed up now,' declared Tapan.

'I am sane. But, if you are, then question the answer,' mumbled Harsh, slurring his words.

'What sort of a question is this? Hell is hell and heaven is heaven,' replied Aadi.

'No, I would like to enlighten you on this topic.' Harsh scrunched up on his abdomen, took a sip and rolled back. 'Heaven is when we have lots of girls and barrels of beer.'

'And what then is hell?' asked Tapan.

'When you come to know that barrels have holes and girls

don't,' said Harsh. Taking off his shirt, he continued. 'I am going to sleep here.' Making a roll of his shirt Harsh substituted it for a pillow. Covering himself with the black blanket strewn with stars, he lay down on the terrace's floor. In no time, others also succumbed to the comfort with the beer knocking down their veins.

Third Semester

THE WHEEL EXISTS

22nd July 2006

Aadi's room, Hall8, IITC

'Hurry up dude!' Standing at the door, Tapan closely inspected Aadi who seemed fossilized on his chair. Laptop, books, pens and notes scuffled for the last available space on the desk. The floor was worse. Cremated under colonies of print outs, sketches of Flymoto and a dozen other things, it looked no less than a graveyard.

Tapan bent down and picked up Flymoto's sketch lying on the floor. Sweeping the loose sheets on his way to one side, he got behind Aadi. 'Can you hurry up? I don't want to get late.'

'Give me two more minutes. I am almost done,' replied Aadi.

'Don't delay me. I have to complete a few experiments by the end of the day.'

'You are not the only one who has got work,' said Aadi standing up from his chair.

Wearing a cotton checkered shirt, Aadi picked a comb to straighten up his unruly hair. Looking at the mirror on the wardrobe door, he said. 'I have a meeting with Subbu. I need to update him on the work I did during the semester recess.'

'When did he come back from the U.S.?' asked Tapan.

'Yesterday,' replied Aadi. He threw the comb on the bed but he was not done yet. Gleaning the journal papers that lay exhausted on the bed, he stuffed them in a bag. Strapping the bag across his chest, he said. 'Let's leave.'

Reaching the lab, Tapan went straight to his experimental setup. In a mechanical manner, he punched a few buttons and stoked his experimental setup to life. Standing on one side, he watched the machine gobbling up the metal pieces from the specimen.

Aadi had to wait as the godrej's 'Shakti Square Padlock' hung by its neck on Subbarao's office door. Fifteen minutes would have passed before a feverish voice tapped on Aadi's attention. 'Are you waiting for me?'

Aadi looked up to find Dr. Subbarao in front of him. Standing up from his chair, he replied. 'Yes sir, I was waiting for you. I wanted to discuss about my thesis.'

'Let's get inside the room.' Cranking open the godrej padlock, Dr. Subbarao pushed open the door to his office. Taking his seat, he continued. 'I have to bring order to my office. This is a total mess.' Exchanging a cursory smile, Aadi took the seat in front of Dr. Subbarao.

Dr. Subbarao swept some books on his table to one side. In the ravaged and plundered city of books, a virgin copy of conference proceedings lay unscathed. 'The proceeding on Advances in Computer Aided Design' glazed in the light available in the room.

'How was the conference, sir?' asked Aadi.

'It was good. There's a huge potential in the area of feature recognition.' Picking up the copy of the conference proceedings, Subbarao continued. 'You can go through this. See if you like something.'

'What is the topic that you want me to go through?' asked Aadi.

'I would like you to read the paper on feature recognition. I want to have your views on the topic.' Subbarao laid his eyes on his wrist watch which had just ticked over to 10 AM. 'I have to leave for a class of B. Tech students. I will be back after an hour. You can sit in the lab and read through the paper.' Subbarao stood up with the godrej padlock in his hand and the notebook hard-pressed in his arm pit.

Feelings of insecurity biked through the aisles of Aadi's mind as he walked into the Manufacturing Sc. lab. It was apparent to him that Subbarao was looking at a different area for his thesis work. Aadi walked his way to Tapan who was busy doing some calculations. 'How are your experiments going on?' he asked.

'Good!' Putting his notebook on guard to the seat he occupied, Tapan asked. 'By the way, what happened in the meeting with Subbu?'

'Leave it! Let's go for a coffee,' said Aadi trekking steps out of the lab.

Catching up with Aadi, Tapan enquired. 'Is something wrong?'

'Subbu has asked me to read this journal. I think he wants me to work on some other topic rather than the flying car,' replied Aadi, flashing the conference proceeding he held in his hand.

'How does it matter if you work on some other project under Subbarao? Now, we all are working towards the flying car. You know that we are not going to stop.'

'Tapan, you are not getting it. We need to have someone who is full time on the Flymoto project,' explained Aadi.

'Yeah, you are right,' said Tapan exhaling audibly.

Once they picked their order from CCD and settled on a bench, Tapan asked. 'Have you submitted the application for the computer loan?'

'I submitted it yesterday. By now, it would have got approved,' said Aadi thoughtfully. 'Remind me to go to the bank.'

After sipping some time with coffee, Aadi came back to the lab and raked his head through the pages of the journal. Once done, his mind picked up the game of possibilities. Was this an omen about something bad coming his way? Was Subbarao planning to pull him onto a topic in the proceeding? … Time flew by while Aadi tried to combat his own savage thoughts.

'Did you like the topic?' Subbarao broke the silence bringing Aadi back from his thoughts. It seemed like a game of 'tic-tac-toe' that Aadi was in. He knew that things will explode in no time but he had to wait and play. Keeping his fingers crossed, Aadi replied.

'Yeah the topic is novel and probably challenging.'

'Why don't you take it up as your thesis topic?' The game got over as Subbarao dropped his words with utmost precision. BoOOOM!, the explosion sound was not heard anywhere though it reverberated in Aadi's mind.

Aadi was also not bad at combat. He took only a split second to retaliate back equally, with a bold **NO**. The passing second turned out to be long as both parties armored themselves with the silence.

'Sir, feature recognition as a research field is already established. We may not get to do something novel in it,' said Aadi breaking the silence. 'Also, my research interest lies in the concept of the flying car.'

'And your flying fantasy sounds sensible, huh.'

'Sir, a flying car is technically feasible and it can be manufactured with the state-of-the-art technologies. If successful, it will compete for the markets currently being served by the light helicopters. The markets that it can serve include emergency services, police and military, luxury transportation ...'

Snatching words from Aadi, Subbarao spoke sarcastically. 'You seem to know more than your supervisor, that's good.'

'Sir, I have been working on this for the last six months,' said Aadi beaming with pride.

'The final choice is yours. I will not pressurize you to take a topic that does not interest you. But, since I have no funding in the related field, I might not prove to be of any help to you.' Subbarao turned his back to Aadi. He pulled the key out of his pocket and screwed it in the padlock. With a crank of the key the lock got its neck, slit open.

'Sir, I already have gone through the state-of-the-art literature on the flying car concept. I have some thoughts on how to formulate the scope of the work,' said Aadi, following Subbarao inside his office.

'Good for you,' said Subbarao, squeezing his eyeballs together, locking them on Aadi. Bearing a scowl, he fired a scornful glance.

'Sir, can you and I sit together with Dr. Mukherjee to discuss the course of my research?' Aadi tried pushing his luck a bit further.

'Not now, I have some urgent work to complete.' Looking at his calendar, Subbarao continued. 'This week I am busy as hell and next week the course registration work will start. Also, I have many academic meetings lined up.'

'Sir, Is 5th of next month fine with you?' asked Aadi.

'Hum … That sounds better. Also, check out Dr. Mukherjee's schedule,' stuttered Subbarao.

'After consulting with Dr. Mukherjee I will send across the meeting schedule,' said Aadi. Coming out of the office, Aadi rushed to the cycle stand. He had to complete a remaining task at the bank.

Finishing all the formalities at the bank, Aadi got the draft against the computer loan. Harsh and Tapan did the same and handed over their draft to Aadi. As their files were processed on different days, no one cared to notice that all of the issued drafts had only one retailer as payee. Also, the retailer didn't belong to Cawnpore city but to a place called 'Pantnagar'.

Aadi had family terms with the retailer against whose name the drafts were drawn. After deducting 4% from the total amount on the drafts, the retailer paid back the rest of the amount to Aadi. Making the transaction untraceable, he updated his ledger for the sale that never happened at his shop.

31st July 2006

Aadi's room, Hall 8, IITC

With a craving for his bed, Tapan dragged his steps in the corridor. The day had been hectic with lectures and lab work. Completing the classes for the day, Tapan and Harsh had returned to the hall when they saw door to Aadi's room open and dashed in. 'Hey Aadi, when did you come back?'

Aadi looked up to find Tapan and Harsh standing in front of

him. Standing up, he greeted them with a warm hug as he spoke 'How are you guys?'

'We are good.' Puffing out rings of smoke, Harsh asked. 'Did you get the money?'

'Yeah, I encashed the drafts,' replied Aadi, exhaling audibly.

'How much did we save for ourselves?' asked Harsh.

Aadi perked up, 'One hundred grand.'

'Let's talk about our next course of action,' proposed Harsh.

'Let's do it over a cup of coffee,' suggested Aadi. The group moved out as did the cigarette smoke. Picking the coffee from the vending machine, they stood in front of the hall's canteen. It was Harsh who started the discussion again. 'How are we going to get access to the wind tunnel facility?'

'Where there's a will, there's a way,' said Aadi.

'Where there's a will, there are relatives,' remarked Harsh.

'The proverb has changed. Where there's a will there are acquaintances,' said Aadi pouring a pint of smile on his lips. Without any pretext, he picked his mobile and dialed a number.

'Whom are you calling?' asked Harsh.

'I am calling the general manager of *Yummylick*,' replied Aadi.

'GM of *Yummylick*,' said Harsh biting his tongue. A big gulp of coffee had burned the oral mucosa. Rolling his tongue over, he asked. 'Did you get another metal scrap in your ice-cream?'

'No, just seeking damages for the earlier one.'

The call got answered after a few rings. Aadi was the one to initiate the conversation. 'Hello, Can I talk to Mr. Anil?'

'Speaking.' Collecting a curt reply, Aadi continued. 'Sir, this is Aadi from IIT Cawnpore.' Giving a pause he added. 'Sir, do you remember me?'

'Can you help me recollect?' asked the voice at the other end.

'Sir, if you remember, we had a conversation a few months back.' Trying to identify himself, Aadi continued. 'I am the one who had raised a complaint regarding a metal scrap in *Yummylick's* ice-cream.'

'Yeah, I remember you now. Are you still at IITC?' asked Anil.

'Yes sir, I am in my final year now.' Weighing his words, Aadi continued. 'Sir, I called up seeking a favor from you.'

'I will be glad to help you. I owe you.' Bringing the voice to a friendlier tone, GM of *Yummylick* spoke. 'You can call me Anil instead of sir. I feel more comfortable when people address me by my name.'

'Sure.' Reading through the expressions that hovered on the faces around him, Aadi continued. 'Anil, I am working on an idea along with my batch mates, Harsh and Tapan.'

'Okay, please help me understand what you guys really need from me,' asked Anil.

'During our earlier conversation, you had mentioned that you know Dr. Bhaskar Saxena.'

'Yes, I remember mentioning that.'

'To investigate our idea further, we need to do a few experiments in the wind tunnel lab.' Giving an intentional pause, Aadi continued. 'Dr. Bhaskar is the custodian of the lab.'

'But, you are students at IITC. Aren't you allowed to use the facility?'

'Anil, this is not an academic project that the institute needs to support us on. We are working on one of our ideas without any involvement of the institute,' replied Aadi.

'I don't know what you guys are up to.' Aadi counted under his breath as the conversation went static for a while. After a long enough pause, Anil continued. 'I won't raise your hopes since I am not sure if Bhaskar would extend me the favor, but I will give it a try.'

'Thanks Anil.'

'You are welcome.' Taxing a pause, Anil continued. 'Aadi, it was nice talking to you. Apart from this if you need any other help, then please don't hesitate to ask.'

'Thanks Anil! It was great talking to you,' said Aadi.

'Pleasure is all mine,' said Anil.

Switching off the call, Aadi looked towards the expectant faces. With a gleam in his eyes, he said. 'Now, we should get access to the lab.'

'You really think so?' asked Tapan.

'Hope so,' replied Aadi.

'Is Bhaskar the same prof who teaches the Flight Dynamics course?' asked Harsh.

'Yes,' replied Aadi. Thoughtfully, he said. 'If I take up the Flight Dynamics course then it would probably be easier for Bhaskar sir to allow us access to the wind tunnel laboratory.'

'Subbarao will not allow you to credit the course,' snapped Harsh.

'I know what I need to do,' replied Aadi with a wink.

5th August 2006

Dr. Mukherjee's Office, IITC

'A well-defined problem is half the work done. I think you would agree with this Dr. Mukherjee,' said Dr. Subbarao dropping the handout prepared by Aadi on his desk. Aadi was sitting opposite to his supervisors forming the third vertex of a triangle.

Looking towards Aadi, Dr. Mukherjee said, supporting his colleague. 'I think Dr. Subbarao has a point. You should seek his help if you lack clarity on your research work.'

'Sir, I have clarity on the work that I want to do but ...' Exchanging a rebellious look with Dr. Subbarao, Aadi continued. 'I think that Subbarao sir wants me to work on some other project.'

'Dr. Subbarao, is there any problem with the research topic that Aadi has chosen for himself?' asked Dr. Mukherjee.

'The research topic is fine but I am not sure if the institute will fund this project,' replied Dr. Subbarao.

'You need not worry about the funds. There are many places from where the funds can be funneled. I will make the arrangements. For me, the student's research interest is paramount.' Being close to the upper echelons, Dr. Mukherjee commanded respect and authority that rested with only a few in the institute. As refuting outright was not possible, Subbarao tried to bail himself out with an excuse. 'Sir, I am already involved in so many projects. I am not sure if I can be of much help to Aadi.'

'I guess we had this discussion earlier also. We need to accommodate the student's interest and if required, I can ask the head of the department to discharge you from some responsibilities.'

'No sir, that is not required.' Stuttering, Subbarao continued. 'If you can do so much to help a student then ...um ... it's my duty to help. I will take care of Aadi's interests.'

Looking towards Aadi, Dr. Mukherjee continued. 'Research doesn't mean that you always have to succeed. Even if you fail, you reveal to the community the existing challenges in the approach you took.'

Before Dr. Mukherjee could have finished his advice for Aadi, his mobile beeped a message. He scrolled through the message and dialed a few numbers. The line was live when he asked Aadi to write down a contact for him. He repeated the number as it was dictated from the other end. Hanging up the line, Dr. Mukherjee asked, 'Aadi, have you jotted down the contact number?'

'It's here,' said Aadi handing over the sheet.

'There's a problem that demands the immediate attention of the director. I need to talk to him regarding the issue.' Dr. Mukherjee saved the number in his mobile before handing back the sheet to Aadi. Bringing the meeting to a formal closure, he continued. 'Aadi, you start your work and stop worrying about funds, resources or failure. We are always there to guide you through.'

'I think you got the idea,' said Dr. Subbarao signaling Aadi that he had to move.

'Yes sir, I got it.' Aadi pushed the sheet of paper back into the file he was holding and sized it up.

'It would not be good for a student to have contact number of the director. Can you give that sheet back to me?' asked Dr. Mukherjee.

Though Aadi laid the paper back on the desk, the concern had aroused his interest. With a sly, he stole a glance at the sheet, transcribing the contact number on the sheet to his brain. 'When can we schedule our next meeting?' asked Aadi scooting his chair back.

'You can schedule a meeting after two weeks. That will give you sufficient time to dig through the literature,' said Dr. Subbarao.

Aadi collected the folder, turned back and walked slowly towards the door. He stopped midway involved in his own thoughts. 'Do you have something on your mind?' asked Dr. Mukherjee.

'Sir, I want to take the Flight Dynamics course during this semester. I am sure it will be helpful for the thesis,' replied Aadi.

'You can't take more than sixteen credits in a semester,' said Dr. Subbarao, arching his eyebrows.

'I already have completed four credits of thesis during this summer vacation. For this semester, I am taking twelve credits against the thesis. With rest of the four credits, I can take the course,' said Aadi looking towards Dr. Mukherjee to intervene.

'I gave Aadi the permission to stay back for the summer recess and work towards his thesis. For his work, I awarded him four credits,' interrupted Dr Mukherjee.

'In that case, you can take the course but I am not sure if it will help you in your thesis,' said Dr. Subbarao, shrugging his shoulders.

'Sir, the course would certainly be helpful,' replied Aadi.

'Okay, as you say.' Subbarao shrugged and nodded in approval.

IT DOESN'T AGE,
IT GETS TOUGHER WITH TIME

10th August 2006

Flight Dynamics Lecture, LHC, IITC

Cross checking the mathematical derivation scribbled on the board, Dr. Bhaskar stood in ragged slippers and lined bell-bottoms. On his bony structure, the professor had an old coat that had lost its color with half a kilogram of dust that it had gathered through the years. His ruffled hair atop an emaciated face gave him a look of some weird bollywood character from the 70s era.

At last, Dr. Bhaskar had found what nagged him all through the lecture. Dusting a portion of the blackboard using his shirt's sleeve, he corrected a mistake. Satisfied, Dr. Bhaskar turned to face the students. 'We will take up further discussion and queries in our next class,' he said, stealing a quick glance at his watch.

Before Dr. Bhaskar could have thanked the class, the students had already started walking out. Collecting his notes, Dr. Bhaskar too walked out of the class. Oblivious to the world, he toyed with an academic problem while rolling down the steps on a skywalk connecting to the library. Today, he was not alone. Someone was following him close on his heels.

'Excuse me sir!'

Dr. Bhaskar turned around to find a student standing in front of him. Before he could have asked, the student spoke. 'Sir, I am Aadi Malhotra.'

Dr. Bhaskar fidgeted with the chalk in his hand. On full

throttle, he searched his mind's database against the name fed. Bingo! He had it. 'Mr. Anil talked about you.' Grinding the chalk with his pale yellowish fingernails, Dr. Bhaskar continued in a thoughtful manner. 'I don't think I can be of much help.'

'Sir, we just need your permission to carry out our experiments.' Catching a breath, Aadi assured. 'I can promise you that we will not cause any trouble.'

'I can grant permission only to the students who need it for their course work,' said Dr. Bhaskar, his fingernails continuously at work.

'But sir, I am already doing a course under you. Can't I take up a term project which allows me to use the wind tunnel facility?'

'That is not possible. The course I am teaching this semester doesn't require the experiments. Only advanced courses require experiments in the wind tunnel facility.' Before Aadi could have proposed anything further, the professor added. 'I am not teaching advanced courses this semester.'

With Dr. Bhaskar throwing up his hands, Aadi was left to wonder his next course of action. He was involved in his thoughts when Dr. Bhaskar hurled a question at him. 'Did you take my course to get access to the wind tunnel lab?'

Aadi kept silent but Dr. Bhaskar was intelligent enough to read through the unspoken truth. Dr. Bhaskar was in his mid-thirties but looked a lot older for his age. His unkempt curly hair had a stock of chalk dust of a week's worth of lecture. His pale yellowish nails, skin tears and gooey eyes safely placed him in the category of eminent researchers.

'What are you guys up to?' asked Dr. Bhaskar.

'Sir,' Aadi hesitated. 'We are trying to build a flying car prototype.'

'Hmm, the flying car has been a human fantasy for almost a century.' Shuffling through the pages of his mind's encyclopedia, Dr. Bhaskar continued. 'Since the time of Wright brothers, people have been trying to build a car that can fly. Henry Ford demonstrated an experimental single-seat aircraft but the project was abandoned after a crash.'

'Sir, there have been many other attempts,' interrupted Aadi.

'Yeah, Yeah, I know.' Picking the gooey substance at the corner of his lips, Dr. Bhaskar continued. 'This is a challenging problem. People have tried rotorcraft, detachable wings and several other contraptions but none has enjoyed commercial success. A perfect roadable aircraft is still a distant cry.'

'Sir, for our model, we are trying wings that can be folded up along the sides of the frame. The design has mechanical locks to bolster the wing at the fold.' With conviction reflecting in his eyes, Aadi said. 'Sir, we are designing a one-tenth scale model for the flying car. We need the wind tunnel facility for testing it.'

'Sounds interesting!' Dr. Bhaskar looked blankly into the distance. Something struck him and with a glitter in his eyes, he spoke. 'I may be able to do something for you but I suspect if you will see that as a help.'

Aadi listened carefully as Dr. Bhaskar continued. 'I am the warden of hall 7. For minor offenses by a student, we assign them community service. Community service includes housekeeping the assigned infrastructure for a period up to 150 hours.'

Throwing the chalk stub, the professor dusted off his hands. Looking towards Aadi, he continued. 'I can assign you housekeeping task for the wind tunnel facility. But, you need to complete your experiments early in the morning, between 6-8 AM.'

'That would be a great help sir,' said Aadi, his heart beating hard on his ribs.

'You guys need to be really nice with the lab assistant,' instructed Dr. Bhaskar.

'Sir, please don't worry. We will not give you a reason to regret,' said Aadi. Adding a pause, he asked. 'When can we start?'

'Today, I will communicate this to the lab assistant. You can start your work from tomorrow,' replied Dr. Bhaskar.

Indebted, Aadi thanked Dr. Bhaskar before picking the trek to the CAD lab. Everything was arranged. He had funds, facilities and the competent resources to turn the idea to reality. When Aadi reached the lab, he had a contented smile spread across his face. Sitting in front of a computer, he started browsing through the journal on the flying car technology.

'Hey Aadi, did you have some lecture?' asked Jaswinder who was sitting next to Aadi.

'I had the Flight Dynamics class.' Without looking towards Jaswinder, Aadi scrolled through the electronic journal.

Before long, Subbarao cranked the key inside godrej's 'Shakti Square Padlock' hung by neck on his office's door. The door crept open as Subbarao stepped inside his office. Throwing his documents on the desk, he came out for an inspection of the lab. He had just entered the lab when his eyes got locked on Aadi.

'Who gave you the permission to work on this computer?' Surprised, Aadi turned around to find Dr Subbarao, his face sullen and red with anger.

Aadi was not able to fathom the reason for Subbarao's rage. Politely, he asked. 'Sir, did I do something wrong?'

'Why are you working on this computer without seeking permission from me?' asked Subbarao in an angry tone.

'I had no idea that I need to ask for your permission,' explained Aadi.

'Where from did you get the login to work on this computer?' asked Subbarao.

'I asked the administrator to create a user account and set a password for me.'

Dr. Subbarao's nose flared out and his eye brows arched. Spitting out his anger, he spoke vehemently. 'How dare you? Don't you know there's a lot of sensitive data on this computer? You are putting to risk the effort of many years. You need to seek my permission before using any facility in this lab.'

Aadi was not able to flush a good expression on his face as Dr. Subbarao continued to bark. With a frail voice, Aadi said. 'Sir, I was not aware. But as I know it now, I will delete my account and will not use this computer in the future.'

'Don't try to fool me with that innocence on your face. I know enough about you, who you are and what tricks you play. In this small brain of yours, you orchestrate every drama of your life.'

Bearing a scorn on his face, Subbarao growled. 'One can sense the quality of a flower just by smelling one of its petals.'

Heads in the lab turned to witness Aadi being ravaged. Holding everyone's attention, Subbarao continued. 'I need you to remove all your data from this computer. Close your account on this.'

'I will do that,' replied Aadi firmly, even indignantly. 'Can I use any other computer in the lab?' he asked.

'First, I need to inspect the damage that you have done on this computer.'

'Sir, you can check my folders. There is nothing wrong in that.' Aadi could barely contain the tremor in his voice.

'No need for all that crap. It's of no interest to me. You better stop using this computer,' snarled Dr. Subbarao. Washing the dirty linen of his grudges, Subbarao left the lab.

Aadi stood stunned for a brief moment and then decided to leave for the hall. With his ego torn to pieces, Aadi dragged his feet out of the lab. He was on his way to the cycle stand when a voice sought his attention. 'Are you going to the hall?' Aadi turned mechanically to face Tapan. Aadi stood frozen in his place, gazing at Tapan. Sensing foul, Tapan came close to Aadi. 'What happened to you?' he asked.

'Nothing,' replied Aadi.

Placing a comforting hand on Aadi's shoulder, Tapan said. 'Tell me what is bothering you.'

'Subbarao scolded me like anything. It felt pathetic,' said Aadi, his eyes already gone moist.

'Why did Subbu scold you?' asked Tapan.

'I was just using a computer in the lab. I don't know why Subbarao expects me to get his permission for that,' said Aadi, his voice shrill.

'Don't feel bad. Let's go to the hall.'

Rolling the wheel down the road, Aadi and Tapan left for the Hall. Aadi was not able to patch up his torn ego and dwelled in silence. Subbarao's words still reverberated between the closed walls of his mind.

'Harsh also uses the lab's computer. Why didn't Subbu ask him to seek the permission?'

'Aadi don't hang on to the issues, just get over them.'

'Yeah but ...'

'Aadi ......,' a stern look was enough to contain Aadi. Both the friends didn't speak for rest of the trek.

Reaching the hostel, Tapan consoled Aadi for some time and then left him in his room to relax. Struggling with his thoughts, Aadi soon fell asleep. Travelling through the aisles of his dreams, Aadi had come out of the block when someone called him for a match of cricket. Picking the gauntlet, he thrashed his anger out on the opponent team. He late-cut the next delivery and ran. Covering the crease in the last minute, Aadi saved himself from a run out. The crowd turned wild as Aadi hit a six next ball. The crowd came cheering and Sid was the only name in the air.

Sid!, but it was Aadi who had played the shot, perplexed Aadi woke up. He could clearly hear the commotion coming from the hall ground. It had already turned dark when Aadi walked out of his room. In the floodlit ground, a cricket match was on. The crowd cheered for Sid who was now at the crease. Unaware of the territory of the game, Aadi sat copiously inside the boundary line.

'Hey Aadi, how are you now?' asked Harsh. Tucking gloves in his arm pit, he loosened up his batting pads and sat by the side of Aadi.

'I am fine. What's going on here?' asked Aadi.

'We are putting together a team for the sports festival,' replied Harsh, looking in the direction of the bowler pacing up for the delivery. A fast pitch ball and Sid flipped it to the fielder on the leg side.

'Take a run,' beseeched Sid. Players exchanged the creases before the ball could cross hands to prove dangerous.

'Tapan told me how the jackass busted you today.' Briskly rubbing his palms together, Harsh continued. 'Try to be impervious to him. Now, when we have the permission for the wind tunnel lab, you should not be thinking too much about him.'

The tempo of the crowd rose as the bowler took a ten step run up to deliver. The ball flew past the bat to hit the stumps. The noise fell from a crescendo to a muted silence.

'We will start the work on Flymoto from tomorrow itself,' said Harsh tapping on Aadi's shoulder.

Tying up his batting pads, Harsh donned the gloves. 'You better be out of the boundary. I will hit nothing under the boundary,' said Harsh with a wink. Moving towards the cricket pitch, he said, raising his bat. 'We will win.'

11th August 2006

Aadi's room, IITC

ching ching ching .... alarm clock came to life as its seconds ticked over to 5:30 A.M.

shhaat... a hand fell like a hammer on the alarm clock, muting it temporarily. Five minutes elapsed when the alarm came back in combat, shrilling high on its pitch.

Finally, alarm clock won and Aadi stood up rubbing his eyes. Switching on the tube light, he kicked Tapan. 'Hey, wake up dude.'

Covering his face with the pillow, Tapan grumbled. 'Is it required to start from today?'

'We are leaving in another 15 minutes,' snapped Aadi.

'I am really tired from yesterday's match. Let's start it from tomorrow,' said Harsh, holding his eyelids open.

'Tomorrow never comes! Now get your asses moving,' replied Aadi.

It took a while for Aadi to get everyone moving for the wind tunnel lab. Out in the campus, it was an entire new world. The morning hours had never felt so cold in the summer. The sun rays had never been so tender. It was a surreal world where birds chirped in melody, the dew sparkled on the grass and the gush of air mischievously tickled the ears. Aadi surely enjoyed the short ride to the lab but not did others. 'Are we going to do this every day?' asked Harsh, parking the bicycle in front of the wind tunnel lab.

'We haven't started yet and you are asking these questions.' Aadi gave a withering look. With a resolve, he pronounced the decree. 'We will follow this schedule till we have something that actually flies.'

'What are we going to do about this?' asked Tapan pointing to the big lock on guard to the wind tunnel lab.

'The lab assistant was supposed to be here by 6 A.M.,' Aadi sighed.

'No one can make it this early in the morning,' said Harsh sitting on the concrete slab in front of the lab.

Aadi didn't bet on waiting and dialed Dr. Bhaskar. The call further got routed to the lab assistant and within 15 minutes the lab assistant was in front of them. In a track and suit, he looked like a perfect zombie. His eyes were still closed when he screwed the key into the lock. Looking back, he asked. 'Can't you guys come in the afternoon?'

As the group didn't have an answer that would please the lab assistant, they kept silent. Probing further, the lab assistant asked. 'How many days will it run like this?'

'Probably two to three months,' replied Aadi.

'Am I supposed to come every day at the same time?' asked the lab assistant, his voice incredulous.

Aadi replied with his silence.

'I will have a talk with Bhaskar sir about this,' said the lab assistant pushing open the door to the lab.

'This is the control panel for the wind tunnel,' said the lab assistant removing the cover from a box with levers, buttons and dot bulbs. 'Bhaskar sir said that you would need basic workshop equipment.'

'Yes, we would need them,' replied Tapan.

'They are placed there,' said the lab assistant pointing to an area on the floor. Looking towards Tapan, he prodded. 'Remove that cover from the bellmouth.'

'Where is that?'

'The one that you have your hands over,' replied the lab assistant, giving a nasty look. 'You guys don't know what the bellmouth is. How are you going to do the experiments?'

'Can you give us a demo on the controls?' asked Harsh.

'I am not liable for it. You need to do it all on your own.' Harsh looked back to Aadi but before anyone of them could have relaxed the favor demanded, the lab assistant said. 'Bhaskar sir has given permission for two hours. I will be back by 8 A.M. By then, you should have packed up your stuff.'

'We will take care,' replied Aadi.

Yawning and stretching his limbs, the lab assistant walked out of the lab.

The wind tunnel was quite a fascinating structure. With its mouth rooted on the wall, it sucked the air from the outside and churned that inside its belly. The exhaust from the giant was routed out of the opposite wall by a similar conduit. Inspecting it closely, Harsh asked. 'How are we going to wake up this giant?'

'Harsh, go through this manual and try to get a hang of the controls,' suggested Aadi. 'Meanwhile, I will try to fit this wing in the test section.'

Tapan could not have sat idle. Picking a job for himself, he announced. 'I am adjusting the camera along the test bed.'

Aadi had been adjusting the wing in the test section when the big fan behind him started rolling. Panic-struck, Aadi shouted. 'Stop the machine,' his voice competing with the din in the background.

Bhoom Bhoom Bhoom … With a thud, the giant stopped its roll. Coming out of the test bay, Aadi shouted. 'Are you a jerk? What did you do?'

'Nothing, I was just trying to start it up,' replied Harsh with spanner in his hand.

'You can't start it like this. First, you need to open up the straighteners,' said Aadi. 'Read through the manual.'

'How do you know this?' asked Harsh.

'I did my homework. We need to understand the set up correctly before we can operate it.'

'Aadi, be patient. We will learn with time. After all, we have to work with this giant every day.' The giant groaned as Harsh hit a spanner on the controls.

'So, you are coming every day then,' asked Aadi cocking a quizzical eyebrow.

'Yes, we are. How will Flymoto be born if its parents do not work through the night?'

Hiding the smile and contriving a serious demeanor, Aadi instructed. 'Harsh, you take photographs of every component of this machine.' Turning towards Tapan, he asked. 'You note down all the engravings on the machine. Pay attention to the specifications and the supplier's name. I want every detail about this machine.'

Opening his laptop, Aadi searched through the web for any information on the wind tunnel setup. Reading through the web and correlating it with the images that Harsh had captured, Aadi prepared a detailed document on the machine. Later in the evening, the group discussed the wind tunnel set up in detail. They equipped themselves for the battle that they had to come out winning every other day for the next few months.

28th August 2006

Football Ground, IITC

Aadi jogged on the trek around the football ground while Harsh sat on the concrete stand meant for the spectators. His face appeared haunted by sleep deprivation. Early morning experiments in the wind tunnel lab and the evening gym session was too much for him.

Completing his jogging on schedule, Aadi joined Harsh. With panting breath, he spoke, high on his volume. 'Wake up dude … spill some sweat.'

'Yeah,' replied Harsh unenthusiastically. Mechanically, he stood up and collected the belongings. Now, he was ready for a walk to the gym.

'We should come to the gym every day,' said Aadi, marching towards the gym. With a smirk on his face, he added. 'You need to get into shape,'

'I am in shape ... well, round is also a shape,' humored Harsh. 'You should have let me sleep. Can't you come alone?'

Sympathizing, Aadi patted Harsh's shoulder and hiked faster. Reaching the gym entrance, he picked the bag from Harsh's shoulder. Sliding his hand inside the bag, he was searching for the water bottle when something hooked onto his attention. Mesmerized, he froze on the ground and so did the world in front of his eyes. With passing moment, everything else on the frozen canvas started dissolving. Only Sonia in her red trousers and a green T shirt was in sharp focus and walked with aplomb towards him. With racing heart, Aadi heaved a sigh. Looking away from Sonia, he said. 'You said it right, I should have come alone.'

Harsh turned back immediately. With a smile on his face, he played lightly. '*Bhabhijaan.*'

'*Bhabhi teri jaan meri.*' Aadi felt weak in his knees as Sonia passed by them. From a corner of his eyes, Aadi tried to steal a glimpse of her but was caught red handed as she looked back, straight in his eyes. The fragrance and warmth of her body was intoxicating. He was involved in his thoughts when Harsh said. '*Bhabhi* looks gorgeous in those trousers and T shirt.'

'She looks gorgeous in anything she wears but you better keep your eyes off her,' snapped back Aadi.

'Why don't you tell her what you have on your mind?'

'I will certainly do that someday.' Heaving a sigh, Aadi continued. 'Just a glimpse of hers feels like heaven.'

'Instead of spending years in the Himalayas, saints should come to IITC and get salvation from your damsel.'

'She is my salvation only.'

Harsh smiled magnanimously. 'Let's move inside,' he said showing the way to the gym.

While veterans in body building pumped iron, treadmills were occupied mostly by novice; or the ones who preferred shape against the bulk. Aadi and Sonia, bathe in their sweats running on the tread mill while Harsh like a skinflint yawned on the bench.

After exhausting himself on the tread mill, Aadi took a break. He now stood by Harsh's side, gazing at Sonia. 'She has got stamina dude,' commented Harsh, looking towards Aadi.

'She runs a lot,' added Aadi, his eyes round as button.

'She is preparing to give you a miss when you go to propose to her.'

'I will manage,' said Aadi slipping on the chest press bench. Harsh gave support as Aadi did his sets. Today, he had reason to pump up his chest more than usual. He went ahead completing barbell push-ups, incline dumbbell flys and machine bench press.

After forty minutes of exhausting treadmill session, Sonia cooled down for five minutes. She miserly sipped water from her glass while sprinkled that profusely on her face. Wiping off the excess water from her face, she stood gazing at Aadi.

Aadi had got his throat dry as he saw Sonia approaching him. Even in a dismal trouser and a T shirt she looked no less than a supermodel. Aadi was under a spell which she broke with her words. 'You are the same guy who sang a song during the 'hall day party'.' Pressing kerchief against her face, Sonia continued. 'Jaswinder is a good friend of mine.'

'Do you come to the gym daily?' asked Aadi changing the track that left him uneasy.

'No, only when my mirror gives me a bad look I step into the gym. What about you, are you aiming for Schwarzenegger muscles?'

'Nothing like that, I don't have a mirror in my room, so I step in here without a cause,' joked Aadi.

'That's funny,' smirked Sonia. She kept quiet for a while and then filled in her words. 'Tomorrow, we have planned a business tycoon game. By any chance, if you are interested in finance, then drop by.'

Before Aadi could have replied, Sonia stole away the possibility to decline. 'You certainly have an interest in finance.' Explaining the assertion, she continued. 'I hope, in the last BIZ club lecture you didn't pick up the mike to impress someone.'

'No, but somebody seems to have got impressed,' said Aadi impishly.

There was a flicker of smile on Sonia's face when Aadi said. 'We will come for the game.' Taking stock of Harsh's reaction, he asked. 'What will we have for the game?'

'I have many surprises ready to roll in the game, so bear with me till tomorrow,' Sonia flirted.

'I prefer surprises. Amuse me,' said Aadi with a mischievous smile.

'You are taking quite a liberty.' Stealing a quick glance at her titan edge, Sonia said. 'I should be going now.'

'Sure,' shrugged Aadi.

'Let's see you tomorrow.' Sonia waved her hand to Aadi and left the gym.

Aadi walked in front of the mirror to take stock of his muscles. Today he envied the mirror, not for showing him a different self but for having the liberty to look straight in Sonia's eyes and admire her beauty. Aadi was still in his thoughts when Harsh breezed in. 'Should we leave now? Sonia has left.'

'Yeah, we can leave. Are you done with your exercises?'

'I was done in my room itself,' humored Harsh.

'There's a difference between shagging and exercising,' snapped Aadi.

Coming out of the gym, Aadi stopped in his way. 'Today I screwed up the lab's scanner,' he said, facing Harsh.

'What other inanimate objects have you attempted to fuck?' Collecting a stern gaze from Aadi, Harsh corrected. 'Okay, tell me what happened.'

'The scanner cover broke while I was taking scans from one of the research papers.'

'How can the scanner cover break by itself?' asked Harsh.

'It's just my bad luck,' replied Aadi.

'Does Subbu know about this?' asked Harsh.

'No. But I have informed the lab assistant about it. I am sure he would have told Subbu by now.'

'It's not such a big issue to worry.' Putting his bag down,

Harsh sat on a step in front of the gym. Allaying Aadi's fear, he continued. 'Subbu can easily accommodate the expense from the funds he gets to supervise the student's thesis. Otherwise, you can also get it replaced. It hardly will cost more than a grand.'

'Right, I can get it replaced,' said Aadi sitting by the side of Harsh.

'Don't worry so much. Mistakes do happen.' Harsh labored with words for a while and then spoke. 'Yesterday while working in the lab, Tapan overheard Subbu talking about me. Subbu does not have a good opinion of me.'

'What did he say?' asked Aadi.

'He thinks that I avoid thesis work and I guess he is correct about that,' said Harsh, shrugging his shoulders.

'Do you have any second thoughts about working towards Flymoto?'

Slipping his hand on Aadi's shoulder, Harsh said with a benign smile. 'It's real hard to get to work on a real world problem and it's even harder to have such a dedicated and resourceful team like you and Tapan.'

'But you have an obligation towards your thesis as well,' said Aadi with a genuine concern. 'You can't ignore that altogether.'

'Yeah, I will take care of that.' Thoughtfully, Harsh continued. 'Aadi, I may need your help in my thesis.'

'Anytime buddy.' Aadi crossed his arm around Harsh's shoulder and stood up. The two of them walked to the hall as the sun dived to his bed, tired from the day's work.

OIL TYCOON

29ᵗʰ August 2006

Seminar room, Computer Sc. Department, IITC

'Friends,' I am Avik and your tonight's host.

'GHOST...,' a voice from the back benches reverberated and with it the whole classroom cracked in laughter.

'Whatever you prefer,' shrugged Avik. Gesturing towards a beautiful lady standing by his side, he continued. 'Meet Sonia, my colleague. She will be helping us with the game.'

In her white shirt-dress, profusely strewn with golden booties, Sonia had nearly caused a scandal. Mercury, finance and then her, the heat in the room was all day high. The junta in the room sized themselves up in the teams of three. The teams were registered, given a name and were ready for the game.

Ramping on the stage, in an ultra-slow motion, Sonia raised the bugle. 'The game is played in four ...' Sonia stopped in her walk and looked towards the entrance. Aadi, Tapan and Harsh had just made the entry. 'Excuse me!' Staring at them, she asked. 'What would be the name of your team?'

The group found itself unguarded with everyone staring at them. It was Tapan who cracked. 'Name ... but ... I came for the beer.' Looking towards Harsh, he continued. 'But you told that it was booze out party.'

The classroom fell in giggle with the innocent admission while Aadi and Harsh stood embarrassed in the classroom. Saving them some grace, Sonia said to a volunteer. 'Register them as

Alcohooligans.'

Once the group settled in the last row in the classroom, Sonia resumed from where she had stopped. 'The game is played in four rounds and is about setting up the biggest oil empire. At start, each team will get a seed capital of 200 crores at an interest of 30 percent. If required, teams can top up their loan,' said Sonia.

Switching over, Avik continued. 'For this round we will auction some of the most promising oil-bearing locations in the world. To help you make a choice, the expert advice is right in the brochure on your desk.'

A five minute break was sufficient for the teams to reach to a choice. Pounding his wooden hammer on the desk, Avik started the auction. 'Here comes the first plot on sale. The civil and exploration engineers are pretty optimistic about it. Let's see how optimistic are the investors on this floor?'

'10 crores, 11... 11.5...,' the room reverberated with the pitches made by the teams.

'15 crores,' pitched Harsh in frenzy.

'15 Crores! Should I consider it the last bid?' Striking the hammer on the desk, Avik continued. '15 one, 15 two ...'

'15.5,' a voice interrupted Avik.

'16 Crores,' another student pitch fervently.

'16 one, 16 two and 16 three ... Well, the land goes to team *Fidayeen*,' said Avik.

The bidding of the remaining plots went through the same frenzy. *Alcohooligans* managed to get their hands on the plot ranked 5th in their preference list.

'You guys have just purchased tons of rock for yourself,' Avik tore apart the sheet of data in his hand and threw it in the dustbin. 'To be true, there's no oil in the lands that I sold to you.'

Surfing on the wave of murmur, Sonia spoke, her voice amplified over mike. 'The oil exists as a chemical formation deep down the earth. It takes an expert to find the right conditions for an oil trap, the right reservoir rock and the entrapment.'

Looking towards Avik, Sonia smiled as she continued. 'While cutting his costs, Avik saved on geologist but ended up digging only rocks.'

'And, I would not like you guys to make the same mistake,' said Avik. Explaining how a geologist can turn a dead well to a gold mine, Avik asked the teams to submit close bids for the geologists available for hiring.

Keeping the information brochure to one side, Harsh spoke. 'A talented geologist can be phenomenal to the success.'

'Also, talent is scarce. If we have it, others are deprived of it,' said Aadi in a slow revealing tone.

'What do you mean?' asked Tapan.

'If we have the best geologist in the market, then others will end up with the less competent ones,' explained Aadi.

'That means they would not be able to exploit their oil wells to its fullest,' completed Harsh.

'What's the bid that you suggest?' asked Tapan looking in the direction of Aadi.

'The amount should be high enough that no one in this room can contemplate,' replied Aadi.

Amidst the hullabaloo, teams submitted their bids. Five minutes had passed when Avik came back on the stage. Looking at the last row in the classroom, he said. 'Unbelievable!'

Musing and strolling majestically, Avik continued. 'Mr. Arnold, who has been voted the best geologist in the industry, has been hired by *Alcohooligans* with a whooping price tag of 150 crores.' With his voice rising with every word, Avik continued 'The bid price is 10 times the second highest bid.'

All the heads in the classroom swung full 180 degree to have a look on the back benchers. Once the murmur died down, Sonia asked. 'Do you guys want to change your bid?'

'No,' replied Aadi plainly.

'Is there any vacancy in your company? I would like to try my luck,' said Sonia smiling impishly.

The financial results after the second round of the game spoke in favor of *Alcohooligans*. Riding on their betted horse, they had the highest production. In the third round, teams had to acquire petrol bunks for selling the oil produced by them. Describing the rules for the third round of the game, Avik announced a fifteen minutes snack break.

Aadi had won the night the very moment Sonia joined the group for a coffee. As Sonia sat in front of him, Aadi didn't indulge in planning for the game. Sipping the coffee, Harsh took the initiative. 'Now, we need to make our moves with more caution in this round.'

'But financial sheets are speaking in our favor.' That was the dumb shot that Tapan played with patties in his mouth.

In an effort to keep Tapan's mouth shut, Harsh extended his share of patty before continuing. 'That's the reason we need to be on the guard. If we sustain our profit through this round then we can win the game.'

'How many petrol bunks are you guys planning to purchase?' asked Sonia.

'Twenty-one,' replied Harsh. 'Limited funds,' he added, shrugging his shoulder.

'Take loan and get more bunks,' said Sonia.

'How many?' enquired Aadi, his eyebrows up.

'Come closer.' Grabbing Aadi's hand, Sonia looked around. Aadi felt an electrical surge running through his body. Sonia's skin was soft and silky. Aadi was all fixed when Sonia whispered solemnly. 'Did you guys notice a catch in the rules?'

'What's the catch?' asked Harsh.

'The maximum sale from a petrol bunk is a factor of the total oil reserves with the teams and the total number of petrol bunks sold in this round,' explained Sonia. Finding others not so convinced, she said. 'Ok, let me write it for you.'

Aadi resumed his senses as Sonia took her hand off and picked a notebook. Scribbling, she said. 'Assume that all of the teams purchase a total of 100 petrol bunks. From the balance sheet of the previous round we know that the total production of oil is about 10 million liters, all teams combined.'

'But ...' Before Tapan could have asked, Aadi passed his patty to him. Scratching his head, Tapan picked the patty, letting Sonia to continue. '10 million divided by 100 ...'

'Is one-hundred thousand,' snapped Tapan.

'Yes,' said Sonia as she completed scribbling the equation in her notebook, *10,000,000 / 100 = 100,000.*

'With 100 bunks with the teams, each bunk can sell one lakh liters.' Crushing the paper that she scribbled on, Sonia continued. 'What good is to have thousands of liters of oil when you can't sell it?'

'You are correct Sonia,' admitted Aadi. Passing second flushed a quaint smile across his face.

Alcohooligans took a loan of 500 crores and submitted their bid for the petrol bunks. Once the balance sheets of the teams got ready, Avik came back on the stage. '*Alcohooligans* did it again,' he said. With his voice rising with every word, he continued. 'This time, they have surprised us by purchasing 250 petrol bunks.'

'Going by the figures, the maximum sale that can happen from a petrol bunk is 30,000 liters. Leaving two teams all others have substantial portion of their reserves unsold,' added Sonia. Looking deep into the crowd, she continued. 'But there's nothing to worry. In the fourth round, teams can sell their surplus oil to other teams who have got enough petrol bunks for retailing.'

Soon, the classroom turned to a trade market. *Alcohooligans* had the monopoly with the maximum number of pumps and they leveraged their holding to batter the oil prices to rock bottom.

By the end of the game, team *Alcohooligans* was the unchallenged winner, claiming the first prize of thousand bucks. It was already six in the morning when students came out of the classroom. Reaching to the cycle stand, Aadi was opening the lock to his bicycle when a mystic fragrance hooked to his attention. He turned back to find Sonia standing in front of him. 'My bicycle is parked in front of yours,' she said.

'Oh, let me take out mine.'

Once Aadi cleared the way, Sonia reached out for her bicycle. Taking her bicycle out, she said. 'Congrats Aadi, you played fantastically.'

'I owe you a party,' said Aadi, hiding the streak of nervousness on his face

'Why?'

'It's because of you that we won the game,' replied Aadi, with a childlike glee.

'So, where are you going to treat me?' asked Sonia, her eyes filled with mischief.

'Tata Inter Continental, our own TIC,' replied Aadi.

'What about the beer party that you promised to your friends?' asked Sonia smiling.

'That can wait,' replied Aadi.

'Are we also invited for the party?' asked Harsh joining along with Tapan. Hesitantly, Aadi replied. 'You guys go ahead. I will join you later.'

'Do you want to get rid of us?' asked Tapan.

'Why would I?' shrugged Aadi, smiling sheepishly.

'You guys also join us,' said Sonia looking towards Harsh. Suppressing her yawns, she continued. 'Let's schedule the treat for the evening. I am tired and sleepy.'

'Okay,' shrugged Aadi.

Sitting on her bicycle, Sonia waved a goodbye and pedaled away. After Sonia left, group drove to the hall, crossing their way through the morning breeze. The sunlight played games shooting off and on from the branches of the tall trees. The dew on the ground counted its last breaths. It was a beautiful day and a perpetual smile sat on Aadi's face.

8th September 2006

Tata Intercontinental (TIC), IITC

'This is not done. This was meant to be my date. You guys are spoiling it,' said Aadi. With his hands folded and an innocent face, he begged. 'Please leave before Sonia gets here.'

'We were part of the game and we will share the rewards equally,' said Tapan in a quavering theatrical voice. 'We already skipped today's Flymoto experiment for you. We can't miss when it's turning out to be fun.'

'Take your share and get lost.' Aadi took out his wallet but Harsh pushed it back in his pocket. Puffing hard the exhausted cigarette, he continued. 'We are here to help you.'

'I don't need your help.'

'But we are together, wherever you go,' said Harsh killing the flamed stick beneath his leather sandals.

Aadi scowled and looked away. His heart filled with ecstasy and his face glowed as he saw Sonia on her bicycle, heading towards them. 'Lock your jaw. It doesn't look good when dropped to the ground,' said Harsh easing his arm on Aadi's shoulder.

Aadi brushed off Harsh and walked towards Sonia who was now parking her bicycle. Before he could have asked, Sonia did. 'Hey Aadi, how was the day?' Aadi smiled tersely and replied. 'Good.'

'You guys must have compensated for the last night's sleep,' said Sonia, swiftly hiking towards the bench occupied by Harsh and Tapan.

'We had a good sleep. But, I am not sure if Aadi slept at all,' replied Harsh, his voice mischievous.

Playing naïve, Sonia asked. 'So, what are we going to have here?'

'Coffee and samosa are the specialty of this place. If you like we can order a pizza also,' replied Tapan, already drooling in his thoughts.

'Is pizza available here?' asked Sonia.

'*Desi*,' answered Tapan.

'Sure, I love *desi maal*,' said Sonia exhilarated.

'But that's not hygienic,' interrupted Aadi.

Sonia laughed and said. 'Let's order pizza, coffee and samosas.'

On the coffee, Sonia stoked the conversation. 'I heard that this is a big *adda* where people come searching for the exotic pleasure.' Clearing the doubt, she added. 'I mean you can get any kind of narcotics over here.'

'I am not sure but here you can get coffee which is really awesome,' said Aadi.

Looking to the group of students sitting on the raised platform around the banyan tree, Sonia said. 'I don't understand how people can burn their own lungs? How can people smoke? Instead of statutory warning on the cigarette packs, Government should grant all smokers an option of mercy killing.'

Harsh froze with the sip of hot coffee in his mouth. Thawing him, Sonia fired loudly her explanation. 'I mean if they are trying to kill themselves then why not give them an option.'

Harsh heaved a sigh of relief on killing the cigarette just in time. But, Aadi was alarmed as many heads around them turned in their direction. Easing the tensions, Sonia looked back straight to them. Heads rolled back and everyone around was now back to their work but Sonia was not done yet. She had something else brewing in her mind. Looking towards the cigarette kiosk, she continued. 'See, matured people like them also come to smoke.'

Aadi turned his attention to the direction where Sonia was pointing. The noise certainly had not rubbed the ears of the person smoking. A tower of smoke still belched out, rising above his head. With back against the group, the man smoked, involved in his own deep thoughts. 'Uncle, don't you think that smoking is bad for health,' said Sonia standing up.

Aadi wished that he could have just disappeared in thin air. He had almost crouched down on his chair when he heard a gentle sorry. He turned back to see how Sonia tamed someone. To his dismay, he found Subbarao killing the cigarette.

Before Aadi could have turned back, Subbarao asked. 'What are you doing here?'

Aadi slowly stood up, trying to steal his eyes from Subbarao. It didn't take much time for Sonia to understand that she had screwed up.

Hauling his steps to the spot where four of them enjoyed a moment ago, Subbarao asked. 'Why didn't you come to the lab? I had sent a message through Sid.'

Aadi kept silent to his benefit. Killing the static, Subbarao charged. 'If you use some facility then it's imperative on you to take care of it. I came to know from somebody else that you broke the scanner. You tried to cheat on me. You lied!' said Subbarao with a rage on his face. The smoke that he had inhaled earlier now pumped out of his flaring nose.

'It was not intentional and I didn't lie,' explained Aadi.

'Why didn't you report it to me?' bawled Subbarao, a spittle fountain busted from his mouth.

Wiping off the droplets of spittle, Aadi rubbed the crispy folded handkerchief on his face. He looked around, gauging his embarrassment, before continuing. 'But, I had informed the lab assistant.'

'I have charge of all assets in the lab and it's me who should be informed. You tried to make a fool out of me,' said Subbarao looking around. Finding that he had drawn attention from almost everyone at TIC, Subbarao brought his tone down to a milder one. 'It's not the way any student of mine has ever behaved to me. I am going to inform Dr. Mukherjee about this.'

Subbarao left but he had raised enough dust that could not have settled easily. Coughing, Aadi strode towards his bicycle. 'What happened? Did I screw up something?' asked Sonia following on him.

'No, I screwed up the scanner in the lab,' replied Aadi without looking back.

'Who was he?' asked Sonia looking towards Harsh.

'His supervisor,' replied Harsh curtly.

Sonia outpaced Aadi and stopped in his way. Aadi was visibly hurt. Before Sonia could have asked, Aadi spoke loudly. 'How can he insult me like this?'

'Aadi, will you tell me what is going on?' asked Sonia.

'I can't. This is a big shit that I really can't explain to you.' Aadi exchanged a furtive glance with Tapan and Harsh and picked his bicycle.

'I want to listen. Tell me, what's going on?' insisted Sonia.

'Who the hell are you to command authority on anyone around you?' said Aadi exasperated.

'I thought we were friends.' Sonia rolled back her steps. Before she could have commandeered her Ms. India, Aadi called her back. 'Hey, I need to share something with you. Let's walk to your hall.'

Strolling towards the girl's hall, Aadi shared with Sonia his misadventures with Subbarao. He briefed her about his interest in the flying car and the work that he has been doing along with Harsh and Tapan.

'What kind of a person is Subbarao?' said Sonia, her words filled with disgust.

'Leave it,' said Aadi.

'Why don't you try to flag a peace with him?' asked Sonia.

'That can't happen. He hates me.' Looking towards Sonia, Aadi said. 'I thought you might be more interested in the flying car than Subbarao.'

'Okay guys, tell me something about the flying car,' said Sonia.

Anchoring his words in the conversation, Harsh asked. 'Have you seen a Volkswagen Beetle?'

'Yeah,' replied Sonia.

'In terms of looks, the flying car is similar to a beetle. The only apparent additions are the foldable wing mechanism and a propeller at its rear,' shared Harsh. 'Basically, it's an aircraft that can run on the road as well.'

'If I am not wrong, you guys had built something similar for one of your course works. Jaswinder used to talk about it,' said Sonia.

'We had built an aircraft. It wasn't a flying car,' corrected Aadi.

'That was just a practice session for the flying car project,' added Harsh.

'And that hit back pretty bad on you guys,' said Sonia.

'It doesn't matter now. We have achieved what he wanted out of that project,' shrugged Harsh. Looking towards Sonia, he continued. 'We have already built a model for the flying car and have started our experiments in the wind tunnel lab.'

'Can I see your experiments?'

'Sure,' replied Aadi kicking a pebble on the asphalt road. 'Maybe someday we will call you for the experiments.'

'What do you guys do in your experiments?' asked Sonia.

'In the wind tunnel lab we do experiments on a scaled down model. We simulate the conditions that the flying car shall see while flying at an altitude of 1,500-2,000 feet,' replied Tapan.

They had neared the girl's hall when Sonia said. 'I really enjoyed the time spent with you guys. Thanks for that. I hope we will catch up soon.'

'Sure,' shrugged Aadi.

Waving a goodbye, Sonia turned back. After she was inside the girl's hall gate, the group picked the trek back to their hall.

WHEN TIME COMES TO A STOP

25ᵗʰ September 2006

Aadi's room, Hall8, IITC

Strolling inside his room, Aadi checked through the list of tasks to be completed for fabricating the flying car. Tapan sat on the desktop preparing the expenditure details while Harsh belched out smoke sitting on the recliner chair.

'One more failure and we are bankrupt,' said Tapan analyzing the report.

'Don't worry it will be a success this time.' Aadi picked up the sketch of Flymoto and inspected it closely.

Flymoto looked similar to a Volkswagen Beetle in appearance. The front wing sat just below the nose of the flying car. The rear wing was supported on the two struts which functioned as rudders for the car in the flying mode. With a custom gear box assembly, the rear mounted engine delivered power to the propeller in the flying mode while in the car mode the power was routed to the wheels. A propeller jutting out of the rear of the car resembled the tail of a tadpole. Flymoto had a streamline body with a two-seater cockpit and foldable wings, framed on the body, by the side of the engine. The foldable wings were the real differentiator between the car and the plane.

Keeping the sketch to one side, Aadi picked up the Flymoto model. 1 meter by 1.4 meter in dimension, the model had wings folded up by the side of its frame. Testing the mechanism, Aadi opened the wings. The mechanical lock at the joint arrested the wings in place.

'Wings seem to be sturdy,' said Aadi cleaning Flymoto's body.

'It's an ingenious mechanism.' Harsh spoke with a cigarette dangling from the corner of his mouth. Winking at Tapan, he continued. 'You are a superstar.'

'A toast for Tapan,' said Aadi, raising his diet coke. Aadi and Tapan clinked their diet coke while Harsh cheered with his cigarette.

Even Mozart would not have enjoyed his own symphony the way Aadi admired the beauty in his hands. Stroking the paint brush on Flymoto's body, he said. 'Tomorrow's experiment will be pivotal. If we can correctly measure the lift then we can finalize our wing design.'

'Don't name it Hell's Angle. That was a failure,' said Tapan. 'We already have a score of 10 failures.'

'We already named it,' said Aadi stroking 'F' of 'Flymoto' on the car. He was not able to carry further as a knock on the door alarmed everyone inside. Slipping the model and other components below the cot, Aadi opened the door.

'Are you guys not going to *Naankari*?' asked Sid coming inside the room.

'What's there?' asked Harsh.

'There's a cultural program organized at the *Naankari* ground. You guys can't afford missing that,' said Sid wearing a smirk on his face.

'We are not interested,' snapped Tapan.

'You are yet not educated enough to be called as IITC graduate,' frowned Sid. Looking towards others, he said with a 10:10 PM smile pasted on his face. 'Today is *Valmiki Jayanti* guys. Go and enjoy the beauties.'

'I have also heard about *Valmiki Jayanti*,' said Harsh almost in a whisper.

'Here, I got my guy. Without any hesitation, I can award him the course certificate,' said Sid patting on Harsh's shoulder.

Sid left in a hurry, leaving others in utter amazement. Judging the question that loosely hung on everyone's face Harsh came to rescue. 'For *Valmiki Jayanti* celebrations, people from *Naankari* village organize dance by hookers.'

'Dance by hookers? What is there in the dance?' asked Tapan as the excitement grew.

Throwing the cigarette stub out of the window, Harsh answered. 'They say it's similar to a pole dance or a lap dance.'

'What?' Tapan's jaw had already dropped to the ground and his tongue rolled out like a carpet. Collecting himself back, he said. 'Let's have a little fun then.'

'I am not coming.' Aadi tried to play spoilsport.

'Well, dude, you don't have a choice, do you?' said Tapan nonchalantly.

'What about the experiments?' asked Aadi pointing to Flymoto's schedule hung on the wall.

'To damn with your experiments. We all are moving.' Passing the diktat, Tapan rushed to his room for a quick make over.

'Aadi, carry Flymoto and the other stuff with you. I believe we will get late at night,' said Harsh.

'Are you planning to go to the lab directly after the dance show?' asked Aadi.

'Yeah,' replied Harsh.

'That can be risky. Though we have the keys, we are only allowed to run our experiments from 6 to 8 in the morning.'

'Don't worry. Nothing will happen,' said Harsh.

Before Aadi could have argued, Tapan rushed inside the room. He certainly was electrified and his spiky hair added to the effect.

'I hope you guys remember that we have invigilation duty tomorrow morning for the machining science exam.' Aadi gave another try.

'I will not take any excuse,' said Tapan throwing the hair gel to Aadi.

Aadi didn't have other option than to follow the resolution from Harsh. He packed the stuff in a bag and kicked his grumpy slave for a ride to *Naankari*, a small village in the heart of IITC's campus.

When group reached the ground, a dance performance was already on the roll. On the tracks of '*kajrare kajrare*', a lady shining from top to bottom danced. She unleashed her beauty in the green colored gaghra, laden with golden embroidery and sequins that reflected light in all directions. Her cleavage was quite visible under 'Demi Cup brassiere', the only revealing outfit covering her upper torso. Her white cream face glazed in the lights.

'Let's move to the front rows,' said Tapan. Locking his bicycle, he strode towards the stage. Aadi and Harsh nearly race walked to catch pace with him.

Making an announcement for another dance performance by Kesar, the protagonist smoked from the water-pipe held in his hand. The crowd cheered and many youngsters climbed on the stage as song '*Beedi Jalaile Jigar Se Piya*' started.

Tapan took bills out of his wallet and climbed up on the stage. Inserting the bills in Kesar's brassiere, he danced with her. Tapan danced like a professional while Aadi and Harsh managed copying him well. Bollywood moves, signature steps of Dharmendra, simmering of shoulders, drumming on the hips of Kesar and their own sharp hip movements, the group did them all.

The show went on till 4 A.M. in the morning. From the ground, the group directly left to the lab.

Placing the model on the test bed, Harsh positioned the sensors. Putting restrictions in place and calibrating the model, he spoke, rubbing his hands together. 'We are good to start our experiments.' Like a commander in-charge, he trundled across the floor. 'Aadi, operate the radio controller slowly. We don't want Flymoto to fly today. We just want to measure the load on her wings.'

Tapan was next in the line of fire. 'Concentrate on the experiment and not on Kesar,' said Harsh snatching mobile from him. 'You need to coordinate with Aadi. Increase the wind speed slowly with an eye on Flymoto. She is learning to fly and can lose her balance. So, never get your eyes off her.'

'Kesar was too good,' Tapan sighed.

A stern expression from Harsh was enough to contain Tapan.

Handing back the mobile, Harsh instructed. 'Concentrate on the experiment.'

Sighing, Tapan put back his mobile in his pocket. Coordinating with hand signal, he started the wind tunnel. Once the flow inside the tunnel became smooth, Aadi flapped the elevators up. Flymoto chattered on its platform. Harsh recorded the readings in his notebook and then signaled Aadi to stop. Aadi adjusted the elevators while Tapan slowed the wind. Coordinating well, they completed the first set of experiments.

'Wing shape is still quite blunt to lift up Flymoto. The flow above the wings is not smooth. We need to make some design changes in the wing.' Almost mumbling to himself, Harsh said. 'You can't elude me for long.'

Harsh took the model out and repositioned the sensors on the body and over the wings. After carefully working for half an hour Harsh had the model ready for the second set of experiments.

'How long will she be around?' asked Tapan taking his position.

'What do you want to do?' asked Aadi smiling.

'Nothing, I just asked.' With a contented smile on his face, Tapan continued. 'She danced pretty well.'

'You are such a jerk,' said Aadi lightly. 'Can't you concentrate on the experiments?'

'Hey guys.' Harsh clapped, seeking attention. 'This is going to be quick. I haven't put the restraints. I repeat again, we just want to measure the lift on the wings. So guys, coordinate real well,' said Harsh.

'Let's start,' signaled Aadi.

Tapan and Aadi started in sync. With each passing second the wind speed increased. Uneven loads on the wings resulted in Flymoto rattling on its bed. Flymoto was chattering considerably when Tapan's mobile beeped in his pocket. With an impulse he screwed his hand in the opposite direction. Sudden increase in the wind speed shook the model.

'Lower the wind speed,' yelled Aadi. Before Aadi could have regulated the radio controller or Tapan could have corrected the wind speed, Flymoto dove down. Coming in contact with the ground, it broke apart in pieces.

'What have you done?' yelled Aadi stomping his foot on the ground.

'I forgot to switch off my mobile. The call broke my concentration,' said Tapan, his face turned to stone.

'We are doomed.' Aadi buried his face in his hands.

'Aadi, I am sorry,' said Tapan. He looked towards Harsh for some help but it didn't come.

Aadi and Harsh sat on the steps outside the lab. Tapan stood a few steps away from the two. With tears in his eyes, Aadi fidgeted with the broken pieces of Flymoto in his hand. After a long silence, Harsh spoke, looking at his watch. 'Let's leave now otherwise we will get late for the invigilation duty.'

'How can he do this?' said Aadi standing up.

'Aadi, cool down. We will work it out,' said Harsh, flagging a cease fire. Stealing a glance at his watch, he continued. 'We should be moving now.'

The clock had already slipped past 8 AM when Harsh, Tapan and Aadi marched towards the examination hall. They entered the classroom to find Subbarao anxiously waiting for them.

Looking towards Aadi, Subbarao sighed, cursing under his breath. 'Here comes the most sincere and studious guy,' Subbarao said loud enough for everyone in the examination hall to hear clearly. 'Punctuality is a sin and we Indians rarely commit it. Am I right Mr. Aadi?'

Harsh and Tapan sneaked inside the classroom but Aadi stood facing Subbarao. Grilling him on the delay, Subbarao said. 'Can I ask why you are ten minutes late?'

'You can ask,' replied Aadi tersely.

There was a sudden burst of laughter in the classroom. The students found the drama reeling in front of them a lot more interesting than the question paper.

'Why are you ten minutes late?' Irritated, Subbarao asked high on his tone.

'Does it make a difference if I come ten minutes late?'

Subbarao's words fretted Aadi who was already fuming over Flymoto's failure.

'You have been assigned a duty. I expect you to be on time. I am not going to tolerate this sort of insincerity,' stuttered Subbarao.

'I am not a NASA scientist that a ten minute delay on my part can fail a space mission.' Aadi's face was now red hot with anger.

'How dare you speak like this to me?' barked Subbarao, a spittle fountain busted from his mouth. 'If I wish, I can make you work for straight eight hours.'

'I already had a lot of shit for the day. I don't care for any crap from you,' said Aadi turning his steps to the door.

'Do you understand who you are talking to?' retorted Subbarao.

'Yes I do.' Aadi turned back, raising his finger at Subbarao. 'Now listen carefully, if you have something other than this to talk about then we are in the discussion, otherwise I am done.'

Dr. Subbarao kept silent. Fuming inside, he looked around. The eyeballs that had frozen on the feud melted with the authoritative heat. Before Subbarao could have spoken, Aadi repeated. 'Are we in the discussion?'

'Aadi, you don't understand the troubles that you are inviting for yourself,' said Subbarao shaking his head. His double chin rolled back and forth like spring-attached head of a bobble-head doll.

'I am done talking to you,' said Aadi walking out of the examination hall. Subbarao had tasted the embarrassment. Stealing his eyes, he also picked his way out of the classroom.

Harsh hushed murmur in the class while Tapan rushed out. He came out to find Aadi sitting on a bench, blank faced. Involved deep in his thoughts, Aadi didn't notice Tapan joining him. Keeping a comforting arm around Aadi, said Tapan. 'I am sorry, friend.'

Coming out of the trance, Aadi glanced at Tapan. He skipped a moment before replying. 'Let's not talk about it.'

Looking from the corner of his eye, Tapan continued slowly. 'You need to abstain from getting in arguments with Subbu. It's not good for you.'

'I really get frustrated with these things. I am making efforts to do something novel but this bloody piece of shit always insults me in front of everyone.' Wiping off the drops of sweat from his forehead, Aadi continued. 'Now, I realize the pressure under which a student attempts suicide.'

'Aadi, what are you talking about? Have you gone insane?' Holding Aadi by his arm, Tapan said. 'Let's move to the hall.'

'No more of teaching assistantship, no more of work under Subbarao. I am done with him. I don't need him,' said Aadi standing up.

That day, Aadi not only lost his dream but also his appetite towards life. He distanced himself from the others, stopped going to the lab and even didn't bother to turn up for his teaching assistantship. Harsh and Tapan tried to help him out of the situation but to no avail.

A WOLF CRY

28ᵗʰ October 2006

Hall8, IITC

Drawing attention of the students coming out of the mess was a world carved out of vegetables. Generally found smashed in mess, today vegetables enjoyed the attention of curious eyes. Dressed in peculiarly Halloween combination, they sat in the corridor in front of the hall's mess. At one end of the display table, a bottle gourd sported sunglasses while at other end a watermelon stood under a sun umbrella. A pumpkin cut to the shape of an idol showered blessings while a brinjal got moulded to laughing Buddha.

'What the hell is this?' asked Harsh, looking through the vegetable collage displayed in front of the mess.

'I guess there was some sort of competition among the mess workers,' replied Tapan.

'That would have been the reason we didn't get enough vegetables in the mess,' said Harsh looking through the strange shapes that vegetables had taken in the collage. Coming to the end of the display, he looked back to Tapan bearing a question mark on his face. 'Has Aadi woken up yet?'

'I haven't checked his room but I am sure he would still be sleeping.'

'We need to push him otherwise he will unduly dent his academics,' said Harsh turning his step towards Aadi's room.

Catching pace with Harsh, said Tapan. 'Aadi's last interaction with Subbarao was really bad. You should have seen his frustration.'

'Subbu is an asshole but he is not Aadi's problem. His problem is the passion that he has lost,' said Harsh. 'I really feel that we need to revive the work on Flymoto.'

'It's not going to be easy. How will we generate the funds?'

'Funds can be arranged. We have sacrificed so much, why not a bit more?' Harsh now stood in front of Aadi's room, staring at the lock on the bolt. 'Strange! Where can Aadi be, so early in the morning?'

'I think he would have left for the lab. We had said enough over the dinner last night.'

'It's good that he is coming back on to the track.' With a contented smile on his face Harsh turned to the cycle stand.

Covering the distance to the Mechanical Department, they were parking the bicycles when Jaswinder crossed their way in haste. She didn't look unusual in her dishevelled attire. Neglecting her presence, Harsh and Tapan carried on. 'Hey guys, have you seen Aadi? I have been calling him for the last twenty minutes but he is not picking up the call,' shouted Jaswinder under a panting breath.

'Is he not here?' In a surprised overtone, Tapan continued. 'We thought he would be in the lab. He was not in his room.'

'He is not in the lab and Subbarao is looking for him desperately. Why is he not coming to the lab for last one month? Is everything alright?'

'I don't know,' replied Tapan.

'You are his close friend and you don't know what his problem is.' Reading through the expression hung on Tapan's face, Jaswinder said, shrugging her shoulder. 'Since morning, Subbarao has asked me several times about Aadi. If he doesn't turn up today, things are certainly going to be nasty for him.'

'Jaswinder, you wait in the lab. We are going to look for Aadi,' said Harsh opening the lock to his bicycle. Without a word, Tapan also joined him on the recce.

'Call me as soon as you find Aadi,' shouted Jaswinder.

Harsh and Tapan combed every corner of the hall, searched cafeteria, dialed every known person and knocked every closed door. After an hour of exhaustive search they were back to the corridor in front of the mess. The vegetables which stood aplomb in the morning now lay emaciated from the heat of Cawnpore sun.

'What's the problem with him? He has never done like this before.' Hanging the call that didn't get connect, Tapan spoke. 'He could have at least picked up our call if he was not in the campus.'

Resting his bum on the step in front of the mess, Harsh exhaled loudly. 'Where can he disappear in just one night?'

'He has taken Flymoto's failure too seriously,' said Tapan sitting on the floor. He stretched back leaning on his arms. The sun's rays flooded his eyes with free radicals, triggering his mind to release somatic cells that relaxed him further.

Chewing his cheeks, Harsh spoke thoughtfully. 'Every problem has a resolution. If he has problem with Subbu, he can ask for changing his supervisor.'

'He was really frustrated after the last interaction with Subbarao. He said things that he should not have.' A thought crossed Tapan's mind and he stood up with an impulse. 'Is everything alright with him?' he asked.

Harsh stood up, his face stern as if he had read the writing on the wall. The worst of thoughts wailed in his mind. Taking charge of the situation, Harsh said. 'Let's get out and search every possible place that Aadi can go to.' Race-walking towards the bicycle stand, Harsh instructed. 'You check in the library and the department. I will look out for him at SAC and the reservation counter.'

Hours had passed since both of them had started from the hall. The sun was making it worse to keep the cool. After failing to track Aadi, Tapan called upon Harsh to take stock of the situation. 'Hey Harsh, any lead?'

'No clue where Aadi has disappeared,' Harsh sighed. 'I have thoroughly searched SAC and just now I have reached the railway ticket counter.'

'I have combed every corner of the library and the department. I too have no clue. I asked many of our colleagues but strangely, no one has seen Aadi since last night.'

'Tapan, now the situation is beyond our control. Let's escalate this.' In an assertive tone, Harsh continued. 'If something wrong happens to Aadi, I am not going to spare Subbarao. I will screw that bastard.'

'Don't lose your temper. Everything will be fine. Let's meet at the department and then we will together have a talk with Subbu.'

Anxiety, anticipation, fear, hatred, love … there were many emotions that swarmed the faces of Harsh and Tapan. They walked their way to Dr. Subbarao's office, struggling with their worst fears. Without indulging in etiquettes, they pushed open the door to Subbarao's office. Unaware of the problem headed his way, Subbarao hurled his first question. 'I had asked Jaswinder to call Aadi and she didn't respond. Where the hell is Aadi? If he wants to play hard ball then I am game.'

'Sir, I think Aadi is in some sort of trouble,' announced Tapan in gushing tones.

'What do you mean by that?'

'Sir, Aadi is missing. We have searched across halls, shopping complex, railway ticket counter and SAC. We didn't find him anywhere. We have dialed every known friend but to little avail,' explained Tapan.

Taking over from where Tapan had stopped, Harsh continued. 'Aadi was disturbed with something. You are aware that he was not coming to the lab for the past few weeks.'

'I haven't done anything wrong to him. I always have been supportive of him, helping him out with his thesis and other academic chores,' Subbarao blabbered as thin line of sweat broke from his head.

'Bastard! Liar!,' Tapan muttered his disgust but Harsh swiftly diverted the attention, injecting his words. 'Sir, we think that IITC's security service should be mobilized. Now, we need to aggressively search for Aadi.'

'If he was going through a rough patch he should have talked to me. I am making a call to SIS,' said Subbarao punching the number on his phone. Subbarao's face was now flooded with sweat as he anticipated the worst that may unfold. He hung the phone before the call could connect. The call to Security Intelligence Service (SIS) would have raised many questions. The hesitation was visible as Subbarao asked. 'Can you guys search again? He might have forgotten to tell you and may have gone somewhere he generally goes. Just check before I raise this issue.'

'Sir, we can again look around for Aadi but we seriously think that the issue should be escalated.' Subbarao was too occupied in his anxiety to fill the pause that Harsh deliberately put in the talk. Sounding his resolve, Harsh continued. 'Sir, if we don't find him soon, we are going to give you a call to escalate the issue.'

Harsh swung around to face Tapan. Beckoning him to follow, he headed out of Subbarao's office. It was time to redo the things. 'Tapan, you keep calling on Aadi's cell. We will search for him at all the places again. Let's hope we get lucky this time.'

Punching Aadi's cell number, Tapan brought his mobile on the speaker mode. He was talking with Harsh when ringing of the mobile stopped and a voice echoed. 'Hi Tapan!'

'Aadi, where are you? We have been calling you since morning. Why were you not picking the call?' yelled Harsh.

'Harsh, is it you?' asked Aadi.

'Yes,' replied Harsh coarsely.

'Actually, in the morning itself I left for the railway reservation counter. I forgot my mobile in the room and just now I saw the missed calls from Tapan. I was about to call.'

'Where are you planning to go?' asked Harsh.

'I am going home for this Diwali,' replied Aadi.

'Have you asked Subbu?'

'No, but I will ask him today. Anyway, it doesn't make any difference to him.'

'Aadi, stay put. We are coming to the hall.' Tapan dropped the call and with it fell the curtain on the whole missing mystery.

'It turned out to be just our anxiety,' said Harsh heaving a sigh of relief.

'Now what should we tell Subbu?' asked Tapan.

'Truth and nothing else,' instructed Harsh. 'You tell him that Aadi had gone to the reservation counter. As he has been disturbed with something for past couple of weeks, his absence from the hostel alarmed us.'

'What about Aadi?' asked Tapan.

'Whatever happens in Vegas remains in Vegas.' Drawing the rules of the game, Harsh said. 'Bury this episode once and for all.'

3rd November 2006

Tennis Court, IITC

'Let's switch to the clay court,' said Harsh looking in the direction of the clay court, which now lay empty, battered from the previous game. Relaxing was not destined to the court as Harsh and Aadi rolled their sleeves to ravage its beauty in the bright sunlit day.

Harsh brushed his shoes against the clay court and placed a sharp serve. With a flick of back hand, Aadi returned the shot which sped past Harsh's ear. A miss from Harsh went as an advantage to Aadi.

'Harsh, finish off this game,' exhorted Tapan. 'If you win, I am giving the treat at PIT Stop.'

Tapan had his eyes fixed on the ball that tossed between the courts. Switching to a double hander shot, Harsh played a strong back hand which Aadi found beyond his reach. A miss from Aadi pushed the game to deuce.

'I will not let it go so easily,' said Aadi bouncing on his feet.

'That's what I expect from you.' Flicking his racquet, Harsh exhorted. 'Look at my arms. That's where the shot starts.'

Harsh tossed the ball up in the air and smashed his racquet. A serve on the edge of court was not easy to take. Aadi missed the shot and lend the game point to Harsh.

'Bravo!' Tapan exulted.

Tossing the ball in the air, Harsh smashed his racquet. The

racquet flew past the ball without making a contact and the ball fell hopelessly on the ground. Harsh had missed the serve.

'Harsh, what are you doing? You had almost snatched the game,' bawled Tapan.

'The game is not over yet,' said Aadi.

'It's not over till you acknowledge.' Harsh placed the serve which Aadi picked up swiftly. The ball flew off Aadi's racquet and made the contact with Harsh's racquet at the last moment. In its own momentum, the ball flew half way to the court and making a contact on the net dropped on Aadi's side. Harsh didn't commit any mistake and converted his next serve to a point and won the game.

After a cool-down routine, the group had their next halt at the pit stop, a small panipuri cart in front of Hall 1. Aadi had started to drool even before panipuri was served to him. The effervescence of the water mixed with tamarind and chaat masala left his mind buzzing. He swallowed a puri which busted inside his mouth. The heat from the chilies mellowed in the sweetness of pani sloshing over his tongue. The volatile oil from the fennel seeds left its tingling sensation while chilies showed its effect on his runny nose and watery eyes.

'Do you guys know what happened with Sid today?' asked Aadi wiping water off his running nose.

'Bring it on,' said Harsh.

'Today, Sid brought his girlfriend to his room. He had everything ready, curtains were fit tight, a nice melody was put on ...' Cutting Aadi in between, Harsh instructed *pani-puri wala*. 'You add lots of spices *bhaiya*. Make it a little less spicy.' Looking back to Aadi, he continued. 'You also add less of spices.'

'It's all true. Sid had a few practice sessions and had saved enough safety caps in his wallet, keeping them handy to use, safe and secure. Talking straight, he had a plot ready to screw his girlfriend.'

'What is a safety cap?' asked Tapan in a hesitant tone.

'Dude, don't say that you don't know what a safety cap is,' said Aadi shrugging his shoulder and arching his eyebrows.

'It's not PSPO that everyone should know,' snapped Tapan.

'Safety cap is nothing but a condom.' Dumping the panipuri ball in his mouth, Aadi continued. 'Sid had his good time only with those practice session. His fortune took an untoward turn when his girlfriend's fiancée barged in his room and roughed him up.'

'I knew his intentions well,' said Harsh squashing the paper cup and dropping it in the bin. After tendering the bill, the three friends moved to the hall, soaked in their sweat. The first thing on the mind of everyone was a cool shower.

The stream of high pressure water jutting out of the shower opened the pores of tardiness and infused a new energy. Standing in front of the mirror, Aadi was scrubbing his head when a knock on the door pulled him back from the act of narcissism.

As soon as Aadi opened the bolt, Sid gushed inside the room. Picking up the water bottle kept on the computer desk he emptied it in his stomach. Settling on the chair, he asked. 'How are things, your thesis and other stuff?'

'Fine. And what about you?'

'Aadi, there's something serious that I want to discuss with you.'

'I am all ears,' said Aadi sitting on the chair, his eyes locked with Sid's.

'Aadi, the academics are important, but, it's not the end. There's a world outside this institute, outside the books, outside the research that we do,' said Sid stepping on a moral beat.

'That is fine. I understand that,' replied Aadi. With the continuing second many thoughts flooded his mind. Breaking through the clamor of thoughts, he asked. 'Is something wrong? You never shared this kind of philosophy with me.'

'This is not a philosophy. You should not consider the trivial matter of studies so seriously when it comes to life,' said Sid, his voice raised.

'It's presumptuous.' Aadi stood up. In an irritated tone, he continued. 'Your concern for me is unwarranted.'

'Aadi, I didn't feel bad because of you being snobbish. I can understand the pressure you are going through.'

'Everyone at IITC has got pressure on them. There's nothing new about it. And, I am not being snobbish, but I am a bit surprised why you chose me today.' Taking a pause, Aadi spoke. 'What have you been smoking?'

'Aadi, I am just trying to help you,' snapped Sid.

'And when did I need your help?' said Aadi, his voice clad with sarcasm.

'Your supervisor has raised a concern with the counseling service. He thinks that you are disturbed because of your studies.'

'I can't believe this,' Aadi sighed.

'What's wrong?' asked Sid surprised.

'First, you need to believe me that I am not disturbed. Second, Subbarao has been harassing me with regard to my thesis and we already had some untoward interactions.' Fitting together the pieces of puzzle, Aadi spoke, half-glancing towards Sid. 'My absence from the lab for last one month might have raised his concern. To cover up his misdeeds, he might have registered a case with the counseling service.'

'He is a thick ass. He creates the problem and then plays safe by registering a case with students' counsel,' said Sid, sighing fervently.

Rolling his head and easing a breath, Aadi spoke indignantly. 'I knew he had double standards, but I never dreamt that he is going to play a foul game.'

'I was also surprised when I was told to keep an eye on you. Subbu is such a hypocrite.' Clinching his fist, Sid said rhetorically. 'Oye Aadi, *Subbu ke batti laga de.*'

'That I will do,' said Aadi, musing, a rage visible in his eyes.

After Sid left, Aadi drifted to Tapan's room. Getting stock of Aadi's conversation with Sid, Tapan spoke hesitantly. 'Aadi, I think you should know the facts. Before I tell you anything, I need a promise from you.' Gauging again his resolve to share the fact, Tapan spoke. 'Harsh should never know that I told you this. For him, you never know this.'

'Tapan, you can have faith in me and for God's sake cut the crap.'

Looking straight in Aadi's eyes, Tapan continued. 'Aadi, you remember the day when you had gone to the reservation counter and had forgotten the mobile in your room.'

'Yes, I remember that. It was quite surprising that you guys called me up a zillion times but had nothing to talk when I actually picked up the call.'

'It was a big mess up.' said Tapan, reeling back in time. Spellbound, Aadi relived the past that has been sacredly hidden from him. He could appreciate the concern that his friends shared for him but was disturbed with one fact. Looking deep in Tapan's eyes, he asked. 'How can you guys think that I can ever do that?'

'Aadi, we were concerned about you. You had taken Flymoto's failure quite seriously. Subbu was creating trouble for you. We may have thought crazy but that wasn't unjustified.'

'I can understand. I had kind of led you guys to think that way,' Aadi sighed.

'You know what Subbu's reaction was when we shared our concern.' Spitting out his disgust, Tapan continued. 'Subbu went on to blabber all sort of nonsense. His first attempt was to save his ass than to help us find you.'

'What are you both doing here?' Aadi and Tapan went practically numb seeing Harsh standing in front of them. But as the chat proceeded it became apparent that Harsh could not have overheard any part of the conversation that went between the two.

'Today I have a dry throat. I am planning to go to NASA for some drinks. Are you guys in?' asked Harsh.

'We can come. It had been a long time since we had beer,' added Tapan, swinging around to face Aadi with the same question in hand. How could have Aadi played spoilsport. He was the one in desperate need of a kick. So, he shrugged his shoulders in a mute acknowledgement.

THE LAST NAIL

10th November 2006

Antaragni, Auditorium Ground, IITC

'This is really pathetic. They have kept us waiting for the last 2 hours. Can't they manage the crowd efficiently?' Aadi said as the clock ticked to complete another hour.

More than 200 students thronged the barricade in front of the auditorium ground, waiting for entry to open for the rock show. The sprawling lawn in front of the auditorium was transformed into an open air theatre with a central stage and a ramp. Temporary bamboo barricades were sowed to herd the crowd to the desired corners. The only entrance was manned by the volunteers from the gymkhana.

'Aadi, the band is going to perform after the fashion show. Security check is delaying the entries,' said Harsh, briskly rubbing his palms together.

Suddenly, the students assorted together in a queue anticipating the gate to open. Two of the organizing committee members slowly walked towards the barricade. Looking deep in the crowd one of them signaled the queue to roll in. After frisking and verifying the entry pass, the students were sent inside.

'Show me your pass,' demanded a volunteer guarding the portion of the ground thrown lavishly with the chairs and sofa. The badge on his chest bore the emblem of the gymkhana club, the student body organizing the event.

After having a close look at the passes, the volunteer remarked, pointing to a direction. 'You guys should go to the other side of the ramp. This side is reserved for the faculty members and their families.'

'Hey, they are my friends. Let them in,' interjected Sid. Being a member of the gymkhana club, Sid also had his duty to discipline the event.

'But, Sid.'

'Don't they look family to a faculty?' asked Sid.

'If you wish so,' said the volunteer shrugging his shoulder.

Collecting back the passes, Harsh patted on Sid's shoulder. 'Thanks dude.'

'Cut the crap and let's settle somewhere. I don't want to miss the fashion show,' replied Sid with a conspiratorial wink. The bleak November evening was warming up to the hot ladies on the ramp. The gentle breeze had turned wild, caressing through the sizzling bodies in the fashion parade.

Jaws dropped to the ground, eyes popped out of the sockets and tongues drooled over the girls from 'International Institute of Fashion Technology Chandigarh.' Bearing plastic face, long tanned legs and short crafted dress, the girls made their own statement. On the beat of 'Tokyo drift', they paraded with the face held high. On the ground many neck bones cracked, trying to steal a glimpse of their beauty.

The background music came to a stop. The last lady in the parade flew a kiss to the audience before going behind the stage. Catching the kiss, the anchor came back on the stage. 'Now we are going to have beauties from our own institute adorn the ramp.' Taking stock of the hopeless faces on the ground, the anchor continued. 'Yes, my dear friends, beauties from IITC are now going to set ablaze the stage.'

'Cover up the stage with smoke,' yelled a student from the crowd.

'What do the girls at IITC know about fashion?' commented another student.

Boos from the crowd were audible enough to be heard over the loud music. Following the beats of passion, the girls from

IITC decked the stage. The audience was left spell bound. No one could ever have imagined that the faces covered with spectacles, pimples and books can be so charming. Leading the ladies was a known face. Pointing to it, Harsh asked, his voice doubtful. 'Is that *bhabhijaan?*'

'*Bhabhi teri, jaan meri*,' replied Aadi looking towards Sonia who was on the ramp. In her satin pencil skirt, she looked no less than a model. 'Sonia looks good in that dress,' he added.

Aadi was not done praising when he heard a voice behind his back. 'Sir, you can have a seat over here.' Aadi turned back in the direction of the voice to find Dr. Subbarao. 'How are you doing Aadi?' asked Dr Subbarao sitting by his side.

'I am fine sir,' replied Aadi.

'How did you guys get entry? You are not allowed in this section of the ground,' said the student volunteer standing by the side of Subbarao. The gymkhana club badge on his chest backed the authority in his voice.

Avoiding any trouble, Sid slid his gymkhana badge inside his shirt's pocket. Exchanging a furtive glance with others, he said. 'Let's move to the other side.' Sid quickly swung himself out of his chair and picked the steps out, others followed him. Before they could reach the aisle, Subbarao commanded. 'Wait a minute.'

Casting a magical spell, Subbarao froze the steps on the run. Thawing them back, he asked the student volunteer. 'Can you leave Aadi with me for some time?'

'But sir, students are not allowed without a pass in this section,' replied the student volunteer. A smile sprouted on Aadi's lips but before it could have blown up on his face, Subbarao spoke. 'I think exceptions can be made.'

Looking to the others, the student volunteer signaled them to continue without Aadi.

Reluctantly, Aadi sat in the chair next to Subbarao. From the corner of his eyes, he had been admiring Sonia when Subbarao spoke. 'I have been thinking about you lately.' Looking towards Aadi, he continued. 'I was not sure why would you stage a suicide drama in front of me.'

Before Aadi could speak up, Subbarao said, bearing a smirk on his face. 'Your friends had nearly declared me a criminal.'

Restraining the Subbarao's creative grey cells at work, Aadi interrupted. 'It was a mistake, sir.'

Ignoring Aadi, Subbarao continued. 'But then I realized you did it to save yourself from my rage after insulting me in front of B. Tech class. Indeed, it was a well-designed plot to gain my sympathy.'

'Sir, it's not like that ...' Aadi was not done when Subbarao pounded his words on him. 'Do I look like a fool to fall for your fraud suicide story?'

'Sir, there is a total misunderstanding.' Aadi found him nearly shouting over the music. Leaving him unnoticed, Subbarao spoke, his words precise and profound. 'I have released you of the teaching assistantship.'

'But sir ...'

'I think you understand that your scholarship would be ceased.' Taking stock of faces around, Subbarao continued. 'You have done what came to your mind but now I will ensure that for the next six months you work on what I want.'

'Sir, I can explain everything,' said Aadi, not fully convinced if he could.

'You better come to my office tomorrow morning. I will wait for you,' said Subbarao noting the appointment in his small diary.

Before Subbarao could have said further, a fair lady in pink zari saree came as an angel. Crossing her hand across her ample bosoms, she held tight the loose end of her sari. Her chiseled face and seductive figure drew attention from everyone around. She bent forward whispering the words heard not only by Dr. Subbarao but by people around him as well. 'Director sir was asking for you. Please follow me. I can show you where he is sitting.'

'I will take your leave now,' said Subbarao extending his hand to Aadi. 'I will be waiting for you tomorrow morning.' Shaking hand with Aadi, Subbarao left with the fairer sex.

Aadi was sitting with a haunted face when someone tapped on his shoulder. He turned back to find Sonia standing in front of him. 'What are you doing here? You were on the ramp,' said Aadi in a surprised tone.

'You are fuming,' remarked Sonia. Grabbing Aadi's hand, she continued. 'We don't have much time. Come with me.'

Aadi literally felt being dragged. He stiffened his hand and asked. 'Where are we going?'

'Quickly, we need to leave.' Reading Aadi's expression which had turned quizzical, Sonia explained. 'I saw Subbu harassing you. So, I asked one of my friends to get rid of him. Now we need to run as director sir is not on the ground.'

'Thanks for saving me from that asshole.' With the passing second Aadi realized that he was with a lady. Regretting, he apologized. 'I am sorry.'

'It's alright. It was due on him,' replied Sonia.

The attraction of the night was the performance by a rock group. Hordes of rock fans from Cawnpore city crowded the road running in front of the auditorium ground. Without a pass they had a limited enjoyment. Coming out of the barricaded ground, Sonia collected Aadi's pass and along with hers she gave it to two lucky rock fans.

'Are we not coming back for the rock show?'

'Do you want to mess with Subbarao again?' said Sonia swinging back to face Aadi. Her piercing gaze was not easy to bear. Stammering, Aadi replied. 'No … I had enough for the day.'

'Let's watch the show from the outside. Anyway, it can be heard from anywhere in the campus.' Sonia had not completed her talk when the 440 volt sound box came to life and the sky got lit with the fireworks. Without any prior announcement a group of seven stormed on the stage. They plucked a few strings before the lead singer of the band took charge on the loud speaker, speaking vehemently. 'It was 11 years ago when we started our journey at IITC. It always feels good to come back to this place. We have travelled a long musical journey and have miles to go but it always feels good to come back home.'

'It would certainly be an awesome feeling to come back to one's alma mater,' said Sonia settling on a bench in the shopping complex, adjacent to the auditorium ground.

'I don't know. Without my friends this place holds no meaning to me. I would like to come back only if my friends are with me.'

'So, you guys are too close, huh?'

'We are certified *chuddy buddies*,' replied Aadi, darting a glance at Sonia. In the crafted dress she looked no less than an angel. The smile that Aadi was able to successfully carve on her face, added to the beauty.

'I think you guys should teach Subbarao a lesson. He needs to be educated,' said Sonia.

'What can we do?'

'I don't know but I think you should do something.' The rock group now had started pouring melody of song *'Dooba Dooba'* by Silk Route. Sonia was all enthralled while Aadi's mind buzzed through her words.

'This song is an acoustic delight. How do they know what I want to hear?' said Sonia plugging in her final ecstasy.

'Sonia, I am leaving.'

'For where?' asked Sonia grabbing Aadi's hand.

'I need to get even with Subbarao.'

'What are you planning to do?'

'You would like to give me a call after mid night.' Aadi took Sonia's hand and writing his contact number on her palm, he said. 'Check your mail before calling.'

Aadi broke away and walked down to his bicycle. Cranking it open, he had sat on the crown seat when Sonia shouted. 'Hey, don't do something foolish. I was just talking rubbish. I didn't mean it.'

'Have faith in me. I am not going to do anything foolish,' said Aadi, reassuring her.

Sonia was curious as she came back to the hall. She tried to contact Aadi but his mobile was turned off. She closed her eyes praying that her provocation prove harmless. In her worries, she fell asleep and woke up five minutes past the mid night.

Waking up, Sonia instantly hopped onto IITC's home page. Her expressions shipped from the island of inquisition to hysteria as she read through the content of the news. Her skin tightened into chill bumps. She now looked onto IITC's home page with awe.

'What the fuck?' talking to herself Sonia stood up as she completed reading the current news on IITC's home page.

Browsing more through the content of the home page got her nuts. 'How is this possible?' Sonia talked to herself aloud as her expressions shipped to the next island, 'island of insanity'. 'Holy Shit, what the hell they are talking about, 'Mc Donalds buys IITC for 40 billion USD'.' Browsing furiously through the home page got her on her toes as she saw the logo of IITC morphed with burger. The mission statement of the institute was grotesquely changed to a hilarious context.

'Dr. Subbarao, Mc Fries R&D has been awarded the George Mccy Fry Gold Medal,' the news on the IITC bulletin now made sense to her. She picked her mobile and redialled the last number on her call list.

'Did you see the IITC news?' asked Aadi picking Sonia's call.

'So, McDonalds has bought IITC for 40 Billion US dollars.'

'Read through the news column of 'Award and Recognition' in the right hand side of the page,' asked Aadi, an excitement mellowed in his voice.

'Aadi, please stop this,' said Sonia indignantly.

'I am now even with Subbu,' chortled Aadi. 'IIT Cawnpore adjudged World's No. 1 Burger Institute,' laughed Aadi reading through the next current news.

'Aadi don't try to make a mockery of institute's e-security.' Anchoring her emotions on the island of exasperation, Sonia continued. 'This can backfire on you badly.'

'You are talking to an expert hacker. They will not be able to track me back.'

'Aadi, you are screwing up your career, an expensive way. For God's sake, stop this,' yelled Sonia.

'Why are you shouting? Were you not preaching that we should teach Subbu a lesson? So, why this fuss now?'

'What do you expect me to say? *Mogambo khush hua!* Don't you have brains?'

'*Nahin,* I thought *sardar khush hoga, sabashi dega,*' giggled Aadi.

'Please stop this nonsense,' said Sonia, her voice abnormally high.

'Stop shouting, I am releasing the server. I never thought that you can't even stand for what you say,' said Aadi.

'I'm concerned about you, that's why I'm shouting and in return you pick on me for not standing up for what I say. It's now over. I am not going to talk to you anymore. You are psychotic, insane and crazy. I am done with you,' said Sonia hanging up on Aadi.

11th November 2006

Dr. Subbarao's Office, IITC

In the wilderness of concrete and machines roamed freely the ghost of 'godrej padlock' hung by neck. Gazing at the padlock, Aadi dozed off sitting outside of Dr. Subbarao's office. The last night was tiring for him. If he had gone to bed, he would not have made it for the meeting. Not betting on his luck, he came down to the lab. While he snored in his sleep, seconds in the wall clock ate circles. An hour would have passed when his sleep broke with some noise. It was Dr. Subbarao locking the spirit of the 'godrej padlock' hung by neck.

With a push Subbarao opened the door to his office. Opening the window blinds he pressed the array of switches that brought the tube light hung on the opposite wall alive. A lizard also woke up and shifted its position for the dark corner of the room. Shoving books kept on his desk to a corner, he switched his glance to Aadi.

'Come on in.'

'How was the rock show yesterday?' asked Subbarao as Aadi stepped inside the office.

'It was good,' replied Aadi, suppressing his yawns that silently yelled for rest.

'Somehow the director didn't have the yesterday's show in his schedule.' From the corner of his eyes, Subbarao tried to read through Aadi's reaction. Taking a deep breath, he continued. 'I assume that you don't know the girl who conveyed me the message from the director.'

'Sir ...' Suddenly Aadi had a cotton mouth. He kept a neutral expression plastered on his face as he continued. 'Sir, I am not sure what you mean.'

'Ignorance is bliss!' With a stern look, Subbarao said, shaking his head. 'I am sure you are also unaware of hacking of IITC's server that happened last night.'

'Sir, I don't have a clue about that,' shrugged Aadi.

'Stop being naïve. Do you think I am a fool? Can't I understand what goes on inside your brain?' said Subbarao, banging his fist on the table. 'I know it was you who did this.'

'Sir, you have got nothing to hold me responsible,' said Aadi, his voice loud.

Narrowing his eyes, Subbarao spitted his words filled with disgust. 'Let me tell you one thing. The day, I get any evidence that speaks about your involvement in this case, your career is finished.'

Trashing the printout of hacked web site in the dustbin, Subbarao strode across to the door of his office. Opening the door, he said. 'Aadi, you can leave now.'

'But sir ...,' stuttered Aadi.

'Get out of the room, NOW,' barked Subbarao.

Oozing out a deep breath, Aadi walked out of the office. Yesterday night reeled in front of him. It was foolhardy of him to challenge the institute. The thought of disciplinary action made him shudder. Coming back to his room, Aadi meticulously negated all the evidence that could have pointed back to him. Aadi didn't get much time to think about his misdoings. As mercury dipped to subzero, he got busy with the academics. The semester exams were not over when the campus placement picked up heat. With cent percent placement in first four days, every student had secured a future for themselves.

Fourth Semester

SHOW MUST GO ON

8th January 2007

Aadi's room, Hall8, IITC

'Hey Aadi, are you going somewhere?' Aadi turned back in the direction of the sound to find Harsh standing at the door. Throwing his comb on the cot, he asked. 'Are you coming from the lab?' Harsh's usual attire of shorts on a red T-shirt was replaced with a more suave dress code. Neatly combed hair on a shaven face yelled that he had just met his supervisor.

'I am coming from the DOAA office,' said Harsh shifting his sight to the ground. A trace of dust on his glistening shoes made him uncomfortable.

'Why had they called you to the DOAA office?'

Raising his left leg, Harsh rubbed the shoe against the trouser on the right stout leg, the dust vanished and so did the question. Looking above, he said. 'I am leaving for home.'

Fitting the loose pieces of talk together, Aadi slung his next question. 'Harsh, is everything alright?'

Picking the tracks out of the room, Harsh cleared the doubts. 'I intend to pack my belongings and need your help. Can you help me?'

'I am coming. Wait!' spoke Aadi high on his volume. Harsh ignored Aadi and trekked back to his room. When Aadi entered the room, he found Harsh busy in disengaging the terminal of his computer. The room was in a total mess. Books and clothes struggled for the last shred of space on the only cot in the room.

Loose wires, shoes, deodorant, water bottles, chip packets, ketchup sachets and their siblings lay abandoned on the floor. Aadi picked up a carton and without exchanging a word started placing the books in it.

'Harsh, please tell me what exactly happened?' asked Aadi after a brief moment of silence.

'I got terminated. Official announcement will be made tomorrow,' replied Harsh plainly.

Aadi found himself frozen in his place. He stood numb while Harsh picked a book from his hand and put it inside the carton. Applying tape on the lid of the filled box, Harsh opened the wardrobe. He brought out a duffel bag from inside. 'Aadi, I created this Flymoto model for us to ...' Extending the bag to Aadi, Harsh said in a husky voice. 'Start the experiments. And don't get angry if Tapan makes a mistake.'

'What the hell? How can they terminate you?'

'My research work was rated as unsatisfactory.' Exchanging a glance with Aadi, Harsh said, his voice remarkably calm. 'Subbarao refused to back me for further research under him.'

'How can he do this to you?'

'Dr. Mukherjee is a nice professor. Stay close to him. Subbarao may try to trouble you after this.' Heaving a weary sigh, he continued. 'And please start the experiments. I believe we are very close to success.'

'We can't succeed without you,' spluttered Aadi.

'Aadi you have already succeeded in life. No one in the institute ever undertook this big a project. Success could have got you in good books of a few but you have already won over your dream,' said Harsh hugging Aadi. Coming out of the comforting arms, Harsh continued. 'Let me show this to you.'

Harsh opened the bag and brought out the Flymoto model. Aadi could clearly see a drop of tear ready to roll from Harsh's eyes. Controlling his emotions, Harsh wiped off his face and packed the Flymoto model back in the bag. Handing the bag over to Aadi, he asked. 'Can you please call the rickshaw?'

'Sure,' said Aadi collecting the bag. He lugged it on his back and walked out to the hall gate. Within five minutes, Harsh and Aadi were pushing the luggage on to the rickshaw standing in front of the gate.

Sitting between the luggage, Harsh bid his adieu. In a poised demeanor, he shook Aadi's hand. Maintaining a tight grip, he spoke. 'Can you do me a favor?' Aadi exchanged a nod of approval for Harsh to continue. 'Don't tell others about my termination.'

'But they will get to know, if not by me, then by somebody else.' Aadi paused, trying to read Harsh's mind. Unsuccessful, he continued. 'I understand that it's tough on you but we all are your friends.'

'Aadi, do me this last favor. Just don't tell anybody about this. Let them get the information from someone else but not from you.' Looking at his wrist watch, Harsh tapped on the shoulder of the rickshaw puller. 'I need to keep going.'

'Wait for a sec, I will get my bicycle.'

'There's no need Aadi, I don't need company. I will call you up once I reach Mumbai.'

'I will take the liberty of coming with you, even if you don't allow me to.' Picking his cycle, Aadi followed the rickshaw. Keeping the duffel bag with the security at the institute's gate, Aadi accompanied Harsh to Cawnpore railway station. Only after Harsh boarded the train to Mumbai did Aadi return.

After coming back to IITC's main gate, Aadi picked the bag and rode to the department, still unsure of how to behave ignorant.

Aadi reached the department and settled with Tapan on a bench sowed in the lawn of mechanical department. 'Do you know where Harsh is?' Tapan asked taking a sip of coffee.

Unaware of the question that stood in front of him, Aadi struggled with the fizz in his glass of cold coffee. He stirred his coffee with the straw till the last bubble inside the glass sunk in the whirlpool. 'Have you seen Harsh?' Tapan repeated his question.

Aadi left the straw and looked above, his face defying any emotion. Avoiding any direct eye contact, he answered. 'No, I haven't seen him today.'

'How come you are in the lab today?' asked Tapan.

'I had come to the library when I thought of catching up with you guys.' Hiding his uneasiness, Aadi picked the coffee mug.

'Is something wrong with you? You look troubled.'

'Nothing,' Aadi tried to flush a calm demeanor on his face, but lost. Hiding his uneasiness, he rummaged through the duffel bag. The Flymoto model sticking out of the bag got hooked on Tapan's attention. Intrigued, he asked. 'Is that Flymoto?'

'Yeah,' replied Aadi, shaking his head.

Drawing it out of the bag carefully, Tapan studied the Flymoto model closely before hurling his next question. 'When did you make it?'

'I haven't made it. Harsh gave it to me.'

'But you said you didn't see him today. Where is he?'

'He gave me the Flymoto model in the afternoon. I didn't meet him after that.'

'Are we starting the experiments?' Tapan's face bore a fantastic exuberance. He stood up as he continued. 'Aadi, this time we are surely going to succeed. Are we starting from tomorrow?'

Aadi replied with a curt nod.

'That's perfect. I will complete my thesis experiments by the evening. From tomorrow, we will start work on Flymoto. We need to get up early tomorrow,' said Tapan putting back the Flymoto model in the bag. 'Aadi, let's get to the lab.'

Tapan went back to his experiments while Aadi sat blankly in front of the computer, trying to kill time that had come to a standstill.

It was drizzling when Aadi and Tapan came out of the department in the evening. Mist suspended in the air refracted the yellow light from the neon lamppost on the sideways. Gigantic trees standing in front of the department seemed dwarfed, lost in the darkness.

'Aadi, I am really blessed. Where else in the world can you have such nice friends? I want all of us to succeed. We have put in a lot of effort into Flymoto,' said Tapan lifting himself on the bicycle.

'We will succeed for sure,' said Aadi, his voice low. Hiding the truth was eating away his conscience but how could he have disavowed his words. Donning a calm expression, he completed the rest of the tasks for the day.

9th January 2007

Aadi's room, Hall8, IITC

'Hey Aadi, are you still asleep?' yelled Tapan pounding hard on the door. Standing in front of Aadi's room, Tapan waited, counting under his breath.

Receiving no response, Tapan decided to try placing a call. He didn't want to ruin the sleep of others in the block. Tapan listened intently the ring tone of Aadi's mobile till the connection got severed. His hopes rose with a creaky noise coming from inside the room. He could hear clearly Aadi shuffling his feet across the floor. Tapan gave a furious scowl as Aadi opened the door. 'Get ready. We are already late,' he snapped.

Aadi tried to marshal his thoughts in some sort of order. He stood gaining sobriety from the inebriated sleep of the previous night. Taking his time, he spoke. 'What are you up to?'

'We had planned to go to the lab. Go and wash your face. You still seem to be dreaming.'

Aadi had too many worries to remember the commitments made. He stood for a while, speculating. Counting the odds, he said. 'Give me five minutes.'

Picking up his towel and face wash, Aadi donned the slippers. Before he could have escaped to the restroom, his mobile rang to hold him back. Picking the call, Aadi spoke. 'Hi, Harsh'

Tapan tried to interpret the monologue as Aadi continued with the conversation.

'Oh, good'......... *'Don't worry, I will handle'* .... *'Will update you on the same'* .... *'Ok, that's fine'*
'Not a problem'
'You need not say that.'

'Isn't Harsh coming to the lab?' asked Tapan as Aadi dropped the call.

Aadi was caught unguarded. Impromptu, he replied. 'Harsh is going to come directly to the lab. He will be there in another 30 minutes.' Stealing his eyes from Tapan, Aadi continued. 'He slept late yesterday night.'

'Where has he been last night? I tried to contact him so many times.' Tapan tossed his notebook from one hand to the other. His face defied any expression though his anxiety lay exposed by his body language.

Ignoring the question, Aadi heaved himself up and hiked to the restroom. Completing his ablutions, Aadi packed the Flymoto model inside the duffel bag. Looking towards Tapan, he said. 'Let's move. There is a lot of stuff that we need to do today.'

It was unusually dark when Aadi and Tapan came out of the hostel. Unruly cold winds ran a shiver down their spines. The climate had turned freezing and making it worse, a thick blanket of cloud covered the skies. Fog on the streets was too thick for the light from the neon lamppost to breach through. Unconcerned of the rogue climate, Aadi and Tapan drove to the lab. They reached the wind tunnel facility, late by 30 minutes from their usual schedule.

While Tapan parked his bicycle, Aadi moved ahead. Standing in front of the lab's door, he rummaged through his bag. He got the key but when he looked up there was no lock for him to open. Surprised, he stood blank while his mind raced to probe a reason. There was enough going on in his mind when Tapan pushed the door open. Stepping inside the lab, he said. 'What are you waiting for? Let's get started.'

The storm inside Aadi's mind was no less savage than the storm outside. Soon, he lost track of the compelling thoughts and got involved with the work at hand. After fitting the Flymoto model in the test section, Aadi adjusted the camera on a tripod. The camera was placed in the control room and through the glass window it could capture every movement in the test section. Through the camera's lens, Aadi could see Tapan preparing Flymoto for the experiments. Dressing up Flymoto with sensors, Tapan came out of the test section.

Room filled with the noises as Aadi started the experiment. In the melee inside the room were participating mechanical shriek from the fan, rumbling air inside the nozzle and Flymoto chattering on the test bed.

Aadi stood up and switched off the experiment. 'There's some problem with the mechanical lock on the wings. Wings are not able to carry the load,' said Aadi looking towards Tapan.

Tapan knew what he had to do. After cleaning the sensors from Flymoto's body, he fixed it in a fixture. Taking out the old mechanical lock, he replaced it with a new one. Completing the job, Tapan fitted the model back on the test bed. Painstakingly, he tied the sensors back on the model before signaling Aadi to start the experiment.

Aadi switched on the camcorder and then started the experiment. A few seconds would have elapsed when Aadi observed something different. He now had his full attention on the Flymoto's model. The model chattered heavily on the test bed. Suddenly, the chattering went dead. Aadi could not believe what he just saw. He went back to the camcorder and zoomed in on Flymoto. Though unstable, the model was airborne in the streamlined flow inside the nozzle. Aadi looked up, his face awash with happiness. Awestruck, Aadi jumped in exhilaration. 'Hey, our Flymoto just flew. It's flying.'

Tapan was next to peek through the camcorder. His heart filled with joy, like a father watching his baby take those first few unsteady steps. With a tenderly expression he turned to Aadi and hugged him tight.

Flymoto would have flown for a minute when Aadi switched off the fan. He rewound the camcorder and saw the recorded movie. Next minute, Aadi and Tapan had tears in their eyes.

'Where is Harsh?' asked Tapan. 'He should see this.'

'Harsh is in Mumbai. He left yesterday afternoon.'

'Why the hell is he in Mumbai?' Surprised, Tapan looked at Aadi.

'He got terminated.' Aadi replied blankly. With the passing second Tapan's face flooded with questions. There were explanations required and Aadi found it tough to hold himself back any longer. He shared with Tapan how Subbarao's critical remarks about Harsh's research work and Harsh's low CPI resulted in the DOAA committee passing a verdict on his termination.

The storm outside the lab had turned violent. The noises from outside now mellowed in the clamor running through Tapan's mind. With the confused expression on his face, he asked. 'Why didn't you tell me?'

'Harsh was not comfortable facing any of us. He moved out on his terms before he could have been served with a notice.'

'It would have been tough on him,' said Tapan with a sigh. With a complaint on his face, Tapan said. 'You should have told me.'

'I was just trying to keep my word to Harsh,' said Aadi, his voice meek.

'Let's leave. I don't feel we can do anything further today.'

'I am also not feeling good,' said Aadi, exhaling audibly.

Carefully removing the devices attached on Flymoto's body, Aadi brought the model out from the test section. Placing the model inside his bag, he joined Tapan. They had taken a few steps to the exit when a sudden thud warranted their attention. 'What was that noise?' asked Aadi.

'I am not sure.' Looking around for the source, Tapan spoke. 'We had left the door open. I think a stray dog might have got inside.'

'The lab assistant will kill us if he finds a dog inside the lab,' said Aadi.

'Let's look for it then,' said Tapan rolling his eyeballs around. The lab came out clean in their search for the source of the noise. After exhausting all the possibilities, Aadi asked pointing to the store room. 'Could the noise have come from there?'

The store room was adjacent to the lab. Aadi picked up an iron bar while Tapan kept pace with him. They came out of the lab and walked slowly towards the store. Aadi could clearly hear the noises. It was apparent that there was someone inside the store. As they got closer to the store room, Aadi could see the lab assistant in chat with a stranger. Finding it unusual, Aadi took cover and swept himself right into the hearing distance. Tapan ducked right behind Aadi.

'It is such a relief. Since the time Dr. Bhaskar allowed those three students to work in the lab, we have had tough times,' said the lab assistant.

'Are they going to start again?' asked the stranger. He was a short heighted, obese, in his early thirties. Under a graveyard of pimples and a mole at the center of the nose, his face appeared plundered. Remnants of hair ran impudently along the temporal lobe while his central skull lay barren. With burly face, round eyes and a big belly, he resembled a rodent generally found in the farms.

'I am not sure. Neither Dr. Bhaskar nor the students ever said a word about that,' said the lab assistant. 'I think they are done with what they wanted to do.'

Aadi peeked in to see the lab assistant opening the iron almirah. Picking up a new packed pitot tube, he handed it to the stranger. 'How much will this piece sell for?'

'Thousand bucks and 50 percent goes to your account,' replied the stranger.

'That isn't fair. The institute purchases this piece for about 10 grand and you intend to sell it out for just one,' the lab assistant argued.

'What's your problem? You just need to say that the piece broke during the experiments. Dr. Bhaskar trusts you.'

'That's correct, but I think I should get more. You should consider the fact that I gave you a bag full of junk as well.'

'Okay, don't worry. You will get thousand bucks for this,' said the stranger with pitot tube in his hand. Tapping on his bag, he continued. 'Just keep getting me the stuff regularly.'

'What the fuck?' Aadi turned back only to realize that Tapan had already marched ahead, inside the store room. 'Tapan, don't do it,' Aadi warned.

Tapan turned back as did the lab assistant and the stranger in the direction of the sound. Exchanging a brief look with Aadi, Tapan continued. 'We will tell everything to Dr. Bhaskar. You steal the instruments from the lab and blame it on the students. I am going to call Dr. Bhaskar right away.' said Tapan taking his mobile out of his pocket.

Aadi rushed to Tapan who was busy scrolling for Dr. Bhaskar's number in his contact list. Before Tapan could have dialed the number, the lab assistant snatched the mobile from him. 'Why are you getting involved in this? You carry on with your experiments as usual. I will help you.'

'We don't need your help,' said Aadi snatching the mobile back from the lab assistant.

Before Aadi could have realized, the stranger shoved Tapan down on the floor. 'What do you think of yourself? Are you some hero?'

From the corner of his eye, Aadi could see the lab assistant taking a step towards him. Aadi plunged to the ground. Escaping the grip, Aadi shouted, his voice rising with every word. 'This isn't happening. We are not going to leave you guys.'

'We will see how you complain against us.' Like a mad bull, the stranger charged towards Aadi. In an instant, Aadi ducked to one corner, putting himself out of the stranger's reach. Taking off the bag from his shoulder, Aadi rummaged for something to fight with the formidable contender. He got hold of the mechanical lock used in the Flymoto's wing. He took it out and slung it up towards the stranger headed his way. The mechanical lock landed on the face of the stranger. The stranger was severely hurt and bled profusely. Like a loose ball, he fell flat on the ground. Seeing the blood, the lab assistant fled out of the store room.

Grabbing the bag and the mechanical lock, Aadi and Tapan rushed to their bicycles. It started raining as they pedaled to the hall. A thick blanket of fog restricted the visibility to a few meters while the downpour made it difficult to pedal fast. Reaching the hall, they slipped to sleep, leaving everything in limbo.

The western winds had brought with them clouds from the Indian Ocean. Rain in the winter was never welcomed by the denizens of the northern states. Under heavy downpour, IITC was literally put on curfew which lifted only in the evening when sky glistened for the first time. A pale sun had seized the control over the clean and crimson gold sky. It stood with his seven-colored bow taut, guarding against another downpour.

Sitting on NASA's terrace, Tapan looked to the sky. It had turned dark and the sky was awash with sparkling gems. At one corner of the terrace, Aadi stood talking on his mobile. Completing his talk, he turned to Tapan. 'Dr. Bhaskar said that he will talk to the lab assistant about the morning issue. He mentioned not to talk about this with anyone else as this can put him in trouble. I guess we need to leave Dr. Bhaskar to handle the issue at his level,' said Aadi.

'It means that nothing will happen to those two guys,' said Tapan.

'I know it's wrong but Dr. Bhaskar has taken a big risk by allowing us the access to the lab. We should think about him as well,' said Aadi, sitting by the side of Tapan.

After a brief moment of silence, Tapan spoke. 'Aadi, I am sad about Harsh. He should not have left without meeting me.' Emptying the pint into his stomach, he continued. 'You should have called me.'

'I am sorry,' said Aadi wearily.

'When we were searching for you on that day, we didn't know what happened to you. We had many bad thoughts crossing our minds. It was Harsh who took the command. He stormed inside Subbu's office and asked him to call SIS.'

'I know if he had been in my place he would have done something. But I don't know what to do,' said Aadi with his eyes soggy. 'We need to do something.'

Aadi stood up and strolled on the terrace. Coming to the edge, he looked up to the rails. Beyond the rails was the institute that had derailed his friend's career at IITC. In an inebriated state, Aadi picked up his mobile and punched a number. 'Is it Professor

Shinde?' he asked as the call got picked up.

'Who is it?' asked the voice on the other side.

'That's not important. But there is something else that you need to be aware of,' said Aadi aggressively.

'What are you talking about?'

'You need to ask Mechanical Department the reason they terminated Harsh. Was a CPI of 6.2 not enough to allow a student to carry on with his academics? Do you really think that Subbarao was fair when he gave unsatisfactory to Harsh against the thesis work?'

'There must be a plausible explanation for all of your questions. Can you help me put a name to the voice I am hearing?'

'I don't think that I can be of any help to you.'

'Help me to help you,' said Dr. Shinde.

'If you want to help me, then ask Subbarao why he advocated termination of his own student. You better come up with some answer or we will get it our way,' said Aadi hanging up on the call.

Aadi walked back to Tapan when his mobile beeped, '*Prof Shinde …*' flashing across its screen. 'You were talking to the director of the institute,' exclaimed Tapan taking mobile from Aadi's hand.

'Yes'

'Are you mad? You will get in trouble,' said Tapan. Killing the call, he switched off the mobile. 'Aadi, if Shinde comes to know about this, you can get into big trouble.'

'Do you really think I care about it? I have seen enough to worry about these trivial things,' said Aadi vehemently.

Aadi opened a new beer bottle and funneled the liquid down his wind pipe. He gulped it all in one breath and hurled the empty bottle to the railway track. With his eyes moist, he shouted, looking towards the sky. 'This system sucks!'

The temperature had dipped more than enough to bear. After dumping a few more pints into their stomachs, Aadi and Tapan came back to the hall. While Tapan was able to catch up on sleep, Aadi missed it big time. With the first ray of light falling, Tapan woke up to find Aadi standing in one corner of the room, staring out of the window.

'Didn't you sleep?' asked Tapan rubbing his eyes.

'Get ready,' said Aadi picking up his boots. Tying them he signaled Tapan to haul off the bed.

'Where are we going?' asked Tapan.

'We are going to SAC.'

Aadi placed a call to Sid and a few other students before stepping out of the room. 'What are you up to?' asked Tapan catching pace with Aadi. 'You already have invented enough troubles for yourself. Don't do anything that can screw you up harder.'

'Tapan, have faith in me,' said Aadi with a resolve on his face.

Before they landed at SAC, a group of students had already swarmed the place.

The architecture of SAC made it apparent that it was one among the first few buildings raised on the campus. Soaked in a clichéd brick red color, the wall of the building served as a canvas for the students' imagination. In one corner, lay a silhouette of man, his legs spread wide across, arms open to the sky. An elderly couple, their faces jutted with the worries of life, retired in the other corner. A beetle also found its way in students' imagination and lived happily among the creatures on the wall. The labyrinth of colors portrayed the energy and students' outlook towards the life.

'Friends, we need to show the institute that we are not a piece of junk that they can scrape off so easily,' roared Aadi, grabbing attention of the students assembled in SAC.

'Was the beer inside Aadi doing the talk?' thought Tapan. He tried to comprehend what Aadi had on his mind. Before he could have thought of any possibilities, Aadi made it clear. 'We are going to make the institute understand that they can't screw our careers like this. I want your support for an indefinite relay hunger strike that we initiate today.'

'We are with you Aadi,' voiced a girl.

Aadi took a pen and paper and scribbled a message on it. Handing over the message to the girl, he said. 'Give this to the local daily newspaper for their editorial tomorrow. Our hunger strike starts from today.'

A few of the students had already spread the mattresses inside the SAC lobby, raising the bugle call for the relay hunger strike.

'Tapan, I want you to come with me to Subbu's office,' said Aadi.

'For what?' asked Tapan as Aadi took him in his stride.

'You will get to know.'

Aadi stormed into Subbarao's office without seeking the permission. Before he could have spoken, Subbarao barked, a rage visible on his face. 'How dare you call Dr. Shinde and blame me?'

'I stated the truth. You need to give reasons for getting Harsh terminated,' retorted Aadi.

'I am not liable to answer that,' said Subbarao retreating.

'You need to say this to the media. The student body has already declared an indefinite hunger strike. There will be a few questions that the media would have. You can't give them these lame excuses.'

'Are you trying to test my patience or mettle?' snorted Subbarao.

'Probably both, and more' replied Aadi. He slammed the door close moving out of the room.

BIKINIS DON'T COVER UP TOO MUCH!

It had been about a fortnight since the relay hunger strike began. A planned and synchronized effort from the students enabled them to be heard at the national level. The media followed the story closely and the students participating were now discussed across different boards. Soon, the spark set ablaze by Aadi had turned into a forest fire. IITC felt the heat but jumped late into firefighting mode.

24th January 2007

SAC, IITC

The sun had flamed out but Aadi's eyes wore a sparkle as he saw Sonia in the parking bay at SAC. He kept looking towards Sonia while she walked along with Jaswinder towards him. Incidentally, Sonia also had worn a black kurti as had Sakshi, the day he met her last.

'Did you guys hear anything from the institute?' asked Jaswinder. Tossing her boots out, she jumped on the mattress, strangling the last breath out of its lungs.

'Nothing till date, but I am sure we will hear something very soon,' answered Tapan. Easing the woes of the mattress, he slipped on to the floor. Looking towards Sonia, he asked. 'Why don't you make yourself comfortable?'

Aadi's eyeballs rolled in sockets, keeping track of Sonia's moves. She sat beside Jaswinder when Aadi asked. 'How are you doing Sonia?' Tapping gently on his heartbeat, he continued. 'It's nice to see you after so many days.'

'Can't you see a 38 size in front of 24?' snapped Jaswinder.

Aadi came out of the trance and switched his attention to

Jaswinder. Before he could have said anything, Tapan intervened. 'Jaswinder, it's really nice that you came. Would you like to sit with us on the hunger strike?'

'I don't want to lead our country towards a food crisis.' Clearing the doubts hung on the faces around her, Jaswinder continued. 'Once I come out of the relay hunger strike, I will surely catch up on eating marathon.'

'I would like to be a part of this relay hunger strike.' Addressing the audience on the floor, Sonia continued. 'I am really impressed with the initiative that you guys have taken.'

'For the next three days, we don't have a slot free. I can book you for Sunday.' Looking above his register, Tapan asked. 'Will that be fine?'

Before Sonia could have answered, Aadi coughed loudly. Taking a cue, Tapan corrected. 'Actually there was some problem with one of the students sitting today for the strike. If you want, I can put you in today's schedule.'

'That should be fine,' answered Sonia.

'I also can join you guys,' voiced Jaswinder. 'On the condition that I am allowed to have my food,' she added.

Smiling, Tapan asked. 'Jaswinder, would you mind signing on the wall as a token of your support?'

'Yeah sure, why not' said Jaswinder standing up. Tapan took Jaswinder with him, easing the woes of the mattress and allowing some private space for Aadi and Sonia.

Scientists claim that an average human mind processes about sixty thousand thoughts in a day. But that moment, Aadi's mind went blank. He found it difficult to think about something to talk. A minute would have passed when Aadi started, not sure what he should be saying. 'I am sorry.'

'For what?' shrugged Sonia.

'I wanted to apologize to you earlier, but better late than never,' said Aadi. Before he could have continued, Sonia said. 'Aadi, let's not discuss the past.'

'Sonia, is there no way you can forget what has happened? I was wrong and I am sorry for that,' said Aadi.

'Aadi, it would be easy for me to be a part of this movement if you leave our past and treat me like any other colleague of yours. We can't undo what has been done. Try to live with it,' said Sonia.

'Save something for the night. We are coming back,' said Jaswinder joining the two. After spending some time at SAC, Jaswinder and Sonia left for their hall.

For Aadi, the next few hours were as long as ages. The sky had turned dark. A mild breeze had started blowing. Aadi was reading a novel by Jeffrey Archer when under the light from the neon streetlamp he saw a silhouette walking towards him. It didn't take much time for him to recognize Dr. Subbarao.

'How are you doing?' asked Dr. Subbarao sitting by Aadi's side. 'Do you think you can make a big dent by this silly relay hunger strike of yours?'

'We know what we can do,' interjected Tapan.

'Why do you guys want to ruin your career?' said Subbarao looking towards the students. Forcing his next words, Subbarao continued. 'You still have a choice. Leave the strike and go back to your studies. I promise nothing will happen to you.'

'Sir, it is really nice that you thought about us. But, Harsh was also one of your students. You could have saved his career,' replied a girl.

'You students don't understand.' Irritated, Subbarao stood up. He shook his head before asking. 'Can I have some space? I want to talk with Aadi alone.'

'Talk in front of us, we are his ears,' replied the girl.

Aadi looked towards the girl. Exchanging a brief reassuring glance, he stood up. 'Let's walk,' he said. Strolling a few steps down, Aadi came to a stop. He stayed quite, waiting for Subbarao to spill words prisoned in his mind.

'Aadi, don't you understand that your hunger strike is damaging the institute's reputation? You have created unrest in the media. An institute is established by the efforts of thousands of people. It can't be put at stake for a single student.'

'Sir, I didn't want to do this but you left me with no other choice. You need to bring back Harsh,' asserted Aadi.

'You said that I didn't leave you a choice. Now I give you a choice. Make your informed decision.' With utmost precision, Subbarao dropped his next few words. 'Either you quit this hunger strike or else you also will be thrown out,' said Subbarao spitting on the ground. 'I will suggest you to save your degree.'

'Suggestions are like arm pits, everybody has got two and most of them stink,' replied Aadi. Before Aadi could have said more, Subbarao came again. 'I will ignore your comment. Think well before making a decision. There's no need to answer now but I need an answer soon.'

Standing at the edge of the corridor, Tapan had been lip reading the conversation. Interpreting that the conversation had come to an end, he stepped towards Aadi. He was a second too early. Subbarao was not done yet. Looking towards Tapan, he demanded. 'You come with me'.

In a few steps, Tapan's mind covered miles speculating Subbarao's intentions. At the SAC gate, Subbarao turned to face Tapan. 'Why are you guys digging yourself a grave? Make Aadi understand that he needs to end this hunger strike, otherwise the consequences can be severe.'

With a concerned expression, Subbarao continued. 'I don't want you guys to ruin your careers. Take an informed decision in your best interests.'

Patting on Tapan's shoulder, Subbarao picked his way. Tapan was turning back when Sonia and Jaswinder crossed him on their bicycles. Tapan walked back with them to the SAC's foyer where Aadi was waiting.

'Thanks for coming,' said Aadi looking towards Sonia. Aadi had forgotten for a split second, the pain and anguish that he had gone through while talking with Subbarao.

'Subbarao took me aside to say ....' Before Tapan could have completed his talk, Aadi said looking in his eyes. 'Don't bother yourself. I know what he would have told you.'

Heaving a breath of relief, Tapan asked. 'Sonia, would you like to see the photographs from our trip to Bithoor?'

'Sure,' replied Sonia.

Sitting on the stairs, in front of SAC, Sonia scrolled through the photographs. A brief smile meandered to her lips as she saw a photograph of Harsh kissing Tapan on his cheeks. Sonia quickly scrolled to the next photograph which had Sid sitting on a bench with his newly purchased SLR camera disassembled in front of him. Another big smile cracked on her face as she scrolled next. It was a photograph of the traffic check post bearing the message, 'I am curvaceous, go slow!'.

'How come you have an interest in photography?' asked Sonia looking towards Tapan.

'I don't have much interest. As you were in the trip, Aadi dragged me,' replied Tapan nonchalantly.

'Do you like photography?' asked Aadi diplomatically dodging the following question.

'I like it. Flashlights turn me on,' replied Sonia keeping the laptop to one side.

'Aadi, how come your interests match Sonia's so closely?' asked Jaswinder.

'It's a nice coincidence,' shrugged Aadi.

'Is something wrong between you two?' asked Jaswinder.

'I am feeling sleepy. Let's get to bed,' said Sonia standing up. Looking towards Tapan, she asked. 'Where can we sleep?'

'For girls, the arrangement is inside the room,' said Tapan pointing to a room.

Aadi took a deep sigh as Tapan assisted Sonia and Jaswinder to the room. The night sped past in front of his eyes while he changed sides on the mattress. His sleep was crushed under Jaswinder's snore and when finally he succumbed to bed in the wee hours, the sun came back, fired up. Aadi gave up on his struggle and opened his eyes to find Sonia standing in front of him.

'We are going to the hostel, will freshen up and join you later,' said Sonia. Standing on one side, Jaswinder resembled a walking zombie, ready to crumble anytime on the ground.

'Wait Sonia,' said Tapan. 'Aadi, you also leave with them. You need some rest. You didn't have anything for the last two days.'

'Tapan is right. You need to take some rest,' said Jaswinder coming momentarily back to life.

'Take some rest,' said Sonia in a plain voice.

'Fine, I am coming with you,' said Aadi standing up.

Along with Jaswinder and Sonia, Aadi picked the track to the hall. Aadi flanked Sonia from the right while Jaswinder drove near to the walkway. They had crossed the main ground and were a few meters away from the girls' hall when a tempo, high on volume, honked behind them. Aadi scooted inside, squeezing Sonia and Jaswinder nearer to the walkway. He looked back signaling tempo to overtake. The vehicle accelerated and before Aadi could have realized a hockey stick came out of the tempo rear. From inside, someone whirled the stick in the air and bumped it hard on Aadi's head. The tempo vanished across the street while Aadi collapsed on the road.

Time had come to a standstill. Sonia saw Aadi falling to the ground, his face covered under blood. Like a bullet shot from the gun she jumped from her bicycle. Yelling, she rushed to Aadi. 'Jaswinder, call the ambulance. Do it quick.'

Sonia took her shawl and tied it across Aadi's head. The wound was severe. Aadi was losing blood profusely. Sonia's hand went wet in blood while her eyes were misty with tears. Looking towards Jaswinder, she exhorted. 'For God's sake, will you call an ambulance?'

Jaswinder placed a call to the institute's hospital. In the meantime, a crowd had gathered around the accident site. From the crowd, a student came forward. Bending down on his knees, he lifted Aadi's head. Looking towards Sonia, he said. 'I can take him to the hospital on my bike.'

With help from a few students, Sonia was able to get Aadi on the bike. Crossing Aadi's leg across the bike, she supported him against the back of the student driving the bike. She herself sat behind Aadi, holding him tight against her.

As the bike neared the hospital, Aadi momentarily gained consciousness. Keeping a tight grip on him, Sonia spoke fervently. 'Aadi, we are going to hospital. Nothing will happen to you. Just have faith.'

By the time Aadi received the first aid, Tapan and Jaswinder along with other students participating in the hunger strike were in the hospital. Bleeding had stopped but Aadi was still unconscious. Head injury was beyond the capability of the institute's hospital and the case was referred to the city hospital. Along with Aadi were Sonia, Jaswinder and Tapan in the ambulance. Speeding across Cawnpore's traffic, the ambulance took about forty minutes to reach Regency hospital.

Sonia's eyes were hooked on the door of the operation theatre while doctors operated on Aadi inside. Four hours of waiting was no less than a lifetime for her. The red light on the door turned green and a group of doctors came out of the operation theatre. Sonia rushed to them, her face flooded with thousands of questions while her throat choked to utter a word. Understanding the worry, a doctor said. 'Patient is safe. There has been internal bleeding and that's the reason patient had lost consciousness. But there is nothing to worry now.'

'Doctor, can we see Aadi?' asked Jaswinder.

'Not now, only after we shift the patient to the private ward.' Pointing to a bench, Doctor said. 'You guys can wait over there.'

Sitting in front of the private ward, Sonia stared, blank faced into the distance. Big tears rolled down her eyes. Heaving a comforting hand around her shoulder, Jaswinder consoled her. 'Don't worry, Aadi is safe.'

After about a couple of hours, Aadi was shifted to the single occupancy room in the private ward. Sid and many other students participating in the hunger strike had also reached the hospital. Coming out of Aadi's room, a nurse motioned that they can meet the patient. Seeing the crowd of students walking towards the room, the nurse added. 'Only two students at a time are allowed to visit the patient. Rest of you, please wait outside.'

The nurse allowed Tapan and Sonia to go inside the room. Reading through the medical report in her hand, she stood in front of the door. She was all involved when Jaswinder tapped to her attention. 'Mam, I am the patient's cousin sister. Can I go in?'

Jaswinder pleaded earnestly.

'Okay,' replied the nurse.

Outside the patient room, Sid waited for the nurse to leave. Ten minutes had passed when he lost his patience and hiked towards the nurse. Contemplating a thought, Sid said. 'Mam, I am the patient's cousin brother. Can I go in?'

'Don't try this *alibaba mantra*. There are 40 other thieves standing in front of me,' said the nurse pointing to the other students. Handing Sid the medical report, the nurse said. 'Don't be sad. Play big brother's role and get these medicines.'

The air inside the patient room was charged with intense emotions. Tapan, Jaswinder and Sonia sat on the chairs kept by the side of the cot. Aadi was sleeping under the effect of sedatives. After a while, he opened his eyes. Looking towards Tapan, he said. 'Don't let it die. We must continue the strike.'

'Aadi, you take rest,' said Tapan.

'Do I look like a monster?' asked Aadi, moving his hand on the dressed wounds.

'You are the one,' replied Tapan smiling.

'Tapan, help me sit,' said Aadi.

Using the crank, Tapan lifted the head portion of the bed. Sitting by the side of Aadi, he asked. 'Aadi, how are you feeling now?'

'I am fine, I guess,' replied Aadi.

'Did you recognize who had hit you?' asked Tapan.

'No, I didn't,' replied Aadi. Looking towards Sonia, he asked. 'Sonia, will you forgive me?'

'Aadi, please don't make me feel ashamed. If you did wrong, I too was responsible for provoking you,' said Sonia looking at Aadi, her eyes swollen and her face tear-stained. She stood up and sidled to the bed, near to Aadi.

'So, have you forgiven me?'

'Yes, I have,' replied Sonia, taking Aadi's hand in hers.

'Jaswinder, let's give them some space,' said Tapan standing up. They had shuffled to the door when Sid barged in. 'Wrong timing, I guess,' he said.

'Sid, you come with us,' said Jaswinder.

Ignoring Jaswinder, Sid said, looking towards Aadi. 'I always thought that you were a virgin.'

'What do you mean?' Aadi winced, sliding his hand from Sonia's.

'Tapan, you have a look,' said Sid passing the report to Tapan.

'Do they do some sort of virginity test?' asked Jaswinder glancing at the report.

'There's no test which can prove one's virginity,' said Aadi, his pitch shrill.

'There's no need to do a test on you. You will die a virgin,' said Sid cracking into peals of laughter. Once his laughter died down, Sid realized that he was laughing alone. 'Guys, it was a joke,' he explained.

'No one dies a virgin,' said Sonia. Smiling impishly, she continued. 'Life screws us all.'

'Well, I succeeded in bringing back smile on Sonia's face at least.' Looking towards others, Sid exhorted. 'Be cheerful guys.'

'How did you come inside?' asked Jaswinder authoritatively.

'It's not so difficult to woo a fat lady. Just tell her she is slim.' Sid did realize but it was already late. Firefighting the situation, he explained. 'I swear to God. I didn't mean you.'

Seeing a smile sprouting on Jaswinder's face, Sid had got on ease when someone held him by his collar. 'Now, I will throw you out of the hospital. Come with me.' Sid turned around to find the nurse with her face red and blotchy.

29th January 2007

Regency Hospital, Cawnpore City

IITC students on the path of rewriting Google story

In an unprecedented revelation, a group of students has left IITC stunned with their faith and perseverance. Aadi, Harsh and Tapan are the names that found their way from the attendance register to the newsprint in the recent past. They again have stunned the academia with the current revelation. The trio have been secretly working on a project that institute had no clue about.

The secret project came to the light when in a dramatic way Security Intelligence Service (SIS) was able to nab the culprit who had hit Aadi, a day before yesterday. Aadi is now stable and the culprit has been booked under the criminal charges.

Is it allowable for students to pull out time from their scheduled study hours and use the institute's infrastructure to develop and nurture their own idea? Each year many ideas go down the drain as institute finds it hard to accommodate them with the existing infrastructure. There is a thin line that these students may have crossed and it seems that the institute has all rights to decide the course of their fate.

With the newspaper folded in her palm, Sonia entered the men's restroom. 'Aadi, did you hear the news?'

Many necks facing the urinals craned back to the shrill voice of a girl. 'You are making the news. Wait for me outside,' said Aadi looking back to Sonia. With his one hand on Tapan's shoulder, he stood relieving himself when Sonia stormed inside the men's restroom.

Sonia cast a cursory glance over the scandalized faces in the restroom and then walked out. 'You better look front,' said Aadi poking on Tapan's shoulder. 'What are you doing? I didn't ask you to look at my joystick.' Aadi turned his pelvic, giving a cover to the unguarded territory.

'Aadi, there's a bad news,' said Sonia as Aadi came out rubbing his wet hands against his pajamas. With his one hand around Tapan's shoulder, he limped towards his ward.

'I know that they have dug up the secret lying in my room.'

'Oh, you know that?' Taking Aadi's hand around her shoulder, Sonia continued. 'Aadi, there's something more that you should know.'

After helping Aadi to lie down on the bed, Sonia continued. 'We don't have the relay hunger strike anymore. Students backing us have given up under the pressure.'

Once Aadi was settled, Tapan picked the medical prescription kept at one side of the bed. 'I will get the medicines,' he said and marched out of the room.

'Aadi, why didn't you tell me about the fight that you had with this guy?' asked Sonia, sitting close to Aadi. She looked at the photograph in the newsprint. A burly looking man with round bobbin eyes and big belly stood smiling in the photograph. A scar mark below the right eye appeared as the latest addition in the face already plundered with pimples and mole.

Taking the newsprint from Sonia, Aadi trashed it in the bin. 'It is not a great thing to talk about.' Aadi looked towards Sonia and finding her unconvinced, he continued. 'Look, I never expected that a guy shall hit me and get caught by SIS. I could never have comprehended that he would be the same person with whom I had a small tussle. Above all, I never assumed that our secret is going to haunt us this big.'

'But Aadi..,' said Sonia, her voice sagging under the complaint.

'Believe me, I never thought of hiding anything from you,' said Aadi grabbing Sonia's hand.

'I believe you,' said Sonia taking Aadi's face in her hand. Aadi felt a shot of adrenalin as Sonia looked straight in his eyes. He slipped his hands up her back. Starved of female touch, Aadi's hand frantically trailed up. Reaching the neck, Aadi tickled her skin. It felt silky and smooth. Bending forward, Sonia gently kissed Aadi's face. Aadi caressed her ears while Sonia locked her lips against his. Next second Sonia started caressing his hands and rubbed her lips furiously on it.

Holding herself back, Sonia stood up. Looking towards Aadi, she said. 'Aadi, I think I have started liking you.'

'I like you too.'

Aadi felt envy as a gush of air stroked Sonia's hair. Chaffing her hair, Sonia asked playfully. 'What do you like about me?'

'Your smile ...' Little anxious, Aadi started. 'Your smile runs miles through my mind.'

'That was poetic,' said Sonia.

Taking Sonia's hand in his, Aadi asked. 'What do you like about me?'

Aadi had his eyes locked up with Sonia's. Like a placid lake lit ajar by the morning sunlight, Sonia's eyes carried his reflection. 'You are dependable, bold and true at heart,' said Sonia. Taking a brief pause, she continued. 'You have become a cult figure in our hostel.'

'What have I done to become a cult figure?'

'You dared to stand up for a cause. What can be more heroic than that?' Sonia's words tasted like honey. Reading deep into Aadi's mind, Sonia kissed him.

Coming out of the breath-taking kissing session, Aadi cupped one of Sonia's breasts in his hand. He could feel her heart thumping against his palm. Nervous, he slid his hand off. Sonia smiled and gently rested her head on Aadi's chest. She was all snuggled up against Aadi when the door creaked. She flinched and spun around. An electric shock ran through her body. Her heart skipped a beat as Dr. Subbarao came inside.

Aadi straightened himself up on the reclined bed. 'How are you feeling now?' asked Dr. Subbarao taking position across the bed. The chair beneath his bums squeaked.

'Confundus,' cursed Aadi closing his eyes. He slowly opened them, hoping that spell from Harry Potter movie would have worked. A confused expression surely surfaced on Subbarao's face but it was not the spell. 'Are you alright?' repeated Subbarao.

'I am fine,' said Aadi giving up on casting spells.

'Aadi, you had asked me the reason for Harsh's termination.' Subbarao waited for the words to sink in. 'You know who was responsible for it,' he said after a pause.

Without collecting any response from the audience in the room, Subbarao continued. 'You were responsible for his termination.' Subbarao stood up and strolled to the only window in the room. Looking back, he said. 'Trailing back from the person who had hit you to the lab assistant of the wind tunnel facility, we came to know everything that you guys have been up to for the past one year. Well, don't you think it's improper to use institute's infrastructure without seeking the permission?'

Subbarao strolled back to the center of the room. Looking towards Sonia, he asked. 'Can you wait outside?'

After Sonia went out of the room, Subbarao said sarcastically. 'If I haven't amused you enough, let me tell you this.' A brief moment of silence elapsed before Subbarao spoke. 'For the gross breach of discipline and the brazen conduct of running a hunger strike, the DOAA committee has terminated you and Tapan.'

'What?' said Aadi, his voice incredulous. With an intense expression, he muttered. 'But, we had asked Dr. Bhaskar.'

'For granting unauthorized access, Dr. Bhaskar has been removed from the lab,' said Dr. Subbarao. Restraining his voice, he continued. 'You still have a chance to save yourself. If you put on paper that you developed the flying car under my guidance, I am ready to consider it as your research work. I can help you seek revocation of the DOAA committee's decision.'

Ten minutes would have passed while Sonia waited outside. With the intent to eavesdrop on the conversation, she sidled up to the closed door and pressed her ear to it. 'Think about the proposal.' A few seconds would have elapsed before a pair of feet shuffled on the floor. Sonia stepped back and turned in the opposite direction.

Coming out of the room, Subbarao looked around. Reaching Sonia, he asked. 'Are you Aadi's friend?'

'Yes,' replied Sonia.

'Then try to impart some sense into him. I want to save him. I don't want another student under my supervision to go out of the institute without a degree in his hand. Try to implant a pea size brain in that big skull of his.' Coughing and adjusting his neck tie, Subbarao strode out of the hospital.

Sonia went inside the room and sat close to Aadi. It was not hard for her to get a whiff of the conversation that she had missed. Aadi's face was still raging with anger when he uttered his first few words breaching the silence in the room. 'How dare he talk like this?'

'Aadi, don't worry, everything will be alright,' consoled Sonia.

'The devil wants me to sell our idea to him. He tried to threaten me,' grumbled Aadi.

'What did he say?'

'I don't know if what he mentioned is true. He said that Tapan and I have been terminated and he can save us if we ...' Aadi stopped, finding Tapan standing at the door. 'Subbarao is not lying,' said Tapan, sweat smeared across his face.

'That was quick,' stuttered Aadi before adding. 'Connect me to Harsh. I want all of us to talk and decide what should be done next.'

Keeping the medicines on one side, Tapan switched on the laptop. Logging on to skype, he placed a call to Harsh. Within seconds, friends were interfaced together on the video conferencing. 'Hey Aadi, how are your bones?' asked Harsh smiling on the web cam. 'They must be rattling.'

'Harsh, there's something that we wanted to discuss with you,' said Aadi.

'Yeah, I saw the video that Tapan sent earlier. The instability in Flymoto's flight may be due to the loose geometric tolerances between the components,' said Harsh.

'It's not regarding Flymoto,' said Aadi in an almost feeble voice. Harsh checked on Tapan who looked devastated. 'What happened to you guys? Is everything alright?' he asked.

'Tapan and I have been terminated,' said Aadi.

'What?' said Harsh visibly shocked.

'They know we were working on Flymoto.' Looking towards Tapan, Aadi said. 'If we give in writing that we did the work under Subbarao's supervision then he can help us revoke the termination orders.'

'Forget Flymoto. It is not bigger than your careers. Do whatever it needs but don't let them terminate you. There is no dearth of ideas in this world but if you lose this degree, it would be a serious loss,' said Harsh. With pain filled in his eyes, he continued. 'It is not safe out here.'

'I will do whatever it takes but I will not let Tapan get punished because of me,' said Aadi taking a resolve.

BREAK EVEN

2nd February 2007

Dr. Subbarao's Office, IITC

'My office is in a total mess. It's not organized and tidy like yours but I can't help it. I am unable to find the time for it,' said Subbarao shoving books on his table to one corner.

'I can understand,' Dr. Mukherjee replied tersely, looking around him. Dr. Subbarao's office was no less than a battleground. Array of unorganized chairs stood as abandoned cannons, piles of books stood as mortars and loose sheet of notes, on the table, lied as martyrs. Plundered, files in the shelf lay exhausted one over the other. The morbid mood inside the room was successfully complemented by the dirty glass panes on the windows.

'I am clueless about what we want to discuss in this meeting,' shrugged Subbarao, his arms folded on the desk. 'The DOAA committee has already terminated these guys. Once the director signs the termination order, these guys will be thrown out of the campus. What's there left for me to do?'

'Dr. Subbarao, these guys have done pretty good work on the flying car. They should not be terminated. Rather, you should veto the DOAA committee's decision,' interjected Dr. Mukherjee.

'Sir, I want to apologize for the mistakes done.' Looking towards Tapan, Aadi added. 'Can we work under your guidance as you offered earlier? We ....' Before he could have completed, Subbarao pounded his words. 'The offer has expired.'

'Sir, we have figured out the problem with our flying car

design. We can surely make it work,' said Tapan gazing at Dr. Subbarao.

'So?' shrugged Subbarao.

Trying to salvage some resolution, Dr. Mukherjee said in an authoritative tone. 'You should rethink your stand. It's not a joke. Two careers are at stake.'

'You have made it a joke. If you had let me control them early on, we would not have had this situation at our hands,' bawled Dr. Subbarao, a spittle fountain busting from his mouth.

'Dr. Subbarao, the flying car is going to be the next big thing. If you support these students then you could be leading the show,' said Dr. Mukherjee, his tone milder. 'Please take this as my personal request and allow these students another chance.'

With expectant eyes, Tapan looked towards Dr. Subbarao. The air in the room felt charged with anticipation. The moment seemed pregnant with prophetic portent. Killing the static, the mobile in Dr. Mukherjee's hand vibrated heavily. 'I am sorry; I need to take this call.'

Once Dr. Mukherjee walked out of the office, Subbarao stared at Aadi, his faced filled with indignation. 'Because of Dr. Mukherjee you have got this far, but no further. I will put a damn stick up your ass. You just wait and watch,' he barked.

'Sir, we are sorry,' said Tapan in a quivering voice.

'Harsh was better than you guys. At least, he had some shame left.' Cursing under his breath, Dr. Subbarao went back to work on his laptop.

For Aadi and Tapan, the two minutes of silence before Dr. Mukherjee returned were worse than a nightmare. Dr. Mukherjee asked, taking the chair. 'Dr. Subbarao, do you consider my request?'

Tearing apart the mercy application, Dr. Subbarao replied. 'You can't force me to change my decision.'

Dr. Mukherjee was good at issuing orders and didn't take insubordination lightly. Collecting his notes, Dr. Mukherjee walked out of the room. Stopping at the door, he looked back.

'You guys come with me.' Once Aadi and Tapan were out of the room, Dr. Mukherjee slammed the door shut behind him.

'I had said it earlier. Subbarao has not got enough guts to defend you guys against the committee,' said Dr. Mukherjee walking out of the department.

'But sir, he only had made the proposal. He wanted us to give him the credit of our work and in return he said that he will save us,' said Aadi.

'And the committee is made of fools? Will they not be able to make out that Subbarao is doing something underhandedly? Subbarao might have said something in the spur of the moment but he understands that he will be putting his career at risk by supporting you guys. He can't support you guys,' said Dr. Mukherjee, his voice fervent.

'Sir, what will happen now?' With a feverish voice, Aadi spoke huffily. 'At least Tapan should not be expelled.'

'It's either both of you or none.'

Coming out of the department, Dr. Mukherjee stopped at the parking lot. 'Now it's time to get some audience. We need to make the director understand the potential of the work that you guys have been doing.'

'What do you mean sir?'

'Prepare a presentation about your flying car project. You guys are going to present your work in the international conference being held by our department. It's two days from now.'

'But can we do so? We already have been terminated?' asked Aadi.

'The director hasn't signed your termination letter. To throw you guys out, Subbarao has to wait till Dr. Shinde is back in the campus.'

'If Dr. Shinde is not in the campus then how can we show him our work?' asked Tapan. The sheer thought of getting terminated had jolted him.

'Don't worry! Last minute itinerary changes do happen. I will make sure that he attends the conference.'

4ᵗʰ February 2007

Auditorium, IITC

Auditorium aka Audi was a massive structure with an equally imposing lobby. With a large foyer and a lavish ground, it stood sturdy in front of the Shopping centre. 'Cerberus of academics', Audi had its eyes set on the future while the intellect brewed in its belly. A veteran host, Audi had accommodated in its past events ranging from the cultural festival to the convocation. Today, it was house to the conference on 'Advances in Automotive Industry'.

The audience present in the auditorium was glued on their seats with pin drop silence, listening intently to the presentation by Aadi and Tapan. The duo shared their innovative design for one of the greatest challenges that was as old as the age of human flight. The audience was spellbound with the simplicity of the design and the prospects that it promised. The flying car held the promises to be the next big revolution after the first controlled flight by Wrights.

After presenting their work, Aadi and Tapan joined Sonia who had been standing by the poster about the flying car, on display in the auditorium's foyer. The video recording of Flymoto's wind tunnel experiments were put in the loop on a laptop. The atmosphere was charged up but there was an unusual silence in the hearts of the three.

'I watched your presentation. It was quite intriguing.' A stranger with a conference ID card hanging around his neck approached the group. 'How quickly can your design switch between the two configurations?' he asked.

'Thirty seconds,' replied Tapan.

'Are the wings detachable?'

While Tapan answered the inquisitive soul, Aadi walked a few steps down the alley. Deprived of sleep for the last two days at a stretch, neurotoxins in his body clouded the mood. The only relief was the air that smelled delicious after a drizzle in the morning. It was 11 AM but the surrounding had turned dark with the cumulus clouds, rumbling intermittently and ready to poop. It seemed the clouds too had a bad stomach today. 'What happened?' asked Sonia, joining Aadi.

'Will I be able to convince them?'

'You will. You should have seen the reaction on the faces of the audience in the conference hall. I noticed Dr. Shinde. He too seemed to be impressed by the work.'

'Really?'

Sonia nodded in silent consent. Craning her neck above the crowd, she said. 'Mukherjee sir, Shinde sir and Subbarao are headed our way. Let's get back.'

Reaching the poster at display, Aadi asked the stranger. 'Can we answer rest of your questions afterwards?'

'No problem. I will wait,' replied the stranger taking a step back.

The group looked earnestly towards Dr. Shinde as he joined them along with Dr. Mukherjee and Dr. Subbarao. 'Despite all the rhetoric against you guys, I found your work pretty interesting,' said Dr. Shinde.

'Thanks sir.' Exchanging a warm smile, Aadi started. 'Sir, the beauty of our design is its simplicity. Flymoto is a roadable aircraft. The automated wing mechanism can fold to convert the aircraft to a car.'

'Can you mention something about the propulsion mechanism?' asked the stranger, brazenly neglecting the request that Aadi had made a few moments ago.

Exchanging a stern look with the stranger, Aadi answered. 'Flymoto uses a Wankel engine for its propulsion. The custom made gear box transfers the power to the propeller in the aircraft mode, while in the car mode the power gets transferred to the wheels.'

The stranger had parted his lips to shoot another question when Aadi shooed him away. Looking towards Dr. Shinde, he continued. 'Sir, the flying car has been a human fantasy since the inception of aircraft. Till date, no one has been able to come up with a feasible design. We took up this challenge and are very close to finalizing our design.'

'Sir, that's only a part of it.' Stuttering, Subbarao continued. 'These guys have not only ignored their academic obligations but also gained unauthorized access to the wind tunnel lab. They faked a suicide ...' After a few seconds, Aadi lost the track of Subbarao's words. The rumbling noise of the clouds annoyed him. It seemed as if someone had been farting in front of a bazooka amplifier. '... I know Aadi. He is a liar, selfish, disobedient and a big manipulator.'

'Sir, that is enough,' interrupted Aadi. Looking towards Dr. Shinde, Aadi continued, a rage visible in his eyes. 'Subbarao sir has accused me of many things which I suppose I am not worthy of. He called me a liar, a manipulator and even ill-cultured. But by any means, I don't hold a reputation of being called as a selfish person. I value my friends more than my dreams and that's the reason I had gone to Subbarao sir for trading my biggest achievement of the past two years.

Sonia and Tapan came close to Aadi. Exchanging a quick glance with them, Aadi continued. 'Now, I stand at the crossroads where I have everything at stake. I have at stake my career, my friends and the thing that I value the most, my belief. But then, I am not a selfish person. If you want to, you can throw me out of this institute but you can't punish Tapan or Bhaskar sir for helping me.' Aadi turned back, his throat had gone dry.

'Sir, since morning 50 odd people have asked us about Flymoto. When others can appreciate our work, why can't our own institute?' Aadi turned back, surprised. Tapan had banged right on the note.

'We are very close to realizing our dream. Rather than constituting a committee to decide our fate, the institute should support us.' With conviction reflecting in his eyes, Aadi continued. 'If the institute believes that thinking beyond the ordinary is a crime, then I have done a crime. And it's only me who should be punished.'

'How close to completion are you guys?' asked Dr. Shinde breaking the brief static.

'They can never complete it,' said Subbarao with a smirk on

his face. Looking towards Dr. Shinde, he continued. 'Sir, don't fall into the trap. These guys are bluffing.'

Ignoring Subbarao's comments, Dr. Mukherjee said. 'I think these students should be given a chance. The whole audience has voted their project as best in the conference. They have done a pretty good work.'

'How close to completion are you guys?' Dr. Shinde repeated his question.

'We need to replace the components with ...' Interrupting Aadi, Dr. Shinde asked. 'Give me a timeline.'

'May be two weeks or probably three,' said Aadi.

'I can't overturn the DOAA committee's verdict based on my opinion,' said Dr. Shinde. Before the smile on Subbarao's face could have grown fully, Dr. Shinde seized it. 'If you demonstrate a working prototype to the committee within a fortnight from today, then I will ask them to re-consider their decision.'

Aadi exchanged a quick glance with Tapan. Before he could express his gratitude, Subbarao interrupted. 'But, we can't delay the decision for that long.'

'I am not available to chair the DOAA meeting for another 15 days,' snapped Dr. Shinde. Looking towards Aadi, he continued. 'In the interim, you both will be on probation and Dr. Bhaskar is reinstated as the in charge of the wind tunnel lab. Get your car to fly.'

Dr. Mukherjee was all smiles when Dr. Shinde turned and strolled towards the exit. Dr. Subbarao followed the director at his own sluggish pace. The feeling of relief had not even sunk in when Tapan asked. 'Aadi, how are we going to make this fly in 15 days?'

'Let's rush to Dr. Bhaskar. We need to start our experiments.' In a jiffy, Aadi packed the flying car model in his bag and tucked it on his back.

'Can you show the animation on the flying car?' asked the stranger who had been intently listening through the conversation.

'Show time is over,' said Aadi, rushing towards the bicycle stand. Tapan followed him while Sonia packed her laptop.

'Will you show the animation?' the stranger repeated his

question to Sonia.

'I guess you didn't listen. Show time is over,' snapped Sonia and made a run to the bicycle stand.

The clouds in the sky had vanished when Aadi came out of the auditorium. Driving furiously, he reached the aerospace department just in time. Dr. Bhaskar was on his way out of the department when Aadi held him back.

'Sir,' said Aadi, catching his breath.

'Hi Aadi, how are you doing?' asked Dr. Bhaskar.

'Sir, there's something that I wanted to tell you.' Before Aadi could have continued, Dr. Bhaskar said. 'I know what has happened is bad but you can't change it. So, let's get over it.'

'Sir, Dr. Shinde has given us 15 days' time. If we can get Flymoto working, the DOAA committee's decision will be revoked,' said Aadi in a single breath.

Dr. Bhaskar stood gazing at Aadi, overwhelmed with what he heard. Sonia and Tapan had also reached the department. They joined the two engaged in silent contemplation.

A minute would have escaped when Dr. Bhaskar said with a terse smile on his face. 'Is this a new season of big-boss?' Shrugging his shoulder, he asked. 'Anyways, what's your plan now?'

'Sir, we would like to start the wind tunnel experiments again,' replied Aadi.

'Can I be a party to this game?' asked Dr. Bhaskar.

'Sure sir,' said Aadi with a big smile on his face.

'Can I see the much hyped video of Flymoto's flight?' asked Dr. Bhaskar.

Opening her laptop, Sonia played the video. After checking out the video, Dr. Bhaskar asked. 'What do you think is causing the flight instability?'

'Sir, we believe the instability in Flymoto's flight is due to loose tolerances between the components,' replied Tapan.

'You are right. That is not the sole reason though. Your design is aerodynamically unstable. There's a pattern in which Flymoto vibrates.' Thoughtfully, he continued. 'Let's go to the lab. We need to start the experiments.'

THE LAST MILE

9th February 2007

Wind Tunnel Lab, IITC

Completing two sets of experiments, Tapan ramped up the flight envelope. Flymoto was now held by aerodynamic lift and pneumatic thrust in the test section. Unbridled from all the restraints, Flymoto was a free bird now. Like an umbilical cord, a loom of wires extending from the roof of the test bed was attached to its rear. The umbilical cables were used for power supply and data transfer. As a fail-safe option, an arresting wire was also hooked to the Flymoto's body.

With utmost attention, Tapan commandeered Flymoto for a pitch up attitude. Flymoto shook in its flight and its nose dipped down instead of lifting up. 'Turn it off. There's some problem with the design,' said Dr. Bhaskar.

Scooting his chair back, Aadi stood up and hiked towards the test section. Through the glass window Sonia watched as Aadi detached Flymoto from the umbilical cords and the arresting wire. Coming out of the test section, he laid the model on the desk in the control room.

'There's something wrong,' said Dr. Bhaskar studying the model. Arriving at some conclusion, he stood and shuffled to the board.

Drawing on the board, Dr. Bhaskar continued. 'Let me explain this to you with an example. You guys must have seen a shuttlecock. Whenever you hit the shuttlecock with your racket, it almost instantly turns around to fly head first.'

Looking towards his audience, Dr. Bhaskar continued. 'The mass of the shuttlecock is in the dome-like cork tip whereas the aerodynamic pressure builds up mostly at the rear, where the feathers are. The point of the aerodynamic pressure behaves as a pivot.'

Dr. Bhaskar picked a ruler and placed it on the edge of the table. Half of the ruler length was overhung from the table's edge. Taking out a chalk from his coat's pocket, he placed it at the edge of the table, above the ruler, at the pivot point.

'Now, if you have played see-saw in your childhood, you will understand where the shuttlecock head will point to.' Dr. Bhaskar moved the chalk on the overhung portion, slowly and steadily till the ruler swivelled on the edge and fell down.

'It will point down, always,' said Sonia.

'Bingo!'

'It means that Flymoto has got a bit more mass than it should ahead of the point where the air pressure is acting,' said Aadi standing up from his chair.

'Do we need to refabricate our model?' asked Tapan anxiously. 'It will take a hell lot of a time and we are already running short of it.'

'I don't think we need to do that.' An idea barrelled through Aadi's mind. Catching it by its tail, Aadi recited. 'Instead, we can put some lead in its back. This way, the center of mass will shift rearwards.'

'That's a nice idea. Let's do it,' said Dr. Bhaskar.

Though tedious, it was an easy solution when compared to refabricating the model. Without wasting a minute, Aadi and Tapan went back to make the required alterations in the model. Tapan drilled a few holes around Flymoto's body at the rear end while working with Dr. Bhaskar, Aadi calculated the amount of lead required to balance the Flymoto's flight.

'Would you like to nibble?' asked Sonia munching on pizza. She passed the pack to Aadi and went out for filling her water bottle. In all small possible ways, Sonia assisted the group through their tough time.

It took two hours for Tapan to size up the holes in the Flymoto's body. Aadi was also done with the calculations. He picked the lead from the stores and hammered it down. Keeping it inside the clay cup, he flamed the welding torch around it.

In the clay cup, the molten lead had started boiling under the arc of the welding torch. Aadi held Flymoto while Tapan picked the cup of molten lead with forceps. Carefully, he poured the molten lead inside the drilled holes.

Once the lead solidified, Tapan dressed up Flymoto with sensors and placed it on the test bed. Taking the controls, Tapan started the experiments. He followed the standard protocols to reach to the first set of the experiments. As the wind conditions in the tunnel reached to the desired state, Tapan unleashed Flymoto to fly on its own. Flymoto was gliding smoothly when Tapan turned its nose up. Everyone in the control room was on their feet as Flymoto flew in a nose up attitude.

'That's it!' exhilarated Aadi.

'We have done it!' said Tapan turning towards Aadi. He was all smiles when Dr. Bhaskar asked. 'Tapan, can you give it a turn to the right?' Tapan did what Dr. Bhaskar had asked. 'Now bring the nose down,' Dr. Bhaskar instructed.

The smile on Tapan's face was gone, replaced by a desperate look. He prayed in his heart while manoeuvring Flymoto. It took only a few seconds for Flymoto to sink down in a spin. The arresting wire hooked on its tail restrained it from diving down to the floor. Under the gush of air, Flymoto swirled in the test section about the arresting wire. Like marbles on the floor, Tapan's eyes rotated in the socket while following Flymoto. The confidence that had soared up over the past few days had hit the ground like a sack of potatoes.

'That was supposed to work,' said Tapan moving towards the test section, his breath heavy.

'I also thought we had solved the problem.' Taking a deep breath, Dr. Bhaskar continued. 'We may need to rebuild the model.'

'What?' said Tapan, his voice filled with despair. Casting gloomy eyes towards Dr. Bhaskar, he asked. 'Is there no other way?'

Dr. Bhaskar kept silent while his brain was at work.

'There should be some way, sir. It's impossible to build a model in such a short time,' said Tapan as beads of sweat broke out and rolled down from his forehead.

'I don't know what can be done,' said Dr. Bhaskar.

'What do you mean you don't know?' Tapan felt the earth slipping under his feet. He propped himself against the wall.

'It's an iterative process. Every experiment tells something more about the physics,' replied Dr. Bhaskar, his voice rising with each word. 'This whole thing goes by experience and a pinch of luck.' Avoiding further confrontation, Dr. Bhaskar moved out of the room.

'What if we are not able to build it on time,' said Tapan, his voice feeble and his throat dry. 'We have just 10 days left.' Suddenly, floodgates of his memory restraining his darkest doubts got open. All of his life's failures came rushing in front of his eyes, reassuring him of suffering. Tapan got inebriated with his own 'what-ifs' as they gyrated in ecstasy in front of his eyes. It seemed to him as if they were carrying out some spiritual code to his doom.

Leaning on the wall, Tapan squatted on the floor. His legs were tugged inside and his face sunk between his thighs.

Aadi and Sonia rushed to Tapan. Sitting on the floor, Aadi supported him on his shoulder while Sonia helped him sip some water. 'We are not going to make it,' said Tapan. 'We can never make a model in 10 days.'

'Nothing will go wrong,' consoled Aadi.

Comforting Tapan, Aadi and Sonia led him out of the lab. At the gate of the lab, on the steps, the three of them sat silently. Sometimes a moment of silence speaks volume.

Unveiling a calm evening, the sun stood at the edge of the day. In the backdrop of the azure sky, the streaks of twilight were fading. The full moon peeked over the eastern horizon. The

Mother Nature had poured all its beauty but still, the three souls sat drenched in deep sadness. 'How can you be so hopeful?' asked Tapan, coming out of his stupor.

'Hope is a good thing, may be the best of things, and no good thing ever dies!'

'*Saala filmi*,' a terse smile broke on Tapan's face while his eyes were silent and smudged.

At a distance, Aadi saw Dr. Bhaskar walking down towards the lab along with someone. As they came close, Aadi recognised the other person. It was Dr. Anubhav.

'Dr. Bhaskar has briefed me on the problem with the flight dynamics,' said Dr. Anubhav joining the group. 'We can do a few preliminary tests on the simulated model before going for the full-fledged wind tunnel experiments,' he proposed.

'But, would this kind of simulation be possible in such a short time?' asked Aadi.

'I can help you guys with the simulation,' said Dr. Anubhav.

'How are we going to fabricate the model?' asked Tapan.

'Once we have the computer model fit for our test conditions, we can fabricate it quickly with the state-of-the-art Rapid Prototyping machine. It will hardly take a day to do it,' replied Dr. Anubhav.

'Sir, this would a great help. I don't know how to thank you,' said Aadi earnestly.

'Aadi, somehow I always felt that I was responsible for Harsh's termination. This whole thing has been started by me and now it's time to put a stop to it,' said Dr. Anubhav.

'Now with Dr. Anubhav's help, we can surely complete the work on time,' said Dr. Bhaskar smiling tersely.

'I am waiting for you guys in the CAD lab,' said Dr. Anubhav picking the trek to the parking.

After Dr. Bhaskar and Dr. Anubhav left the place, Tapan took Aadi in his hug. 'Hope is certainly a good thing,' he said with full grown tears in his eyes.

18th February 2007

Wind Tunnel Lab, IITC

Running scores of simulation, the group identified the problem with the flight dynamics. They had resolved quite a few handful configurations and the final design was frozen in close consultation with Dr. Bhaskar and Dr. Anubhav. The chosen configuration was sent for fabrication with the rapid prototyping machine. The two weeks of time had gone in the blink of an eye and now the group stood at one of the decisive points in their lives.

'The model will take about 5 hours to set. We will assemble together the components first thing tomorrow morning,' said Dr. Bhaskar. It had turned dark when the group came out of the CAD lab. The weather had turned ferocious. The thunder roared as the lightening illuminated the sky.

'Sir, how is the new design different from the earlier one?' asked Sonia as the group marched towards the cycle stand.

'The wings of Flymoto are not straight anymore, they are swept backwards. This should help in stabilizing the flight,' replied Dr. Bhaskar.

'Sir, is it going to work this time?' asked Tapan.

'You are invited to the show. Come, watch it yourself,' said Dr. Bhaskar sporting an infectious smile.

'Sir, I think I should stay back. I will start the work as soon as the model sets. This will give us some headway,' said Tapan.

'No way, you guys have been stretching like this for the last many days. You will wear yourself out. You need to take some rest,' said Dr. Bhaskar.

'But sir …'

'Do as I say,' snapped Dr. Bhaskar. Looking at his watch, he asked. 'Can one of you come with me? I will hand over the keys to the wind tunnel lab. I have an early morning class to take and I don't want to hold you back.'

'Sir, I will come with you,' said Tapan joining Dr. Bhaskar to his office.

Aadi and Sonia stayed back at the department, rewinding through the experiences of the last few days. The air felt unusually tender and filled with fragrance. Taking a deep breath, Aadi brought his duffel bag forward. Rummaging inside it, he fetched a beer can. 'Sonia, this is for you.'

'Oh Shit! How can you carry a beer over here? It can be a problem if anyone notices.'

'Hide it before anyone can see it,' said Aadi flinging the can towards Sonia.

Sonia quickly collected the beer can and tucked it inside her T shirt. For himself Aadi had already extracted the beer in a coke can. So, he didn't need to budge while Sonia had to keep a keen eye around her till she was done. It was Aadi's own private little entertainment.

'What's the occasion?' asked Sonia finishing her can. She crushed it before throwing in the dustbin.

'I could not have mustered enough courage to propose to you when sober. Also, I am chucking my odds.' Aadi reached for the ring in his pocket, his heart revving faster than a F1 car's engine.

'Is this supposed to be a ring?' asked Sonia looking at the metallic contraption in Aadi's hand. With stacks of thin slips and some alphabets scrambled, it looked no less than a piece of junk.

'Yes, actually I didn't know the size of your finger. So, I devised this universal ring, which can fit in anyone's hand but is still meant for one.'

'How?' Sonia asked intrigued.

Aadi slipped the ring in Sonia's hand. Being bigger in size, it slipped in easily. Cautiously, Aadi pulled a metal thread coming out from the center. The stacks of thin slips started rotating, taking up a floral shape. When the shank of the ring sized up with Sonia's index finger, Aadi cut the thread with a cutter. The ring head now had a flower with 'Hell's Angel' imprinted on it.

'This is an ingenious design. But don't you think this proposal comes at an unusual time.'

'Sonia, I don't know what will happen tomorrow. Whatever be the result, I want to let you know that I love you.' Getting down on his knees, Aadi asked. 'Will you marry me?' He felt butterflies in his stomach, nervous and yet excited.

'Yes, I will,' said Sonia with tears in her eyes ready to roll.

The surroundings had gone mushy. The air blowing had suddenly gained pace; competing with Aadi's already racing heart. Aadi grabbed Sonia's hand and rushed towards the bicycle stand. Reaching the stand where their bicycles stood flagging their reigns, Sonia said. 'It's going to rain heavily.'

'Nice observation,' remarked Aadi. 'But now we need to rush.'

Struggling against the rogue weather, they reached the Girl's Hall just in time. The showers had tamed the storm. Aadi and Sonia rushed inside the Girl's Hall cafeteria as countless water droplets poured down. Over a plate of onion pakoras and coffee, they enjoyed nature dancing to an unsaid rhythm.

'Aadi, let's move to my room. Once the storm subsides, you can leave,' said Sonia holding Aadi by his arm.

Coming inside the room, Sonia opened the window. A sudden gush of shower rushed in, getting them equally wet. 'Aadi, take this towel and dry your head,' said Sonia extending the towel.

Squeezing out excess water from her hair, Sonia asked. 'I need a fan. Do you mind?'

'Go ahead,' replied Aadi, darting his glance around. Sonia's room was in total harmony. Suave, neat and tidy, no corner of the room had a liaison with the dust. At one corner of the room, Sonia stood in front of the wardrobe mirror, brushing her hair. She looked beautiful with a blob of hair over her ears. Her dark hairs running down her shoulder smelled of lilies. 'You are looking good,' said Aadi.

Sonia looked back, surprised at Aadi's comment. Exchanging a smile, she continued combing her hairs. In an unwarranted move, Aadi picked her hair and brought that close to his face. The water dripping down her hair set ablaze the desires in Aadi. He wanted to be close to her, to hold her, to love her.

Aadi was caressing her hair when she turned back, annoyed. 'Aadi, what are you doing?'

Tentatively, Aadi stood up and kissed her cheek. With an impulse, Sonia slapped Aadi. The next moment, she caressed and kissed the face she had punished. She pulled Aadi against her breasts. Catching his breath, Aadi listened to her heartbeat. Coming out of the grip, he gently moved his hand beneath her left breast. Holding it up, he planted a kiss on it.

Switching off the lights, Aadi took Sonia by her arm. In the faint light of neon bulb across the street, Sonia's lips glinted like gems. Caressing her hair, Aadi slid his lips gently over her face, picking on the eyes first and then checking out her eyebrows and cheeks. Taking her nose in his mouth, he pecked at it. He further fondled her ears before drifting towards her mouth. His excitement grew as he swept his tongue over her upper lips. 'I am going to kiss you all over,' he said.

Aadi's lips glided down her throat. Kissing the small dip at the base of her neck, he undid first few buttons of her shirt. He rested his mouth on her cleavage while Sonia moved her fingers in his hair. Relaxing his hands on the contours of her body, Aadi trailed down. On a winning streak, his hands covered the territory of her breasts. Gliding on the waist, his hands trailed back before being punctuated by her ass cheeks. Aadi rubbed his hands over her hips, splitting and squeezing them gently.

'Let's get the shirt off, shall we?' said Aadi softly, unbuttoning her shirt, unveiling a flawless skin. The reticence of her front covered under black bra tantalized Aadi. Moving his hand between her cups, Aadi unhooked her bra to reveal the full round breasts with pink button shaped nipples.

'You fit my hand perfectly,' said Aadi nipping each of her breasts. He kissed and gently sucked her nipples. His tongue explored every bit of her mammary before cruising down. Like a docile river, her midriff awash with tanned skin flowed down her body before turning to an untiered cascade, plunging into her marvelous navel. Reaching her navel, Aadi dipped his tongue inside, and gently nibbled her belly.

Before Aadi could have further explored down, Sonia arrested his head in her hand. 'Let me have some fun,' she said. Aadi stood admiring her half naked body while she undid his shirt. Pushing Aadi on the bed, Sonia quickly removed her trouser. Aadi gazed over her as she stood in front of him in her panties. Aadi relaxed as Sonia got over him, planting soft, featherlike kisses all over his chest. Licking his belly, she grabbed his trousers and unzipped it. Pulling down the trousers, she now had Aadi in his briefs. Her hair falling on his legs, titillated him.

Sonia caressed her hand over his brief before grabbing his erection. Aadi felt an adrenalin rush down his spine. Relaxing her grip, she pushed his thighs apart. Anticipation was more erotic than the act. Aadi enjoyed as Sonia got between his legs. Kissing and caressing she made her way up his thighs. Her breaths hot on his skin meandered upwards, slowly but steadily. Reaching his groin she stared at his erection and then looked at his eyes.

Aadi quickly removed his briefs as he could not bear it any longer. Sonia fondled him with untamed desire and then lay on his chest, her breath accelerated. She grabbed his lower lip within her teeth and bit him hard. 'What are you doing?' asked Aadi.

'This is to show the world that you belong to me.'

'The female of the species is more deadly than the male,' said Aadi, moving his hands on her hips.

Sonia smiled and pushed Aadi back on the bed. She kissed his chest and bit his nipples. 'Woof! God damn, it's hurting.'

'Don't worry! I will give you the pleasure of your lifetime.'

'Now it's my turn,' said Aadi rolling on his back. Sonia was now below him. He tugged off her panties and threw that on the floor. Smelling her pubic hairs, he said. 'You smell too good. Spread your legs,' he instructed.

'Let's see how you do this,' smiled Sonia.

Taking a beer can from his bag, Aadi opened it. He dropped the beer in the basin between her legs. He sipped the beer complete and then explored her depth with his tongue. Kissing over there, Aadi aroused her till she pleaded to end the torture. Very slowly he eased into Sonia and started to move.

'Ah,' Sonia moaned. She had grabbed his hips as Aadi started thrusting faster and harder into her. Before the rush could have flowed down, Aadi came out. Sonia rolled and sat on her knees.

'I like the dimples on your hip line,' she said as Aadi moved behind her.

Leaning forward, she supported herself on her arms. She moved a pillow between her chin and breasts and bent down with her waist raised up. Aadi got between her legs and took her from behind. Like a conductor in an orchestra, Aadi ended the symphony in a crescendo. After making love, Sonia settled by Aadi's side, her hips against his pubic. Picking Aadi's hand, she wrapped it against her breasts. 'Was I near to your fantasy?' she asked.

'Why did you ask this?'

'Boys always fantasize for the girl they can't get into bed.'

'You were my fantasy and I am in bed with you.'

'I was your fantasy before I went in bed with you. Do you still find me beautiful?'

'You are more beautiful than you were before we made love.' With a mischievous smile, Aadi crossed his legs around her naked body. 'I think your sex quotient is a factor of the love we make to each other.'

After fondling her body, Aadi stopped, involved somewhere deep down in his thoughts. 'What's the matter? What are you thinking, darling?'

'We made love once and I got promoted from Aadi to darling. Let's do it once more. It's a pretty fast promotion.'

'Relax! I am with you only,' said Sonia. 'What were you thinking?'

'I hope everything goes fine tomorrow,' said Aadi. Taking a deep audible breath, he continued. 'I feel really sad about Harsh.'

'You tried your best,' said Sonia.

'Harsh wanted to be a part of our final effort towards Flymoto. But we could not involve him,' said Aadi. Something snapped in his mind and he glanced at the table clock. 'It's already 11. I should be leaving otherwise it would be a scandal.'

'Don't worry, relax for now. We still have an hour left before the visiting hours end,' said Sonia kissing on Aadi's hand. Sonia moved her hand between his legs. She stroked his desires till he sank into her. Aadi and Sonia explored the depths of their love while the storm drenched every corner in the campus.

19th February 2007

Wind Tunnel Lab, IITC

On the desk in the control room of the wind tunnel lab were the pieces of the scaled down model of the flying car. Keeping required equipment on the desk, Tapan said. 'Let's assemble it.'

Aadi and Tapan stood in tandem, assembling Flymoto. While Aadi worked on the automated wing mechanism, Tapan assembled Flymoto body. Completing their part, they assembled the body and wings together. Fitting together the structure, Tapan installed the motors and wired them to the control surfaces on the Flymoto. A propeller was fitted to the motor's spindle jutting out of Flymoto's behind. The 1.4 meters by 1 meters model weighed about 12 kilograms when finished.

The crowd in the control room swelled while the group prepared the model. Dr. Shinde had himself come to witness the final trial.

Anticipation was visible on the faces of Aadi and Sonia as Tapan dressed Flymoto with sensors. Placing it on the test bed, Tapan arrested the model using the restraints. Dr. Bhaskar checked the relay of the sensors being displayed on his laptop before signalling a go ahead. Dr. Bhaskar joined Dr. Mukherjee and Dr. Anubhav while Dr. Subbarao stood at one corner of the room.

Like a ritual, Tapan was on the controls of the wind tunnel while Aadi handled the radio controller. 'Test Number one,' said Tapan pushing the button on the controls.

The gigantic fan at one end of the test-section started rotating. With every passing second, the speed of wind in the tunnel increased. Everyone's attention in the room was hooked on Flymoto when it swivelled on its platform, its tail facing the wind.

'What the fuck,' said Aadi looking towards Tapan.

'Oh Shit!' With utmost alacrity, Sonia switched off the wind tunnel.

Tapan held his head with both of his hands. The platform supporting Flymoto had yielded and blown away with the wind. There was a deep dent at the place where it had hit on the wall.

Aadi rushed towards the gate opening to the test section. 'You will get hurt,' said Dr. Bhaskar picking Aadi by arm.

'But sir, if Flymoto falls off, it will break.'

'Don't worry. It's restrained at three points. Let the wind slow down,' said Dr. Bhaskar. In a blatant defiance, the wind broke one of the arresting wires. Flymoto now hung loosely on the remaining two restraints.

Aadi looked around. His eyes met Tapan who had already sunk in the chair. Standing at the entrance was Dr. Subbarao, smiling contemptuously. Pushing Dr. Bhaskar to one side, Aadi entered the test section. The wind speed was still very high. It lashed against his body casting ripples on his skin, like waves on the water. His skin tightened into goose bumps. It felt that the wind will tear him off to bits. Walking upright was not possible. Aadi crouched on the floor and crawled his steps to the test section were Flymoto was hanging.

Standing up, Aadi grabbed Flymoto and cuddled it against his body. With his back facing the fan, Aadi stood firm on the ground till the fan stopped. Tapan and Sonia rushed inside the test section. Removing the restraints they kept Flymoto on the floor.

Taking control of the situation, Dr. Bhaskar instructed the lab assistant to fit a new platform. It took about an hour before Flymoto was back on the platform, prepared to fly.

'Let's start,' said Aadi exchanging a furtive glance with Dr. Bhaskar. He looked towards Tapan to find him visibly shaking. 'Let's start,' he repeated.

'I can't do it,' said Tapan, stepping back.

Dr. Bhaskar left his laptop with Sonia and took over the controls from Tapan. In close coordination, he released the wind in the test section. Aadi had his full concentration on Flymoto. In a self-reassuring manner, he said to himself. 'Let's not play anymore.'

The first three manoeuvres involved translations in the three directions. The next three were rotations in the three directions. It took about 10 minutes for Aadi to complete the preliminary experiments. Flymoto was now due for a free flight.

Aadi slowly brought Flymoto in a nose down attitude. His heart skipped a beat as he prepared to turn Flymoto to its right. The air flowing on Flymoto's body felt passing by his ear. In the silence of his heart, Aadi could hear air talking to Flymoto. It tried to intimidate Flymoto and gushed louder, brushing past its body. Aadi could feel Flymoto being bullied down by the wind bumping on its body.

'Let's show it to them,' said Aadi, in almost a whisper. Suddenly the chaos in his mind faded. Aadi turned Flymoto to its right and stared at her response. The moment seemed pregnant in nature. It was a split second of turbulence that Flymoto successfully handled and was back on the stable flight.

The air in the tunnel glided effortlessly on the body of Flymoto while it soared like a free bird inside the tunnel, yearning for an open sky. Aadi didn't lose the sight as the crowd in the room roared in claps and cheers. Recording two minutes of the flight, Aadi switched off the wind tunnel. He turned back to find Tapan standing in front of him, his eyes wet. Coming out of his momentary stupor, Tapan took Aadi in a hug.

Aadi quickly darted his eyes around. In one corner of the room, he could see Dr. Mukherjee along with Dr. Shinde discussing intently, their composure benign. A few steps away, Aadi could see Dr. Subbarao. Hiding his face in embarrassment, Dr. Subbarao slipped out of the room. Coming out of the hug, Aadi and Tapan walked down to Dr. Bhaskar who was working on his laptop. Sonia stood by his side, assisting him. 'Sir, how did she do?' asked Aadi.

'She was impeccable,' replied Dr. Bhaskar.

From the corner of his eyes, Aadi could see Dr. Mukherjee

and Dr. Shinde approaching him. In an unassuming manner, he turned around. 'Congratulations Aadi,' said Dr. Mukherjee joining the group.

Aadi smiled tersely, waiting to hear it from Dr. Shinde. 'Congratulations to all of you,' said Dr. Shinde. Putting a deliberate pause, he continued. 'This is a matter of pride not just for you guys but also for the entire institute, nothing ever like this has been done before. Measuring the magnitude of positive impact this project will have on this institute, its students and faculties and the world at large, I revoke the DOAA committee's decision with immediate effect. Now, I want you guys to take it out to the world,' he said, pointing to Flymoto in the test section.

'Sir, we haven't done this alone,' remarked Aadi.

Taking the cue, Dr. Shinde added. 'Dr. Bhaskar, we need you more than ever before.'

Dr. Shinde took great interest in the discussion on the flying car. Sating his inquisitive self, Dr. Shinde took leave. After seeing-off Dr. Shinde and Dr. Mukherjee to the parking lot, the group headed back to the lab. Coming close to Aadi, said Sonia. 'Your wish came true.'

Taking a step back, Aadi linked his arms into hers. 'Ours,' said Aadi smiling and looking at her.

A WALK TO REMEMBER

26ᵗʰ April 2007

Farewell Party

Applying the brakes, Aadi brought his bicycle to a sudden stop. Putting bicycle on the stand, he rushed to the volleyball court. Climbing to the last row of the theatre style seating, Aadi parked himself between Tapan and Sid.

'Shuffle to your right.' Cameraman instructed a student. Sitting on the benches by the side of the volleyball court, the entire batch of mechanical engineering students had assembled for a farewell photograph.

Aadi was adjusting his neck tie when a rumbling sound drew his attention. Looking towards Sid, he asked. 'What was that?'

'That was my stomach roaring,' smiled Sid. 'I skipped lunch for the evening buffet.'

Exchanging a terse smile, Aadi adjusted slightly, assuming a suitable pose. He held his breath still when Sid asked. 'What's the last thing that goes through the bug's mind before it hits a windshield?'

From the corner of his eyes, Aadi scowled at Sid.

'It's butt,' answered Sid, a wide smile spread across his face. 'How do you say the word hunger in Hindi?' he asked.

'Is this another joke?' asked Aadi.

'No, seriously.'

'*Hawas*,' replied Aadi. A terse smile sprouted on his lips as he added. 'Wish you a *bone* appetite!'

'Look towards the front, you jerk.' Sid kicked a student craning his neck back, intrigued by the conversation.

'Cheers!' said the cameraman. Like a military parade, everyone straightened up in attention. Covering the lens in less than 1/100th of a second, the shutter froze all that was in front of it. Jumping off the staircase, Tapan thawed what camera had frozen. 'Let's move for the farewell party,' he said.

'Wait, I need to do something.' Relaxing his neck tie, Aadi walked over to Dr. Mukherjee.

'So, the great day has come,' said Dr. Mukherjee looking towards Aadi.

'Sir, this was not possible without your support.'

'It's all your hard work,' said Dr. Mukherjee. Smiling, he continued. 'Did you know that Subbarao has taken a year's sabbatical?'

'Good for us,' said Aadi.

'Good for him. Leave it, what are your plans after college?'

'Sir, we want to take our research on the flying car further.'

'I happened to meet a few guys from 'Whole Motors'. They seem to be quite interested in your project. If you wish, I can talk to them.'

'Sir, that will be a great help,' said Aadi.

'Let's discuss it at the party,' said Dr. Mukherjee, brushing off the imaginary dust on his shoulder.

'Sure sir,' replied Aadi.

Along with Dr. Mukherjee, Aadi and Tapan walked down to the SAC where a farewell party was being organized for the graduating students. After enjoying a short performance by the junior batch, Aadi and Tapan came out of the building to the ground where a buffet was arranged. Sitting in one corner of the ground, Tapan asked. 'When is she coming?'

'I don't know. Her mobile phone is not reachable,' replied Aadi.

'Let's hope she comes before Jaswinder declares jihad on food,' said Tapan looking towards Jaswinder who was headed their way.

'Did you guys have your dinner?' asked Jaswinder, joining them.

'No, we are waiting for Sonia,' replied Aadi.

'Lucky her,' said Jaswinder. Looking earnestly around her, she continued. 'I have no company. I will also wait with you guys but can we move out of the ground. The more I see the food, the worse my appetite gets.'

Aadi, Tapan and Jaswinder were hiking across the ground when Sid crossed them. Chewing the betel leaves in his mouth, he asked shouting. 'Are you guys not going for the dinner?'

Stopping in position, Jaswinder sneered towards Sid. The mention of food annoyed her.

'Not now,' replied Aadi.

'I would go ahead then. *Mujhe bahut hawas lagi hain,*' said Sid, heaving a sigh of relief. Before he could have turned his steps, Jaswinder asked. 'What did you just say?'

Sid's mouth was filled up with red spittle which was beginning to dribble out. 'I will go ahead ...' Before Sid could complete, Jaswinder snapped. 'Say it in Hindi.'

'*Main chalta hoon. Mujhe bahut hawas lagi hain,*' replied Sid.

'I think one slap was not enough for you,' said Jaswinder. 'You sleazy sex maniac. You have nothing else than sex to think about.'

Aadi shoved his knuckles into his mouth, his eyes wide as saucers. Saving his position, he winked at Tapan.

Sid found himself uncomfortable under the constant gaze of Jaswinder. He stood with his mouth agape. A thin stream of red spittle dribbling down his mouth had now reached over to his shirt. 'Get all that poop out of your mouth,' snapped Jaswinder.

Spitting and wiping off his mouth with his shirt's sleeve, Sid asked. 'But, what did I do wrong?'

Aadi got a call from Sonia just in time. Walking beyond the earshot of others, he asked. 'Where are you?'

'Come down to the lobby,' said Sonia. As Aadi reached the lobby, Sonia further instructed. 'Take the stairs and come straight to the terrace.'

'What's on your mind?'

'Don't worry, I am not going to take advantage of you,' chuckled Sonia. 'Be a man, Aadi,' she exhorted.

'Are you thinking about that?' asked Aadi, picking the stairs going upwards.

'You boys can't think beyond it. So cheap,' said Sonia indignantly.

Climbing a flight of stairs, Aadi enquired. 'What are you up to?'

'Come to the terrace and then we shall talk,' said Sonia and disconnected the call.

Aadi was huffing and puffing by the time he reached the top of the building. An adrenalin shot ran down his spine as he saw Sonia walking towards the edge of the building. With his senses heightened, Aadi yelled. 'Please stop. Don't go near to the parapet. It's dangerous.'

'Aadi, if you want me to get back, you need to kiss me here,' said Sonia lifting herself on the parapet.

'Don't be stupid. Get down,' said Aadi slowly walking towards Sonia. He reached near Sonia and grabbed her hand. With his heart pounding hard inside his chest, Aadi raised himself on the parapet. Taking Sonia in his arms, he smacked her down under his lips. A flash of light broke his concentration and he trembled on his legs. Jumping onto the terrace's floor, Sonia pulled Aadi back, saving him from falling.

'What was that?' asked Aadi.

Sonia smiled and walked towards the entrance to the terrace. Picking up her camera, she collected the photograph. 'Check this out,' said Sonia passing onto Aadi the photograph with both of them smacked together against a backdrop of dark sky with a full bright moon.

'This is the best photograph I have ever seen,' said Aadi taking Sonia's hand. He trundled with Sonia towards the exit when a sound coming from the ground alarmed him. Taking a quick glance at the ground from the edge of the terrace, Aadi turned back towards Sonia. 'Someone has probably seen us. Let's quickly get down before they are here.'

Climbing down the first flight of stairs, they stopped, listening to the sound of footsteps which was increasing with every passing second. Grabbing Aadi's hand, Sonia said. 'Not this way. Let's pick the stairs meant for fire escape.'

'What about the exit door? Will it be open?' asked Aadi.

'It always is.'

Coming down the fire escape staircase, Aadi and Sonia joined the crowd in the lobby. They were swiftly walking out of the building when someone called them. 'Hey guys, are you coming from the terrace?'

Aadi turned back to find Jaswinder standing in front of him. 'Sonia, you look beautiful in this dress,' said Jaswinder.

'*Palangtod,*' added Sid, joining along with Tapan.

'You need to unlearn what Aadi has taught you till date. That's all crap,' snapped Jaswinder.

Aadi quickly darted his glance around, checking on others. Sid's face bore a scowl of frustration and anger while Jaswinder's face held an apologetic rage. As always, Tapan was all smiles and Sonia had a confused expression pasted all over her face.

'Did you guys see something on the terrace?' asked Tapan.

'Nothing,' shrugged Aadi.

'I saw two shadows on the terrace. It must be the ghost of the student who committed suicide last semester,' said Sid.

'But there were two shadows,' said Jaswinder.

'He might have got a ghost girlfriend by now. Nowadays, girls don't go by looks,' said Sid half-glancing towards Aadi.

'Guys, stop this. Don't scare me. I live alone in my room,' said Jaswinder.

'You should not worry. It's the ghost who should be afraid,' said Sid impishly.

'Let's get the dinner started.' Looking towards Sid, Jaswinder said. '*Mujhe bahut bhookh lagi hai.*'

Jaswinder marched out while others followed her. Coming out of the building, Aadi turned towards Sonia. 'You look beautiful. Can I have the privilege of clicking a few pictures of yours,

Madam?' he asked.

'I am all yours,' said Sonia running a finger through her hair.

Aadi bent down on his knees and adjusting the camera he clicked a photograph. With a smile running across his face, he said. 'You are now imprisoned forever in this 6 by 4 cell and more importantly in an equally sized heart of mine.'

'This would be the first time that one would have rejoiced so much on a life sentence,' Sonia chortled with mirth. Clinging on to Aadi, she said. 'Aadi, I love you.'

31ˢᵗ May 2007

Auditorium, IITC

Preparations for the convocation ceremony were at their best. Every minute detail had been given the utmost attention. Negating any threat, the campus was combed thoroughly. Temporary posts were rooted for the army to take command. Officers with sniffer dogs patrolled the streets. Police personnel outnumbered the civilians in the campus which had turned into a military cantonment overnight.

In front of auditorium's main gate, Aadi stood with Tapan and Sonia in a queue. Dressed up in the convocation robes, the students sweated in the burning sun. At the other end of the auditorium, in front of the Shop C, a taxi stopped. A person in the convocation robe came out paying the change. His tall frame held a heavy face resting on broad shoulders. On his long legs, he leaped forward towards the auditorium. Covering the distance, the stranger now stood low in the tall column of grasses. The next second he took out a cutter from his robe and swiftly slit open the barbed wire securing the auditorium. Without tripping on any alarm, the stranger slipped inside the premises. He raced towards the backside of the building while the main gate got open, letting inside the graduating students and their guardians.

'Why is this rigorous check in place?' asked Aadi to Sid who was manning the first chest of the security.

'The security has been beefed up in lieu of the threat received for the event,' answered Sid. Taking the passes, he tore it off in two and signalled Aadi to roll in. While Aadi moved inside, Sid moved away to answer a call.

Sid had covered the length of the auditorium while on the call and now he stood at the back side of it. He hung the call as the stranger who had tripped inside Audi, stood in front of him.

'Are you sure about what you intend to do?' asked Sid.

'Yes,' replied the uninvited guest.

'Ok then, I will assist you to get inside. We will move once the entrance gate is open. Keep this card with you,' said Sid handing his counselling service pass to the stranger. 'If someone stops, you can masquerade as a counselling service student.'

The entrance opened after a while and the crowd of students sailed inside. Sid and the stranger walked together to the entrance and then they split. Sid went to the main gate, while the stranger mixed with the crowd. After another hour, the entries got closed. The whole area was cordoned off and police vans patrolled on the circuit of IITC.

A motorcade wailing high on sirens stopped in front of the auditorium. Ms. Gandhi, Prime Minister of the country came out, flanked by black cat commandos. At the entrance was Dr. Shinde, the director of the institute to receive the premiere of the nation.

Everyone was settled in their seats. Ms. Gandhi, Dr. Shinde and many other stallions of the institute adorned the stage for the day. Dr. Shinde took the podium to deliver his speech. Seeking the attention, the director of the institute began. 'By virtue of my qualification, I should not be standing in front of this elite audience sitting here. But from my experience, I would like to give a piece of advice to the graduating students.'

Looking deep in the crowd, he continued. 'The three pillars on which gets laid the foundation of one's career are expertise, knowledge and integrity. Above these pillars one needs to create the platform of credibility. If you deliver on your words, you build upon the credibility. ...'

Dr. Shinde further talked about the institute and the place it holds in the nation's progress. He went ahead recounting the feats the institute has achieved. Concluding, he said. 'I have armed you with all of my suggestions. I will not take much of your time and would like to wish you all success in the life.'

Dr. Shinde stepped off the podium and a girl anchoring the event stepped up. Giving a terse review of the schedule, she called upon Ms. Gandhi to deliver a speech to the students. Ms. Gandhi stood up and from the crowd of students stood up the uninvited guest. Walking briskly, he neared the stage. In his convocation robe, he drew no unwarranted attention. He swiftly covered his way to the stage.

'Where are you going?' asked a security personnel.

'I am with the counseling service of the institute. I need to look at the arrangements,' replied the stranger flashing the counseling service card with him.

'You can go inside,' said the security personnel.

Climbing the stairs, the stranger now stood on the stage. The next second he was sprinting towards the podium where Ms. Gandhi was about to step on. Seeing a sudden flurry of action on the stage, the black cat commandos got into action. A line of commandos jumped forward and sealed Ms. Gandhi inside a human wall. The stranger blatantly rushed to the podium and picked the mike. 'I want to speak in front of all the students and in front of the secretary of the state,' yelled the stranger, high on his volume.

The black cat commandos now had their gun angled towards the uninvited guest. Before the stranger could have realized a commando yanked him on the floor. Grabbing the stranger's arm, the commando pulled it around the stranger's back, seizing him in place.

Aadi stood up and yelled as he recognized the stranger. 'Leave him. He is not a terrorist.'

Heads in the vicinity turned at Aadi's words. A few more students stood up as they recognized the stranger. The words spread among the crowd of students like the fire in the forest.

'This is insane,' shouted Aadi. 'He is not a terrorist. Leave him,' Aadi was now running towards the podium.

Giving him a warning, some commandos rushed towards Aadi. They had to retract back as now he was not alone but had gathered a mass of students with him. The commandos now stood aiming at the students who had left their seats and were walking towards the stage.

'Please stop at your place. We can't compromise the security of our premiere and in case we need to fire we won't hesitate. Please stop.' In an unsaid rhythm the students looked towards each other and continued their walk.

'He is not a terrorist,' yelled Aadi.

'I request all of you to please stop. Don't push me to give the orders,' yelled the major of the army. Aiming their guns on the students, the commandos took their positions.

The eye balls inside the auditorium were glued to the bizarre episode reeling in front of them. The convocation hall turned into a center of attention for the nation as various channels tuned on the event unfurling inside.

Outside the auditorium, CRPF personnel were taking their positions. Taking cover, they scrambled to the auditorium gate. A paramedic team kicked into action. Another team of black cat commandos pulled up in front of the auditorium. Spearing through the crowd, they crossed through the gate manned by the state police. They wore bullet proof chest and held an AK-47 each. On nimble feet, they stormed inside the main gate.

'Keep them away,' retorted the Captain. Two gunmen took the charge at the auditorium gate, pushing back the spectators assembled in front of the auditorium.

'You all keep out of this,' bawled the inspector.

Using the hand signals, the Captain asked two commandos to clear off the area till the Audi entrance. Keeping low, they climbed the distance to the entrance. Covering their positions, they signaled the team to roll in.

The commandos waited for the signal from the Captain while he took instructions from the major, inside the convocation hall.

'Major, can you give me the position of the target,' asked the Captain.

The conversation went blurred as an explosion occurred inside.

'What's the situation inside?' asked the Captain.

'You need to wait,' came the response.

'What? Are you sure we need to stay put,' the Captain retorted in his walkie talkie after hearing the response from the other side.

'Positive and wait for further instructions before taking any action.'

'What was the explosion?' asked the Captain.

'It's nothing to worry about. That was just a shot in the air,' replied the major at the other end of the walkie talkie.

The captain signaled everyone to take cover and stay put, waiting for further commands. The melee outside the auditorium had settled. 'I am coming inside alone,' said the Captain. Stealthily as the Captain stepped inside the auditorium, he saw a male, about 25 in age, being surrounded by the commandos.

'I had come to say something. I have nothing on me to be considered a threat,' said the stranger as he was being frisked.

'Captain, please put down your arms and be at ease. There's nothing to worry about,' said the major.

Ms. Gandhi breached the human wall of commandos and took the mike. 'Students, I request you all to be at your seats. We will give him a chance to speak. Commandos, please leave the guy,' said the premiere pointing to the stranger.

'But madam, he can be a threat. Are you sure we should leave him?'

'Yes.' Pointing to the stranger, Ms. Gandhi said. 'You can talk your mind.'

The commandos had left the stranger who now stood aplomb on his one foot. Limping towards the podium he took the mike from Ms. Gandhi and spoke. 'Thanks Ms. Gandhi, for allowing me my right as a citizen.'

'Say it, whatever you want to say,' said Ms. Gandhi.

'I would like to first clarify that I am not a terrorist.' Looking to the students, the stranger spoke. 'I was a student of this institute who has been thrown out in his fourth semester. My name is Harsh.'

Quickly surfing on the crowd's attention, Harsh continued. 'As we are celebrating our success in academics, there are parents weeping for their loss. Today, a girl attempted suicide because her parents were here for her convocation while she had failed in a subject twice and thus had to lose her degree. It's not the first case but in my counting it's the sixth case that has happened here.'

The commandoes were alarmed as Harsh slipped his hand inside the pocket. Putting them on ease was the hanky that came out. Wiping off the sweat from his face, Harsh continued. 'It seems as if this institute is waging a war for the intellect. They think of us as warriors, expendable in their war against ignorance. Every semester, many of us are trashed out in the name of the academic performance and some, who can't bear, pay with their life.'

Killing the brief silence, Harsh spoke loudly. 'The world is not about making all people think in a single direction. Let us choose our own path rather than something imposed upon us.' Banging his fist on the podium, Harsh continued. 'I question the logic behind making such subjects mandatory that have a reputation of killing a student per semester. I question the relative grading system that often penalizes a student by 20 percent for a difference of one mark.'

Relaxing his words, Harsh said, his voice losing the tempo. 'I can't speak for all the fallacies but they are there and we need to put in some action before it's too late. We can't celebrate our achievement when some parents are mourning.'

Harsh stepped back from the podium. The captain shifted his position and stood behind Harsh as he still saw threat in him. Ms. Gandhi now stepped on the podium and taking the microphone she spoke. 'I am amazed how these things never reached my ears. But now, I am determined to dig up the truth.'

'A nation needs to remember that the lowest common denominator, its citizens, is what takes it up. The nation breathes with its citizens and dies with their pain and ignorance. Every nation has the responsibility to groom its citizens for a better tomorrow. You can't wake up one fine day and say that you need to excel. It's a gradual process and institute like IITC are there to take us towards that goal.'

The room fell in a moment pregnant with silence as Ms. Gandhi paused in her speech. Putting across her thoughts, she delivered. 'But, sometimes greatest of minds commit the mistake, they become blinded with their vision. Sometimes, we are so focused about our goal that we strive for it too hard. Every day, we move an inch or two towards our own demise. How can we forget that destination is a moment while journey is a lifetime? One should enrich the journey instead of hiking always for a goal.'

Looking towards Dr. Shinde, who now stood at one corner of the stage, Ms. Gandhi asked. 'I would like to be furnished with the information over the suicides in the recent past. Also, I would like to have a list of complaints from the students against the academic rules. We will make positive plans to wash away fallacies in our system and come out clean in the eyes of the future of our nation.' Taxing a brief pause, Ms. Gandhi spoke. 'Before moving ahead with the convocation, I would like to thank Harsh who took the courage to risk his life for a cause. We need this passion among our citizens.'

The convocation went further without any chaos. Harsh was there to witness when Aadi and Tapan received their degree. Coming out of the auditorium, Tapan and Aadi hugged Harsh. There were tears in everyone's eyes as they realized what each one meant to the other.

31st May 2007

Hall 8, Terrace, IITC

Under the roof of stars sat friends on the hall's terrace. With champagne and beer bottles in hand they boozed the moment, holding it to pass.

'We never thought you could do this.' Raising his toast, Tapan continued. 'I am happy that you surprised us.'

Harsh raised his glass. In a profound acknowledgment, he said. 'I always wanted to live this moment again. All of us sitting on our block's terrace and boozing up.' Making errata to his wish, Harsh continued. 'Sonia was not in my equation but that's a lovely addition to have.'

'That's not the only change. Tonight, you are shining brighter than any of the stars in the sky.' Sipping from his bottle, Aadi continued. 'Harsh, you did a great job.'

'I wanted to tell the truth to the world,' said Harsh sipping a big gulp of his pint.

'Guys, give me your hand,' said Sonia grabbing both Aadi's and Tapan's hand. Taking a cue from Sonia, Harsh clenched the hands together and said tenderly. 'Friends forever.'

'Aadi, how far have the talks about funding our research reached?' asked Harsh, opening a new bottle for himself.

'Discussions with Whole Motors have been quite promising. Let's hope things conclude to our benefit,' replied Aadi.

'What's in it for them?' asked Tapan.

'They will partner us in the sale. They will have a decent share in the profits,' said Aadi. 'Dr. Mukherjee has already filed patent in our names.'

'I want to come back to IITC to fly our real car,' said Harsh with excitement visible on his face.

'The day will come,' said Aadi. 'And let me promise you guys, I will do the first flight of our flying car.'

'Will Dr. Bhaskar and Dr. Anubav consider our proposal?' asked Tapan.

'I hope they will,' replied Aadi. 'It will be a dream team if they join us for the research.'

'Sonia, don't take anymore,' instructed Aadi as Sonia picked another pint.

'I am with my Aadi. I have nothing to fear about. Aadi will take care.' Like a kitten, Sonia unzipped Aadi's jacket and snuggled inside. She opened a pint and drank that with her head in Aadi's lap.

'Sonia you should go to sleep now,' said Aadi intervening. 'I need to drop you back to your hostel.'

'I am not going anywhere. I will sleep here only,' insisted Sonia.

'She is now fully drunk,' said Aadi.

'No I am not. But I wonder what a place like me is doing in a girl like this?' said Sonia, her eyes wide as saucers and her voice incoherent.

'Now she is out,' declared Aadi.

In one corner, Aadi and Sonia slept under the naked sky while Tapan and Harsh continued dumping the pints inside their stomachs. Aadi relished his final sleep in IITC as a student while Harsh shared his stories with Tapan.

EPILOGUE

05th August 2010

Airstrip, IITC

On a sun drenched summer morning, the tarmac appeared a puddle of molten mercury with shadow of objects in the surrounding shimmering on it. Sailing across the puddle was the flying car speeding on the airstrip of IITC. The rumbling noise of the propeller broke the stillness of the air. The noise reached a crescendo before the front of the car tilted up and the car started its climb to the sky. The moment just after the wheels were off the ground was seized by array of cameras standing on the side of the airstrip. The very moment got etched in human history as a symbol of an extraordinary accomplishment.

In the backdrop of a crimson sky, the flying car looked like a legendry Unicorn. A chase aircraft followed it in the wake, capturing the video of its maiden flight. Flymoto on its 25 minutes flight plan hovered over the spots of importance in IITC. Completing the flight, Flymoto descended for the landing. It flared out before touching the tarmac and then rolled for a stop at the spot where media and other dignitaries were present.

Covering the important event in human history was present national and international media. The very second Aadi and the Captain stepped out, a surge of reporters rushed towards them. Slitting the moment in innumerous frames, the camera shutters filled the silence. A horde of journalists jostled to catch a glimpse of the two pilots who rode the flying car. A battery of microphones was thrust in the face of Aadi and the Captain.

'Sir, how was the flight?' asked a correspondent from CNN.

'Remarkably unremarkable,' said the Captain. 'It was one of the easiest planes to ride in my entire career as a pilot.'

'Sir, did you ever feel it being risky?'

'Not an iota. Though, with Aadi as co-pilot, I could not have avoided the thoughts of our previous crash.' With a terse smile, the Captain said. 'It was a glider that we had crash landed, somewhere 4 years back.'

'How did different aircraft systems perform?'

'The data gathered on the different systems was up to our expectations.'

'Sir, please tell us something about Flymoto,' asked another reporter thrusting mike towards Aadi.

Harsh and Tapan had been standing out of the media barricade. Signaling them to join, Aadi continued. 'Harsh, Tapan and I have worked towards this dream of ours for almost 5 years. The flying car has got continuous variable transmission, a liquid based cooling system, a custom design gear box for switching the power from the engine to either propeller in the aircraft mode or wheels in the car mode. This innovation of ours shall surely make world a more accessible place.'

'Sir, tell us something about wings,' asked another reporter.

Aadi passed on the question to Tapan who answered. 'In the car mode, the wings of Flymoto fold up along the sides of its frame. The automatic wing fold mechanism is real time. You just push some buttons in the cockpit and the wings come out. The mechanical lock on the wings arrests it in place when fully deployed, enabling it to carry the air loads that Flymoto shall see in the flight.'

'How much will it cost?'

'It should be costing near to a small sports plane but over the time the price will come down and it will be in the range of high end cars available in the market,' answered Harsh.

'Sir, can you talk about the joint venture with Whole Motors?' asked another reporter.

'Whole Motors is funding us for the research. They are also going to help us with their distribution chain to market Flymoto,' replied Harsh.

'What is their sharing in Flymoto Inc.?' asked a reporter.

'No Comments!' snapped Harsh.

'Rest of the questions will be answered during the press conference, later this evening,' said Aadi.

Swimming across the human barricade of reporters, Aadi, Harsh and Tapan reached the hangar where a small celebration party was organized. Sonia already occupied a table waiting for the others. With sparkling and dazzling colors on her face and mascara in her eyes, she looked beautiful. Joining Sonia on the table, Harsh asked. 'Did you like the show?'

'It was amazing,' she replied.

'There's a piece of good news that I want to share.' Filling a toast for Sonia, Aadi cheered. 'Soon, we are going to tie the knot.'

'Sonia, I wish you have a great and exciting life ahead,' said Tapan.

Easing his arm around Sonia's shoulder, Aadi said. 'Without you guys I would never have realized my dreams. I can't ask for more.'

'So guys, what are your plans for your honeymoon?' asked Harsh.

Sonia blushed. Taking a sip from her drink, she wafted the question to Aadi. 'I would like to go to Ladakh for our honeymoon.'

Easing his hand inside his coat's pocket, Harsh brought out a packet of cigarettes. Lighting a cigarette, he puffed out the smoke balls as he asked. 'Sonia, what are your plans?'

'A short trip to France after our Ladakh trip is done,' replied Sonia.

'The ticket to France is on me,' said Harsh. A smile spread across his face. He felt happy for Aadi and Sonia.

'Let's have a photograph with Flymoto,' proposed Sonia.

'Why not,' said Harsh. He stood up extinguishing the cigarette in the ash tray and walked with the group towards Flymoto parked in the hangar.

Aadi followed Sonia from one corner of his eyes. He saw her swiftly picking up the cigarette box kept on the table. Throwing that in the bin she leaped forward catching pace with the group. Innocently, she eased a hand on Aadi's shoulder as group walked towards Flymoto. Smiling tersely, Aadi rolled back his eyes.

The Research and Development division of Flymoto Inc. under the guidance of Dr. Bhaskar and Dr. Anupam successfully completed 10 proto-vehicle trials. Flymoto cleared all the criteria laid down by Federal Aviation Administration (FAA) and was certified later in year 2011 as a vehicle safe enough to fly. Flymoto was made available for public purchase by 2012. Technologies like fly-by-wire, glass cockpit avionics made Flymoto not only easy to command but also safe to fly.

Sonia and Aadi got married after Flymoto was made available to the public. For their invention, the group got felicitated by IITC. Honoring Harsh for his suggestions to the academic counsel, IITC felicitated him with an honorary degree. The invention of the three friends went ahead winning accolades across the globe.

www.ingramcontent.com/pod-product-compliance
Lightning Source LLC
Chambersburg PA
CBHW070110030726
47506CB00002B/679